FAREWELL
HORIZONTAL

To Les and Rita Escott

When he awoke, he saw angels mating overhead.

For a few seconds longer, Axxter watched them, fragments of a dream. The sun broke over the distant edge of the cloud barrier below, tinting red the metal wall against his shoulder. All through the night his body had huddled close to it, as though his acrophobic spine had been trying to burrow through the building's skin and back to the remembered safety of floors and ceilings. His own dreams were of falling, spinning free of the great curve and impacting into clouds filled with small, biting faces; or, pleasantly, of sleeping itself, cradled by gravity and solid steel. But never of floating, of drifting locked in embrace, turned slowly by a bed of winds. Thus it flashed on him that the angels were real.

"Shit." Teeth clamped to lip even as he twisted about in the narrow sling, to silence any further outburst. Gas angels were notoriously skittish; they could decouple and

■ ■ ■ 1

split, flight membranes deflated for a parawing dive down-wall and overcurve, before he could get a lens on them. And he needed the money, equally real. The little, biting faces in his dreams were the zeroes on his bank account readout.

He came up with the camera, out of his gear bag grappled onto the cable below the sling—for a dizzying second he had hung half out of the swaying fabric, head down toward the clouds and the big step to them, as he'd fumbled around. Mercenary spirit overrode the usual nausea; he rolled onto his back, the sling's pithons adjusting to shifting weight, their triangular heads finding and biting into holds tighter than those needed for corpselike slumber.

A scan across, from the upwall bulk of Cylinder to open sky. There they were, centered in the camera's view-finder. Axxter sighed, shoulders unknotting. They didn't hear me. Coital oblivion apparently equal among all species; he focused, hit RECORD, and crawl-zoomed in on the airborne lovers. Hold it right there, you beauties.

The sun had risen far enough that all the air had turned gold. The spherical membranes behind the angels' shoulders were filled with light, radiant, as though the hemo-dialyzed gases that kept them aloft had ignited with the friction of the two forms between. Axxter went in closer, his hand trembling at the controls, until the camera filled with intricate red lace, the angels' veins swelling taut the papery skin.

As if in sympathy, another vein pumped through heavier, gravity-bound flesh. Axxter ignored it; he knew how long he had been vertical, out here hustling business. *Knock it off, already; don't remind me.* He went on taping, rolling onto his shoulder to follow the angels' drift.

The golden-and-pink knot turned, their waists the equator of a bifurcate planet. At the dark margin of his vision,

2 ■ ■ ■

the camera's data fed through the metal contact on his fingertip to the display feed spliced into his optic nerve: distance to subject ranged between 100 and 125 meters. The red digits effectively tracked the eddy currents at the building's atmosphere boundary. Axxter, squinting and likewise tracking, wondered if the angels enjoyed that effect. Maybe it enhanced the pleasure, like being tickled all over by invisible fingers. Who knew?—Ask & Receive's files on angelic sex were pretty thin. Something to think about, though. Christ, not now, he pleaded to his own distracting flesh.

In the distance above, the male's downward rotation brought the female's face into the viewfinder. Axxter zoomed in tighter. They did look like angels, what angels should look like, beyond the simple floating in air. Where no vertical or horizontal existed. The fragile bodies, substantial only against the translucent membranes ballooning from nape to buttock; the golden light seemed to pass as well through the female's small, delicate breasts as she arched back from the other's chest, her eyes closed and mouth soundlessly open, her small hands gripping the male's fulcrum hips to her own. A shining trail of kisses and sweat spiraled over her throat and face, and his, that slow moisture being the only response to gravity's tug as they had turned and pivoted about.

So pretty; Axxter, slung and bound against the metal wall, taped and watched. The thin wands of the angel's collarbone above her luminous breasts; he could almost believe there was no flesh at all, only fragile and weightless skin, taut with the blood's tracery, the same as the two buoyant spheres that held the two aloft. In the viewfinder a deeper blush welled up into her face. Her lashes trembled against her cheek. Instinctively, Axxter pulled back, reverse zoom, until there was sky all around the couple. On tape he caught the shudder that ran through

■ ■ ■ 3

their limbs, a shimmer echoing in the inflated membranes behind each of them, a seismic event in that light-permeated world.

They moved apart, drifting on separate currents. Though the male was in sight longer, angling on a slow diagonal out from the building's face, Axxter kept the camera on the female. A stronger wind lifted her farther overhead; she stretched her thin arms above herself, smiling, eyes still closed. A sleepy nude against the sky. Hair all tangled, dampened black. When she became a speck, untrackable, and then gone, Axxter lowered the camera. The machine had sweated in his hands, but he found—it took him a moment to realize what was missing—that other urgencies had been forgotten. As if the flesh had also been disarmed by the angels' beauty. "You know—" He spoke aloud, put in a good mood by the morning's omen, hugging camera to chest. "Maybe—just maybe— you aren't *completely* forsaken, after all." A string of cold electrons ticked over in the camera, downloading to his internal archive; he tucked the machine beside himself in the sling and gazed out over the cloud barrier to the lifting sun.

Feelings of universal benevolence dissolved when he remembered his bank balance. The angels were gone, evaporated back into Cylinder's surrounding atmosphere. Except on tape, Axxter reminded himself. For which we are truly grateful. That, in itself, was not enough of a break to save him from bankruptcy. But it would put it off awhile longer, in which time all sorts of things could happen. The little gem of hope radiated in his heart, as if a drop of the angels' sweat had fallen and crystallized there.

The sling rocked uncomfortably as he scrambled to his knees. He had left the deadfilm for his terminal pinned to the building's metal wall, right where he'd be able to find it first thing in the morning. For most of this excursion

4 ■ ■ ■

he'd been traveling off-line, the Small Moon being over-curve, all signal to or from it being blocked by the building itself. And in this scurfy territory, the building's exterior desolate and abandoned in every direction, Ask & Receive hadn't been able to sell him a map of plug-in jacks. So finding this one had been a break, as well. Maybe that's when my luck started. Axxter rattled his fingertip inside the rust-specked socket; a spark jumped from the tiny patch of metal to the ancient wire running inside the building. Last night, when I found this; maybe it's all going to just roll on from here. At last.

YES? The single word floated up in the center of his eye, bright against the deadfilm's black drain of ambient light. More followed. GOOD MORNING. "THE GLORIES OF OUR BLOOD AND STATE/ARE SHADOWS, NOT SUBSTAN-TIAL THINGS/THERE IS NO ARMOR.—"

"Jee-zuss." Axxter's gaze flicked to CANCEL at the corner of his eye. The trouble with buying secondhand; his low-budget freelancer's outfit had all sorts of funky cuteness left on it from its previous owner; he had never been able to edit it out.

VERY WELL. Sniffy, feelings wounded. REQUEST?

He hesitated. For a moment he considered not calling anyone up; just not saying anything about the angels at all. His little secret, a private treasure. That would be something. Something nobody had except me. He nodded, playing back the tape inside his head corresponding to the one inside the camera. So pretty; both of them, but especially the female angel. Slender as a wire. A soft wire. And smiling as she'd drifted away. That smile was locked away, coded into the molecules inside the camera. And in my brain—burned right into the neural fibers. As if soft, dreaming smiles could burn.

It'd be a kick: angel footage rare, of any kind. You had to get out into these wastewall areas of the building's surface to have a chance of spotting them at all, and just by chance. Elusive; a gas angel expedition, just for that purpose, a ridiculous notion.

Except maybe they hang out here, in this zone. Axxter rubbed his chin, thinking. Like a nest, or something. The great angel rookery? Who knows?—surely they don't give birth in the air as well? How do they, then? He made a mental note to log the wall coordinates, downwall by left-around, so he could find the place again. Some other time.

Angel stuff being rare also made it valuable, however. Beyond the mere smile. That decided the issue. "Get me Registry."

After he'd zipped the footage from his archive to Reg and got a File Check, Clear & Confirmed Ownership—thank God that much service came free—he asked if anything else had come in lately under the heading Angels, Gas, Coitus (Real Time). For all he knew, whole orgies had been taking place in the skies around the building's morningside.

Two cents pinged off the meter panel in the corner of his sight, Registry's charge for the inquiry. The sight/sound made him wince.

NOTHING, JACK. TOTAL NADA. The Registry interface had a flip personality. YOU MIGHT TRY UNDER HISTOR-ICAL AND/OR POETRY. "I WANDERED LONELY AS A—"

Another eyeflick, to DISCONNECT. He didn't want to get tagged for another charge. Not for ancient nonsense, some pre-War file dredged out of Registry's deep vaults. "Screw that."

PARDON?

"Get me, um . . . get me Lenny Red." By contract, Axxter should have called his agent Brevis. But Brevis took a ten-percenter bite; and any idiot working out of a toplevel office could peddle hot angel love stuff. *I could*

6 ■ ■ ■

do it, from here—Axxter knew Ask & Receive had a call out, all angel footage bought top-price. But Ask & Receive also listed their stringers in a public file; if Brevis found out—and he would—he'd take the whole wad paid, not just ten percent. Contractual penalty. So Lenny's usual five made him a bargain.

SHIELD LINE?

"Naw, don't bother." No sense in paying the extra—he had his Reg confirm. "Just call him straight in."

YOU'RE THE BOSS.

The cranky wire quavered Lenny's face. "Howdy, Ny."

He squinted at the image overlaid in his sight. Lenny's forehead smeared to the left; his mouth was a rippling loop. This far downwall, you took what you could get. "Got something for you."

"Oh?" *Oh?*—the line echoed as well. "Like what?" *Kwut?*

"Angels."

A distorted eyebrow lifted like an insect leg at the edge of the film. "Really." *Lee-ee.*

"Catch this." Axxter engineered a smug smile into his own face. *"Angels having sex."*

"Yeah?" No longer bored; Lenny's hand came into view, tapping a control panel at the edge of his terminal. His face pulled together, brow stacked on top where it should be. It hadn't been distance/transmit problems at all—he'd taken Axxter's call through some low-rate line filter. The little shit—Axxter smiled and ate his resentment. Only greed, the push to cover his operating nut, kept him from disconnecting over an insult like that.

"Yeah." The word tasted good, with its juice of money. "Fresh this morning. I thought of *you* first, Lenny."

"Flattered." Lenny, in sharp focus now, tried to reassemble his dealer's cool. "I . . . *might* . . . be able to help you out. Possibly."

■ ■ ■ 7

"Cut the crap." Not screwing me on this one. Axxter blinked on PLAYBACK from his archive. "You're gonna love it."

Registry's confirm number shadowed miniscule across the bottom of the image in his eye's tiny editing segment; Axxter shifted his gaze back to center and caught the small sign of disappointment the Reg number produced on Lenny's face as he watched the tape on his own terminal. Bastards like him made such precautions necessary.

They watched in silence, image on wire linking them through the building's vast corpus, thread in subcutaneous mesh. Even in miniature, at the corner of his eye, the entwined figures caught him. Floating in their rectangle of recorded sky. Axxter's heart drained, became hollow, as he gazed. I shouldn't even have kept it for myself. Mercantile victory soured on his tongue. The angel faces, small dots at this resolution; he couldn't see the female's trembling lashes, but remembered them. I should've let them go and drift away, off-tape. Just in memory. Need the cash, though. Shit.

He snapped out of his reverie when the image suddenly jittered ahead in time, the taped angels comically flailing and whirling in flat air. Lenny, on-line to the archive, fast-forwarded through the tape, catching a few bits in real time, then running ahead again. Axxter bit his lip. This bastard's got no soul at all.

End of tape; the square of empty sky vanished as Lenny's face, at center, came back up. He nodded, not even trying to hide how impressed. "Not bad."

"Unique." Axxter smiled around the bone in his throat. Sell, you sonofabitch; the advice he'd given himself a million times. Be a bastard and eat. "The word is unique."

"Well . . ." Lenny's hand crawled into view and waggled on edge. "There was that Opt Cooder find a few years back. Along the same lines."

8 ■ ■ ■

"What? Your ass." Axxter shook his head in disbelief. "The one Cooder found was *dead.*"

"Yeah, but Ask & Receive got wild accessing off it. Death tones are always big in the horizontal levels. That tape's still bringing in money for them."

True enough; Axxter knew. He'd been on the horizontal himself, saving up his grubstake, when the Cooder tape had gone on market. And he had bought it, too. First the minimum charge for one-time access; then, when he hadn't been able to get the image of the dead angels out of his mind, paying for permanent zip into personal archive. Through the long months—Christ, years if totaled—of working in the piss-factory types of jobs he could get without signing a lifer contract, and the nights on end of honing his would-be graffex skills, sketching out ideas for warrior decs and military ikons, building up a working archive, buying little scraps of biofoil to practice implanting; sweating every nickel toward the used freelancer gear he'd locked onto—unable to afford superstition about residual bad luck from the guy who'd gone bust running it before—and worrying that some other young hopeful would snatch it up before his account reached the precisely calculated level where he could chance going vertical . . . through all of that, he remembered watching the Opt Cooder tape of the famous dead gas angel. Watching, thinking, and waiting. Or waiting with no thought at all. Kept me going; Axxter nodded to himself. Maybe because, even dead, the angel had represented a certain freedom. A creature of the air, neither horizontal nor vertical. Cooder, top-rank wanderer that he had been, had lucked out in that find: no sign of violence on the angel's body. Anyone watching the tape might have thought the female angel was sleeping, until the reverse zoom from her tranquil face revealed the torn and deflated membrane, no longer a sphere behind her shoulders. She had lain swathed in the billowing folds, which when taut with blood-rendered gases would have borne her aloft. Caught by that delicate tissue alone, she would never have remained bound to Cylinder's wall; as Cooder's camera had watched, another translucent scrap had torn loose in the wind and fluttered away. But one of the dead hands had snagged in a transit cable loop; Cooder's lens had moved in on the dried trickle of blood running down from her wrist under the gray metal, just enough to dispel the mystery of how the nude form had come to this rest. If closing his eyes would have blanked out Lenny's face, Axxter could have replayed it, watched it all over again from memory; it lay parallel and so close to this morning's living, mating angels that the images had bled into each other, one section of time superimposed over another. As if the lovers had coupled all unconscious of the corpse framed in the same shot with them, tangled in the building's cables, diagonal from the open air in which they turned and clasped.

Opt Cooder had made the most of the rare chance; no one else had ever gotten so close to one, alive or dead. A certain aesthetic sense that went with his rep, catching the fading light as the sun went over Cylinder and on to the eveningside—so that the red tinge on the angel's cheek had almost made her seem alive. But sleeping. Because if she had been dead, wouldn't she have disappeared where all the other dead angels go? And where was that?— something that Axxter still wondered, along with every- body else who watched the scanty archives, over and over. Maybe there was some one spot on an unexplored sector of the building's surface where all the pretty corpses came to rest. Leaving behind not a whitening layer of bones— those would crumble away like dust, figured Axxter—but of something like tattered silk, gray where the blood had once made the tissue into pink lace.

10 ■ ■ ■

Or maybe they just fall, he thought. Down through the cloud barrier, and whatever's below that, if anything. Maybe all the dead angels are still falling.

"So you want me to peddle this stuff for you, or what?"

Axxter refocused, the image resolving back into Lenny Red's face. For a moment he didn't speak, then, "Sure. That's why I called you. What d'you think you can get for it?" Questions like that indict your heart. Sell, you sonofabitch.

Lenny shrugged, the thin points of his shoulders coming up into the image. "Lemme run it past a few people. I'll get right back to you." The face vanished.

He passed the couple of minutes—that's all it ever took with fast Lenny—looking out across empty sky. The line chirped inside his ear; Lenny's features could just be made out, light against brighter.

"High quote was two thousand, Ny." A conspirator's wink. "But I jacked 'em up to twenty-two-five."

He stared at the bright, overactive face. "Twenty-two-five? That's all?" Jeez—now I *know* I should've kept it for myself. "You gotta be kidding."

"Hey, that's after my cut, man. That's all straight to you. Come on," wheedled Lenny's image. "You know you want it, you need it—just sign me over the confirm number, and we'll do the deal."

The realization hit him. "You're getting yours on the other end. You're lowballing me." Fury welled up in his throat. "Fuckin' lowballing me."

That little shrug again. "It's a fair price, man. None of the scientific data agencies had any interest in it—everybody knows already how angels do it. You're not making no big contribution to human knowledge, all right? So it has to sell just on aesthetics, I shop it around to Ask & Receive's entertainment division and their guys go, *'Ten minutes? Whaddya think we can charge for accessing ten minutes of tape?'"* Lenny's finger, a pink dot, jabbed toward him. "And *that's* why two thousand."

"Twenty-two-five." It's what you get, thought Axxter, for dealing with people like this.

"Twenty-two-five was before you pissed me off. *Now* it's two thousand."

"I should've gone straight to my own agent." He looked back out at the sky. Serves me right, I suppose.

In his ear, Lenny's voice went blunt. "Two thousand is also so your agent doesn't find out about all this. Non-info costs, just like real info does."

It's what I get. Axxter punched out the confirm transfer without looking, screwed it up, then got it right. From a distance he heard some parting shot from Lenny. Should've kept it for myself—the thought became bleaker with repetition. To cheer himself, he blinked up his bank account.

The payment had already gone through, zipped in via Lenny. The numbers crawled across his sight, digits kissed by the two thousand wad. He was afloat again, at least for a little while. Maybe that's what my luck is. The cheerful edge had already worn off the morning's event. Maybe just getting by, hugging the wall with the wind at the back of my neck. Getting hungry lets you cling even better, spine tight to the metal.

MESSAGE FROM REGISTRY. The words crawled into view. NOTIFICATION, TRANSFER OF OWNERSHIP, FILE BLAH-BLAH-BLAH; YOU DON'T WANT THE REAL NUMBERS, DO YOU?

"No." Screw it. At least he wouldn't have to pay to see the mating angels, as everyone else would; the original images were still inside his archive. At least I've got that much. "Call up Brevis, okay?"

His agent's face came up in his sight, in sufficient-enough resolution. In the corner of his eye, the Wire Syndicate's call charges nibbled away at his bank account.

"Ny—I was just about to call you." Brevis smiled.

And pay for the call from his end?—that'd be the day. "Yeah? Why?—got a lead on some new clients?"

Brevis's eyes closed above his smile, as though he'd just been nicked by some pleasurable bullet. They opened again. "Working on it, Ny. Promise you—there's going to be something coming up that's going to make you very happy. You can count on it."

"Yeah, right." Brevis being a smoother, cooler version of Lenny Red; for this he gets ten percent? Axxter heard his own voice harden: "I'll nip aroundwall to Linear Fair and pick up some supplies I need. When they ask about getting paid, I'll tell 'em you said they could *count on it.* How's that?"

A tilt of the head, acknowledgment of witticism. But still smiling: "Just . . . be patient a little longer, Ny. You'll see."

You'll starve; for a moment he thought that Brevis had actually said that, until he realized it had been a glitch on the line. Or in his own head, out too long on the vertical. You're starting to lose it, he warned himself.

"I'm trying." Axxter kept the hard edge in his voice. It was either that or start whining. "I really am. But I'm cutting it a little thin out here, you know. I'm down to the *bone,* man. If some money doesn't come in pretty soon, I could wind up defaulting on my Moon and Wire charges." The words emerged from his mouth like all the words before them; in his throat a thick clot of nausea formed. Pure fear: both of Cylinder's communications agencies reacted unkindly to defaults. Fat chance of operating as a graffex, or anything else on the vertical, without them. "I *need* something to come through." Hard edge gone now, having scared himself.

Brevis's expression changed to one of woeful sympathy. "What can I say, Ny? None of your holdings have paid a dividend or a bonus in . . . quite a while." The smile again, manfully facing up to his client's imminent ruin.

"Yeah? And whose fault is that? Jesus *Christ.*" He heard his own voice screeching, worn brake on cable, still unable to stop himself. "Pull up my portfolio." A quadrant of his sight filled with words and numbers; in the center, Brevis's gaze shifted to the right, seeing the same data. "Just *look* at that crap." The back of Axxter's hand rapped against the wall, the metal ringing hollow. "That's why I'm going broke."

He could watch Brevis's eyes ticking down the list of holdings. "Ny . . . what can I say? These are your clients; like you're my client. I've got faith in *you;* you've got to have a little faith in them."

"These," said Axxter, "are the flakes you stuck me with. Warriors, my ass. Bunch of wankers, is what they are. They couldn't rape and pillage their way out of a plastic bag. I mean, of all the tribes in my whole portfolio—tribes that *you* set me up with—who do you think's doing the best? Huh?—out of this whole wimpy lot?"

Brevis shrugged. "I suppose . . . those young guys— what were they called?—Stylish Razorteeth; something like that. They were pretty hot, weren't they?"

"Mode of Razorback." Axxter shook his head. "*Were* hot—precisely. *Now* they get their butts kicked on a regular basis." The mention of the tribe's name grated on his nerves. He had done a full graffex workup for them, from the wall out, all the combat visuals and PR regalia that a brand-new military tribe required. A solid month's work, without even any upfront money for it—Brevis had sold him so hard on the new tribe's prospects that he'd swal-

14 ■ ■ ■

lowed this major inroad into his operating capital. Receiving for his labors a good-sized chunk of the Razorbacks' initial issuance of stock. *Preferred* stock, he reminded himself. He'd get his share of whatever loot, ransoms, or other spoils the tribe brought in right at the initial divvying-up, zipped straight into his bank account. A cut of the gross; that was always the condition attached to one of these start-up deals, why the attraction for freelancers— not just graffices like him, but the whole panopoly of caterers, campfollowers, tacticians, everything a military tribe needed to operate on Cylinder's vertical wall. Attractive enough for freelancers still on the hustle—*like me,* thought Axxter. Hungry for those high returns on the investment of time and labor. Blood and sweat—

"I really *worked* for those suckers." He muttered his thoughts aloud.

"I know you did, Ny." Endless meters of sympathy from Brevis. Part of his job. "First-class work. Terrifying stuff; just *terrifying* as hell."

"Yeah, right; terrifying." His gloom deepened. "All they had to do was go out and terrify somebody with it. You know, get out there and do their *job.* Act like goddamn warriors. But did they? Tell me—did they?"

"That's not quite fair, Ny. Their first couple of sorties went pretty well, all in all. For new guys. You made money off them, remember? You didn't mind that so awfully much, now did you?" A waggling finger, admonishing a sulky child.

Axxter grunted. "About enough to sneeze on. And how've they done since then, huh? Eaten their shorts. Give me Stats. What's the ranking on Razorback, Mode of."

After a moment's search came the response: THAT TRIBE IS UNRANKED AT THIS TIME. UNDER THRESHOLD

■ ■ ■ 15

LEVEL FOR TRADING; INITIAL OFFERING PERIOD
ELAPSED.

"Combat, historical quickscan, same tribe."

PRECEDING SIX MONTHS FROM PRESENT DATE: THREE
ENGAGEMENTS; TWO CHALLENGE SKIRMISHES, ONE
RAID. LOST BOTH SKIRMISHES, HEAVY EMBARRASSMENT
DUE TO FLEEING WALL SECTOR DURING WIRE SYNDI-
CATE'S "UP & COMING" BROADCAST, LEADING TO DUMP
OF HOLDINGS BY ALL SPECULATORS, THUS LOSS OF
BOARD RANKING. RAID INCONCLUSIVE DUE TO MAP ER-
ROR BASED ON INADEQUATE INFO: HIT UNOCCUPIED
SECTOR. MORE DETAIL OR FURTHER BACK?

"Christ, no," said Axxter.

"Come on, Ny." Brevis lifted his hands, pleading. "I
admit they've had some bad luck. They'll pull out of it."

Axxter glared at the image. "I doubt it. And they're the
best of the lot I'm stuck with. What about Straight-Line
Ravage? Huh? What happened to them?"

Brevis winced. "Please . . ."

They'd gone over this before, more than once, but like
probing a broken tooth, he couldn't leave it alone. The
particular black hole disaster of his freelancer portfolio.
All that work down the drain . . . the thought of it still
made him ache with fury. "Right off the board." Dis-
tantly, he heard Brevis's weary sigh. "Right off the goddamn board."

Straight-Line Ravage had suffered the final ignominy,
the ultimate possible for a military tribe. Too inept to
even manage getting killed in a challenge with another
tribe, unable to scrape together enough credit to feed
themselves, they had sold themselves *en masse* on a long-
term labor contract. Axxter supposed they were making
plastic-extruded widgets in some grim horizontal sector
factory at this very moment.

"Right off the board." He said it wonderingly this time,

16 ■ ■ ■

anger having ebbed away. Right off the board and off the exterior of Cylinder itself, wiped from the vertical wall as if they had never existed, had never swayed on the transit lines or hung in their thin bivvy slings, boasting to each other and the open air of all the blood and havoc they were about to wreak on the great building's unsuspecting inhabitants. Beating their fists on the warror decs that Axxter had worked into their armor and into the very skin over their pectoral muscles, along the swollen biceps. When he had sent the coded animating signal to the Small Moon and the appropriate response had been narrowcast back to the Ravage camp, the decs had writhed through their simple five-second cycle and the tribesmen had howled with an equally simple joy. Well, that's over; Axxter could almost taste the sourness of the thought. Ain't no joy in working the lever and pushing the button, putting out those widgets. You proud warriors. He managed to feel sorry for them, beyond the economic loss to himself, their selling out having left him and the other freelancers with shares in an enterprise gone bust. Sorry, and a certain chilling kinship.

Vertical was tough. Anybody could fall off the wall. One way or another; either the big step, right down into the cloud barrier below, or . . . back the other way, inwall to the horizontal. Where some fuming widget machine waited for him as well.

"Ny . . ." Brevis's voice slid under his bleak meditation. "Can we just . . . *put* the Ravage thing behind us? And . . . look ahead?"

"'Look ahead'—Jesus." Axxter turned his gaze toward the sky, managing not even to see it. "I'm looking ahead to starving out here."

"Hey—it's not any easier for *me,* Ny." Finally, Brevis's lubricated armor had worn through. His voice rose in pitch. "I got operating costs, too, you know. *You're* getting nothing? Fine—I'm getting ten percent of that nothing. My other clients—" Bitter now. "What they bring in isn't paying the comm charges, either. We're *all* hurting, Ny. Can I help it if that Ravage bunch, and all these others, they turned out to be such wimps? They *looked* good, man; I had scouting reports up the *ass* on those guys. At the level we're operating at, we can't plug into some sure-bet outfit. We have to go with the chancy ones."

"Yeah, yeah, I know." He rubbed his brow, feeling a twinge of guilt. I don't even know why I called him up, except to just bitch and whine. Which doesn't come free, idiot. "I don't have to put up with this freelance bullshit. I could've gone to work for DeathPix. They said they wanted me." His oldest whine of all, invariably dredged up when he was feeling sorry for himself. The big topside corporation, which handled not only all the graffex work for the Grievous Amalgam, the ruling tribe of Cylinder, but also for the Havoc Mass, their main rivals for power— he had passed their hiring exam, been offered an entry-level job with them . . . and had turned it down. So he could go freelance. So bitch about it, asshole.

"Ny . . . you want to call it quits . . . you want to see if the DeathPix job's still open . . . I'll understand." Brevis had recovered his smooth, soft ease again. "I don't want to lose you, but . . . I'll understand. I think you could make it, if you could just see your way to hanging on a little bit longer. But if you don't think you can . . . Hey. It's all right. I know it's tough out there."

You slimebag. Axxter knew he was being conned, his own buttons being pushed. But a *good* con; he knew that as well. Tying right into his own thoughts on the matter. Giving up on the vertical—giving up the whole freelancer shtick, starvation and all—that's giving up everything I dreamed of. Dreaming while watching the tape of the dead angel, over and over. Dreaming and waiting.

18 ▪ ▪ ▪

"All you need is the one break, Ny." Brevis's soothing patter went on. "Just the one. Your stuff's *good;* you've really got it."

"You really think so—don't you." He lifted his eyes hopefully, bringing the agent's image back onto the dead-film. This, he knew, was why he'd called him. Just to get that little pump of life into his heart again.

"You got it, man." So sincere; radiant with emotion. "All it takes is one tribe with your designs on them; they pull off some heavy shit, get some attention, some good line coverage, and then *you* are the hot number in the graffex biz. All you need's the exposure. With your stuff—I guarantee it, Ny. When it happens, we'll have clients all the way to the top calling us up. You'll write your own ticket after that. You just gotta hang in there a little longer."

Foolish hope. And vain desires, thought Axxter. He could still taste them, welling up under his tongue. Well, shit—if you can still be jerked around by a two-bit lube artist like Brevis . . . then maybe it really is all possible. Or at least you still think it is.

"All right." He nodded, Brevis's face sliding up and down his vision. "I didn't say I was giving up. I'm not at that point yet. I just wanted you to know what my situation is out here, that's all."

Brevis's smile tightened at the corners, wink above, a signal acknowledging this gritty attitude. "I knew you wouldn't crap out. You got what it takes."

"Yeah, yeah . . . you bet." He glanced at the corner of his vision where the charge for the pointless call racked up, and sighed. "Look, I'll give you a ring after I get hold of this new bunch—what're they called—"

"Rowdiness Combine. They look hot, Ny; I wouldn't bullshit you about this. But they got real blood-lust. They just may be the ones who're gonna do it for us."

■ ■ ■ 19

Simmer down, for Christ's sake. "We'll see about that. Catch you later." Flick to DISCONNECT, letting the Wire Syndicate take its summed-up bite out of his bank account.

The sun had lifted higher over the cloud barrier, moving along the course of the morningside's day. Full light now, no longer filtered red. Time to get moving on his own small segment of the building's circumference.

For a moment he considered watching again the tape of the mating angels. No—don't. Unnecessary, anyway; he could still see them, as if some brighter radiation had burned them into the empty sky, or his own eyes.

2

Methodically, with elaborate care, Axxter broke
down his small camp. Taking more pains
than necessary; I know, he told himself once more, as he
watched his hands going through routine. Mind working
on two levels about the subject. On top, right up against
curve of skull, the old subvocal litany: *Careful; have to be
careful; weren't born out here like some of them; until you
get your wall-legs, better, smarter to be careful still.* But
underneath, not even words: fear, not caution, slowed his
movements. As narrow and cramped as the confines of
the bivouac sling were, it was at least something underneath him, a bowed floor of reinforced canvas and plastic
beneath his knees as he knelt, or shoulder and hip when
he slept, and the empty air beneath. That was as safe, he
knew, as you got on the vertical. He could have stayed in
the sling forever, hanging on the wall. Money, the lack of
it, compelled otherwise.

Eventually everything—not much—was packed into two panniers, and a larger amorphous bundle. He closed his eyes for a moment, gathering strength, then stood up, the sling's fabric stretching beneath his feet. He whistled for his motorcycle.

For close to a minute, as he leaned against the building's wall, holding onto a transit cable for balance, he heard nothing, no answering roar of the engine as the motorcycle came wheeling back to his summons. Thin green on this sector of the wall; something to do with Cylinder's weather pattern, Axxter figured. The motorcycle would have to have grazed for some distance to have filled its tank. Just as he was about to whistle again, he heard the rasp of its motor, growing louder as it approached.

Over the building's vertical curve, due rightaround from where he stood in the bivouac sling, the headlight and handlebars of a Norton Interstate 850 first appeared, then the spoked front wheel and the rest of the machine behind. Bolted to the motorcycle's left side—the uppermost side now, as the machine moved perpendicular to the metal wall—the classic blunt-nosed shape of a Watsonian Monza sidecar came with the motorcycle, its wheel the parallel third of the whole assemblage. A typical freelancer's rolling stock; he had eyeballed it for so long back on the horizontal, when he'd been saving up his grubstake, that he'd memorized every bolt before he'd ever actually wrapped his fist around the black throttle grip. Even now, after this long out on the vertical, the sight of the riderless motorcycle heading toward him—accelerating as if impelled by love, though he knew it had only taken a visual lock on his position—affected him, rolled on a sympathetic throttle inside his chest. A notion of freedom, as much so as angels, living or dead.

The Norton swerved as it approached, circling below the sling and then turning upwall by one of the sling's an-

22 ■ ■ ■

chor points so that the sidecar was within easy reach. It halted there, headlight pointing toward Cylinder's far-distant toplevel, engine idling with a throaty murmur. Axxter gripped the ridge of the sidecar's hatch and pulled himself up to see the gauges between the handlebars. The perfect resemblance to a real, ancient 850 Interstate ended beneath the instruments' circular glass: a row of LCD readouts indicated the state of the machine's internal processes. That, and the thin black pithon cords that had whipped out of the hubs of the spoked wheels as the Norton sped across the building's surface, the triangular heads at the ends of the lines striking anchor points on the transit cables and the pitted metal surface of the wall beneath them, holding and then releasing when each line reached full extension; snapping back into the hub and darting out again . . . Like nests of hyperactive snakes, it had seemed to Axxter, the first time he had seen, in some kiddie TV show, a freelancer rig scooting, gravity-defying, along Cylinder's exterior.

Nearly a full tank. He pushed himself back from the gauges. All through the morningside's night, while the sun had been on the other side of the building, while Axxter had slept, the Norton, with a machine's faithfulness, had scoured the nearby sections of wall, scraping up with its extended butterfly proboscis the thin green fur and overlapping plates of lichen. From somewhere in the motorcycle's ovoid tank came the soft gurgle and hiss of conversion, organic matter into fuel. In his gear, Axxter had a kit for rendering the green into something edible, or at least nutritious. The remembered taste of the distilled slime made him shudder. If death itself had a taste, he thought, it would be something like that. One more reason for praying that some more money came in before his current stock of supplies ran out.

As he began loading his gear from the sling into the

sidecar, strapping everything into place with bungee cords, he heard a sound rising over the Norton's idle. Another engine, barking and rasping, and, up in treble, the singing of pithon lines zipping around transit cables. Axxter looked over the edge of the sling, and saw another freelancer heading upwall toward him.

"Hey! Sonofa*bitch!*" A shout and gloved hand waving above the approaching motorcycle's handlebars. "How ya doin', Ny?"

He had thought he recognized the clatter of her ill-tuned Indian replica. "Guyer—where'd the hell you come from?"

She pulled the Indian and sidecar rig up alongside the sling's other anchor. The words GUYER GIMBLE—I DELIVER were painted on the sidecar's flank; on the motorcycle's tank, a three-quarter profile of her when younger, and the most in-demand campfollower anywhere on Cylinder's surface. Or at least the known morningside of the building. The years since then had pared her face down to a more intimidating sexuality, as if leaning into the wind of her full-throttle passage had stripped away all but the most necessary flesh. One knot loosened at the base of Axxter's gut while another tightened with a pleasurable fear.

Guyer leaned away from the Indian's handlebars, her silver hair thus coursing straight back from her knifelike profile. "Here and there." She smiled sideways at him. "Just making my rounds. You trying to run down that Rowdiness bunch?"

"Yeah—you seen them?"

"'Bout a week ago." Her eyes shifted, following some interior calculation. "Yeah, that's right. They should still be downwall from here." One hand waved toward that quadrant. "Gonna try and sign 'em up?"

Axxter shrugged. "What else?" Guyer had inside

24 ■ ■ ■

sources, having become well-known for her key position on the freelancers' gossip net. Though you wouldn't need that, he thought, to figure out what I'm doing in these parts. "What'd you think of them?"

The smile extended, turned upside-down by her position. "Nice boys. Hey—at this stage, who can tell? They all talk tough when they're starting out. Gonna set the whole building on fire." She leaned forward, spreading her hands on the motorcycle's tank. "They're worth a shot—I picked up a couple shares of their initial offering, and an option for a block later."

That explained her feline aura of self-satisfaction. A woman who enjoyed her business. And the Rowdiness bunch wasn't a week's travel away from here—Axxter looked into her hooded eyes and got a confirm. She'd serviced them yesterday; he could almost smell it on her, not an odor but an echo of adrenaline charges going off under her practiced hands. The itch moved across his shoulders, to get his Norton loaded up, to track down the tribe for his own business proposition. Maybe they're just hours from here; they could be.

Another impulse sparked against the first. "Hey, Guyer—you want to see something neat?"

She swung one leg over the Indian's tank and ambled toward him. The easy grace of a long-time freelancer, born on the vertical: a twinge of disorientation nausea clenched Axxter's stomach as he watched her walk, perpendicular to the wall, the pithons from her boots catching and releasing with each stride, whip lines from just below her knees to the metal surface. Under her skin the muscles tightened to keep her straight as a flag in wind.

He dug the camera out of the sidecar and brought up from his archive the tape he'd shot that morning. He watched her screening it in the camera's tiny viewfinder; kneeling above him, her hair just tracing across his own cheek—in the center of her pupils the figures twined and drifted across two small skies.

"'S nice." She straightened, away from the edge of the sling, and smiled at him.

His hands fumbled with the camera, the power LEDs winking out. He didn't know why he had wanted to show the tape of the mating angels to Guyer. Maybe I was hoping for something. The usual action, I suppose. A repeat of his initial encounter with her, when he'd first been making slow and nervous progress across Cylinder's exterior, a few kilometers downwall from his exit point. It was well known that Guyer had long ago built up her portfolio to the point of comfortable retirement; she did what she wanted now, including such nonmercantile acts of initiation. A welcome to the vertical.

The memory of it faded as Axxter gazed at the dead camera. The replay of the angels, reflected in the woman's eyes, stilled that ordinary desire. He turned away from her, stowing the camera back in the sidecar's hatch.

Guyer could read some tendon's semaphore in the back of his neck. He felt the warm sympathy of her regard, even before her hand stroked the hinge at the top of his spine. She hadn't gotten to the toplevel of her field without these more tender abilities. How many warriors had lain in those thin arms, listening to the percolation of blood beneath her minimal breasts, watching the stars in their slow revolve around the building?—more than I could guess, thought Axxter.

"Guess where I've been." Distracting him. "Over at the Fair."

"Yeah? Which one?" Not that it mattered; the prospect of hot rumors from either Linear Fair, the twin rivers of commerce and gossip running down the sides of the building, was sufficiently enticing. The Fairs' merchants, sitting

26 ■ ■ ■

on the demarcation lines between the known world and all the mysterious eveningside, heard everything.

Guyer signaled with a tilt of her head. "The Left." The gesture went to her own right, perched upside down as she was. "Heard all kinds of good stuff."

"Like what?" Angels forgotten for the moment.

She leaned down, closer to him. "The Havoc Mass." Her voice a whisper, for the sheer pleasure of conspiracy; they were alone on the barren sector wall. "They're putting on a big recruiting push. For the grand alliance they're building up. Signing up all sorts of little tribes, two-man outfits, battalions, everything. Cutting deals all over the place, to get 'em signed on. You talk to this Rowdiness bunch when you finally run 'em down: betcha even they've been approached." She rocked back on her haunches, butt in the web of her boots' pithons. "The Mass—" Her eyes narrowed, as though she was savoring the word. "They're making their move. At last."

The sudden fervor in her voice unnerved him. What's it matter to her?—all that heavy squabbling for control of Cylinder's toplevel seemed distant in more ways than one to Axxter. Like the passage of the sun over the apex of the building, casting the morningside into deep shade and then deeper night, when the cloud barrier below the eveningside swallowed up all light. Not much you could do about it—you lived within the constraints of light and dark like everyone else on the vertical exterior. If the Havoc Mass wanted to square off against the Grievous Amalgam, who had been squatting on top of Cylinder since long before Axxter, or Guyer, had been born—hey, let 'em, he figured. Cynical enough to believe that it wouldn't make a rat's ass difference to him personally, yet the sight of Guyer with her eyes closed, dreaming of some golden future, made him wonder.

■ ■ ■ 27

"Yeah, well—" He shrugged. "Best of luck to 'em, I guess."

She looked at him with a sad reproof. "You really have to care more about it than that, Ny. It's important."

The maternal tone irritated him. "What's important to me is hustling up some business, getting some real earners into my portfolio. Right? I'm gonna be out here on the wall doing that, no matter what happens between Grievous and Havoc up on top. They don't mean shit to me, sweetheart."

Guyer said something back to him, but he didn't hear it, overridden by the shout of his own thoughts. *Important to me.* Money, always money. The Havoc Mass had plenty of it, being the roughest and toughest military tribe currently operating, and good politicians with overlapping layers of alliances and treaties among all the other hardcase tribes. Collective force pressing up against the Grievous Amalgam—generations away from being the military tribe they had started out as. Now into the sheer Byzantry of power, raking the big licence fees in from the toplevel agencies such as Ask & Receive, the Wire Syndicate and the Small Moon Consortium. Mucho bucks there. A throughflow, to pay for the legions of mercenaries, the diplomatic and intelligence corps, all the machinery to keep the Amalgam court, in all its glittering pathology, right up where it had been for so long. The meaning-heavy phrase *mucho bucks* circled around in his thoughts again. If I could just squeeze out a few dimes of it—then I'd be happy. Christ, I don't want it all. Or much. Just enough. And dimes were dimes, no matter who ate the dollars.

Guyer's voice broke in. "So that's why I did it."

"Did what?"

She regarded his blinking, up from fog, and sighed. "Cashed in all my Amalgam holdings, the preferred, the

28 ■ ■ ■

options, every single blue chip—and sank it into the Mass."

"Jeez." Heard twice, and still unbelievable. She must *mean* it. Beyond mere faith—talking money now. One thing for her to dream of A Better Age, when those clean and hard-limbed warriors have kicked out the effete, sneaky politicos—Guyer being nuts, in a sweet way, he had decided long ago, with her still traveling and doing her business out in these godforsaken wastewall sectors. But for her to roll up her entire wad and bet in on that rosy prospect . . . Axxter shook his head, whistling his breath in through clenched teeth. Thought she was smarter than that. Just never know about people.

"Gotta split. Catch you later."

He looked up to see her standing, perpendicular to the wall. From his crouch in the sling, he had to tilt his head back to meet her gaze. She turned and strode to her rig.

From back aboard the Indian, its headlight pointed straight up: "Give us a good-bye kiss, Ny." And the same indulgent smile as before.

He knew what she wanted, the kiss a pretext. She had seen him before, when he'd been a hundred percent new to vertical. Clinging white-knuckled, chest against the wall like a flattened spider, pithons taut from shoulder and hip. Pitied him, gave him something . . . Now she wants to see how I'm getting along with it. A little test. He swallowed against the pulse in his throat, and pulled himself up out of the sling.

In his kneecaps he felt the snap of his boots' pithons catching their holds on the wall as he stood up. Straight out, his shoulder to the cloud barrier far below. One line from his belt for balance, but that was all right; nothing uncool about that. Walk and don't think, he told himself. All there is to it. Pithons stretched as he lifted his foot, the leader lines releasing and whipping ahead for the next grip. All there is.

All there was. Axxter stood beside the Indian, pulse still high. But there. He regarded her narrow face for a moment before he bent down to kiss her.

He felt the brush of her lashes and the shift of her gaze. He leaned back and turned his head to see what it was she saw.

One hand had locked onto the nearest transit cable, every tendon in his wrist drawn tight as the metal line. Holding on, shameless, against the fear of gravity.

Axxter looked back into Guyer's smile. The Indian's motor coughed as she twisted the throttle.

"Take care, Ny." A wink. "See ya again sometime."

The engine's rasp came to his ear long after she had disappeared upwall by leftaround. On her ceaseless errands. He gripped the cable with both hands, no one to see him now, and pressed his burning cheek against the cool metal, only a little harder than the woman's face and kiss.

■
■

Just before breaking camp, he went back on-line, calling up Ask & Receive. The Small Moon, in its orbit around Cylinder, had finally appeared, a silver nail-paring coming around the building's leftedge. Cheaper to connect when only enough relay surface for audio signal; that was all he needed. He blinked on his transceiver.

"Update on previous request." His jawbone buzzed with the echo of his own voice. "Estimate of current position, Rowdiness Combine, military tribe. Scale reliability down to . . . oh . . . twenty-five percent." An old trick that he'd picked up from the more experienced freelancers. If you took a high enough reliability on initial location requests, seventy-five percent or higher, you could cheap

30 ■ ■ ■

out on the updates. You'd still get close enough to your target to do a physical scan of the sector. Though twenty-five, he knew, was pushing it.

The info agency ran through its location factors—previous sightings, speed of travel and direction, analysis of raiding strategies. Rowdiness hadn't reached the point—might never—of having a PR service advertising its whereabouts, recruitment points, the big-league stuff; otherwise he would've dinged them for the call and info.

At twenty-five percent reliability, it didn't take long. Axxter detected, or imagined, a condescending tone to the coordinates reeled out in his ear.

"All right." As if addressing the Norton, no one else on the empty wall. He pulled the transceiver lead free from his wrist, folded up the dish and stowed it in the sidecar. His boot pithons came free as he mounted onto the motorcycle, the seat line zipping around his waist. A moment of vertigo as he gripped the handlebars and looked straight down the building's long vertical fall. "Time to roll."

He didn't stop until the motorcycle's shadow stretched down Cylinder as far as he could see. Hours of traveling: sun right overhead, the leading edge sliced off by the building's top rim. Only a bit more pure light before the sun's zenith and the deepshade falling over the morningside. Whatever lay on the eveningside could come creeping out into the light then, on whatever unknown circuits might be pursued there. Axxter stood up on the pegs, easing the cramp in his butt, the vibration fatigue in both his thighs. The cloud barrier looked as far below as ever.

Making good time, he figured. The transit cable the bike had locked onto had run free and clear all the way down here. And farther: the cable, thick around as his head where the wheels grappled onto it, dwindled down to spider-silk before disappearing into the clouds. A few kilometers more—he gazed around, estimating his position—and he could steer the Norton off the cable, tacking left. Lateral travel, across the vertical cables, always slower. The Rowdiness bunch should be pretty close, though; might not find 'em before dark, but tomorrow I will.

He settled back down in the seat and gunned the engine. Satisfied with a day's travel, almost completed; the angels had proved a good omen, besides the cash into his account. A certain representation of freedom. That's why you became a freelancer. That, and starving to death. He let out the clutch and rolled again, picking up speed downwall.

Shadows on the wall. He spotted them, half a kilometer to the right of his own lengthening smear. All dimming; he glanced over his shoulder at the sun, three-quarters obscured by the top rim. He'd be on whatever threw the shadows before they were swallowed up by the advancing deepshade.

His heart sped up, as his fist rolled back on the Norton's throttle, when he spotted the jagged edges of metal curling up from the wall. A solid darkness lay inside, just visible past the ripped segments of wall.

This is a bad scene, Axxter. Just turn round and . . . *roll* away. His warning sounded inside his head as he halted the Norton at the edge of the torn zone. A section of wall, twisted and blackened, reached out into the sky, its sharpest point circling back on a line even with his head. It looked mean enough to rip open any angel that might chance to drift by.

Split on out of here. These War sites, cold and abandoned echoes of that ancient violence that had wracked the building, always spooked him. He hadn't known that there was one out here; some of these wastewall sectors

32 ■ ■ ■

had zero files on them, producing just question marks and a refund of your money when you queried Ask & Receive. Some people got off on them; the ancient battle sites nearest to the heavily populated horizontal sectors drew a certain number of tourists. Some people got off on anything. Axxter heard the wind whistling past the jagged point in the sky, and shivered. A papery, skeletal note a hungry bird might make. Fat chance of getting a good night's sleep, conducive to effective business negotiations, around here. Time to split. Go make your camp somewhere else, a long ways somewhere else.

He reached out and gripped the edge of the metal curling up alongside the Norton. The chill inside him died, fell away into a hole under his gut.

The metal was warm, hot at its core. The retained heat of the violence that had torn the wall open passed into his palm.

He jerked his hand back, the fright finally penetrating through his surprise. "Jee . . . zuss." No more than a whisper. When he breathed again, he smelt the trace of smoke drifting out of the darkness ringed by the ripped wall sections.

If they were still here—the ones (*and you know who,* he told himself) who had blown open the building's skin, and had put that sickening smell into the wind, sickening with the knowledge of what it was even if you had never smelled it before—if they're still here, thought Axxter, *inside there,* it's no use pouring on the throttle and splitting on out of here. Because *they* don't work that way. How far would he get before he felt the same heat that had charred and twisted the metal wall on his own back? Not far enough—Christ, he thought, sick with dismay. What happened to all that good luck?

Of course, they might not still be here. Watching him from inside the gaping hole, with their hard little eyes, or

■ ■ ■ 33

whatever they might have instead of eyes. In which case, by their absence, he would be allowed to scurry away with his deeply treasured little life.

In which case, also—the thought rose unbidden, an automatic mercantile reflex—you might as well see what's *in* there. *In* as in *information*. Which can be peddled; that's what being out here on the vertical does to you, thought Axxter, amazed at the track of his mind.

Greed beats fear anytime. Axxter slung one leg over the Norton's tank and let his boot pithons snap onto the wall's surface.

Cautiously—though he knew there was no point—he gripped the torn edge of the metal and peered around it. The heat inside the metal soaked through his jacket to the skin of his stomach. Lying on the curved shelf the wall segment formed, he could look across the gaping hole torn into the building. Or out of—the explosion, or whatever it had been, had come bursting from inside. That alone proved it hadn't been the work of any military tribe rampaging around on Cylinder's exterior, but something else.

Through the viewfinder, Axxter estimated the jag-rimmed hole at over a kilometer across, a gaping cavity in the building's side. Turning the camera to the interior, he taped the twisted girders of a horizontal flooring level jutting out. Farther inside, only blackness, the walls of the broken corridors blackened with smoke.

He reattached the camera to his belt, right behind where the gun's handle protruded. A lot of footage, more than he needed. If he was going to sell this—and there was no question of that; he needed all the cash into which other people's misfortunes might translate—it wouldn't be on the basis of aesthetic appeal. The thought of what had done this would be, as for him, just a little too much for people to bear. That thing that everybody's afraid of,

34 ■ ■ ■

back in the darkness, way inside the building—Axxter shivered. Maybe that's why I like it out here, one way or another. At least it's *out here*. Away from that. He craned his neck and looked back inside the charred hole.

Something looked at him. He felt it before he caught sight of it. A white face, right at the edge of what had been a floor. He lifted the camera and zoomed in on it.

He lost it in the viewfinder, panned across the black metal, and found it again. He felt no surprise, nausea more than fear.

Empty eye sockets gazed toward the camera. Flamescabbed remnants of another stuff, the odor the outside winds hadn't yet cleansed from the atmosphere, blackened the withered neck and cage of ribs behind the skull. A hand, unmarked, clutched the broken edge of steel.

You too. The skull grinned as it spoke inside Axxter's head. *Watch out.* The smile licked out and relished the knot in the still-living gut. *Watch out, watch out, watch out . . .*

3

He'd fallen asleep among corpses. His fatigue had caught up with him, in the burnt-out sector. Dreaming of bad things; Axxter cradled his head on his wrist, back of hand against ashes and concrete. The familiar comfort of sleeping on a horizontal floor, no matter how torn where it ended in air. An even more comforting weight of metal on his chest, finger curled against sickle trigger. A space cleared among the grinning things, so they wouldn't whisper in his ear. But he was dreaming of them nonetheless.

"You too!" Dancing in a circle around him. "Even as we are! You too will be!" From their white faces and spider ribs the charred-tissue remnants flutter, black rags. (In sleep, Axxter moaned, clutched the gun tighter.) A skull squared off with a mortarboard cap turns to its audience, hand rattling like dice, the thin end of the pointer tapping on Axxter's breastbone. The lecture-hall lights come up, blinding him, standing naked on the podium.

The pointer flicks his nose, then draws a line down to his navel. "We see the front side." The skull's voice is Guyer's, oddly, but no longer kind. "The sun comes up on this side. We see this side, we *know* this side."

"We see! We are! Will be!" White grins swaying in the seats. (The crosshatched handle sweats in Axxter's grip.) "You too!"

"The sun goes up and over—" The pointer traces vertical between Axxter's eyes, bisects his forehead. He strains to hear the skull's words; some analogy here, but he can't make it out. "Then it's on the other side, the rear side. We *don't* see that side, we don't know what's on it— we don't even care!"

"Don't care!"

"But ah! The center! The core!" A flourish, and an overhead mirror lights up. Axxter rolls his eyes browward, to see what the pointer stabs at. And observes, with sick surprise, the reflection of a circular hole at the top of his own head. A flat hat of darkness that drops away into a hole parallel to his spine. The reflected light falls into it, with only a few glimmers as echoes. "*That* we know— *something* about!"

"We know!"

(Sleeps and draws a bead, but all the grinning things outside the dream stay prudently quiet.)

Skull, Guyer's voice: "Something we don't *want* to know! Something *inside*—where it's dark!"

"Dark! Dark! You too! Dark!"

(Twitches and mumbles, sweating.)

Dream-Axxter stares at the hole revealed in the mirror, the darkness running down inside him, the hollow core.

■ ■ ■ 37

The lecture goes on. "*Something*—it's where *they* are! The—"

He shouts at the voice, just a grin behind the glare of the lights, warning it to shut up. But it doesn't, he knows with dream-certainty that it won't. It's going to say *the name*.

Chorus: "You too! You too!"

". . . *the*—"

Then the gun is right there in the dream—you're never completely naked with one—and he squeezes it with both hands as the white face screams in triumph.

"—*the Dead Centers!*"

In the corridor of ruins the gunshot slapped against the wall and bounced back into Axxter's ears. He jerked awake, the gun in his hand scraping across the floor as he scrambled upright, just in time to hear the bullet's clanging echo against the wall.

"Shit!" He ducked instinctively, head down between shoulders. "God-*damn.*" The bullet clattered into silence somewhere along the corridor. Gun warmth seeped into his palm; he dropped it with a start, as if seeing the weapon for the first time. Looking down, he saw a burn mark across the front of his jacket. Prodding his ribs, he found nothing amiss. A mutter, as he shook his head: "Fuckin' dreams." Could've killed myself. What I get for falling asleep, down here, of all places. His hand still shook as he reached for the terminal jack he'd found when first looking about the place.

As soon as he waggled his finger in the socket, the words zipped into his vision.

WHERE YOU BEEN? GOT ASK & RECEIVE HOT FOR YOU.

"Oh—yeah. Right." He blinked away a bit more sleep muddle. Dark enough in the corridor, the exterior visible through the torn-open wall already fallen into deepshade, that he didn't need the deadfilm. From the time readout in the corner of his gaze, he made a quick calculation: he'd only been asleep and locked into the dream for a couple of minutes or so. He'd called Brevis—no way of avoiding him, since the info value of the find depended on giving the ruined zone's location—and Brevis must have called, as a good agent should, the numero-uno toplevel data agency. And sold it for a lot of money, Axxter hoped. "Put 'em through."

Ask & Receive's animated logo—hand with mouth in palm, then eye, then mouth again—came up on the terminal. Followed by a softly modulated female voice: "Please send location coordinates. Will credit to your account the sum of—" A male voice broke in, clipped and bored: "Two hundred dollars."

"What?" Axxter stared at the mouth, eye, mouth pattern.

The words looped in repeat. "Two hundred dollars."

"You must be joking."

The male voice came again, a real-time override. "The price was worked out by your agent, fella. You want to check with him—"

"You bet your ass I'm checking with him. *Hold* this sucker," Axxter instructed the line. "And get me Brevis."

His agent's face came up, one pacifying hand already stroking the air. "I know, I *know*—"

"Two *hundred*—what are you *doing* to me, for Christ's sake?"

Brevis's other hand rose, warding his client away from his throat. "That's all they'll pay, Ny. Believe me. They don't even want your tape, man. Somebody beat you to it."

"Somebody what?"

"Somebody else already got the info to Ask & Receive. And copped the initial report fee for it. Two hundred bucks is the standard payment for a confirming report from a second-on-the-scene. There isn't *any* money for anybody who comes after you, Ny."

"Two hundred bucks." Axxter gritted his teeth, bitter spit under his tongue. They're screwing me. First the angels tape, now this. He looked around, Brevis's face floating superimposed over the charred corpses, the walls bowed and blackened by explosion, the torn skin of Cylinder itself. He had climbed in and taped it all, greed circuits kicking in at the sight of so much destruction. You get paid—you're supposed to get paid—lots for info like this. The unprofitable corpses went on grinning at him.

"They're screwing me." Out loud. "There's no one else around here who could've reported it. I'm the only one out in these sectors." Except maybe Guyer Gimble, he noted to himself. And she would've told me if she'd spotted anything like this. "And the metal was still *hot*. From . . . whatever happened." Still reluctant to speak it, the name the skull had shouted. "Nobody else could've come across it before me. They're cheating me of the initial report fee."

"Hey." Another wave of Brevis's professional sympathy. "I know that. You know that. But what do you want to do, get a bad rep with Ask & Receive? You're gonna have to deal with these people long after this. They want to cheap out on you—just let it slide, Ny. You won't be able to get as much money from anyone else."

"They're screwing me." Axxter closed his eyes, but Brevis's face didn't go away. "Shit."

"Take the money, Ny."

The voice behind Ask & Receive's logo sounded smug when Axxter got back to him. "Two hundred dollars all right, then?"

"Yeah, sure." Your ass. He read out the coordinates for

the zone, and logged off. Not even bothering to check his account for the deposit of the fee.

It was a moment before his spirits rose again. "Not yet," he replied to the nearest corpse's grinning comment. "Soon enough, but not just yet." Hadn't been a total waste of a day. Two thousand for the mating angels, another two hundred—those fuckers—for coming across this place . . . Not bad; not really. "Puts me ahead of *you*." A fly in search of unscorched nourishment crawled over the white face.

The dream came back to him as he reached across the floor and retrieved the gun. I get it now. The spooky lecturer, the hole in the top of his own skull, the darkness running down inside. Everything except the point of it all. He stood up, the gun heavy in his jacket pocket, and started walking back toward the exterior, the deepshade lighter than the ruined interior. His boots, pithons nulled on the horizontal, raised little clouds of gray dust.

At the jagged floor edge, the welcoming corpse lay across his path, white face turned toward where he had spotted it in his camera's viewfinder. He stepped over it— bony hand reaching for his ankle, unable to grasp it—and looked back inside. He could still smell the burnt odor.

That's what happens. Stupid shits—gave your lives for me, and all I got out of it was two hundred bucks. The people who had lived in this horizontal sector—bumpkins, this far from toplevel; machine tenders—had made their little deal with the Dead Centers—the name finally spoken inside Axxter's head, the dream skull having broken the ice—and had made their final payment for it. That's what happens. Even if you don't think it's going to happen to you.

He wondered what had made them decide to do it. How long they had thought about it, talking during their

■ ■ ■ 41

lunch breaks at the widget factory, first *sotto voce*, then right out loud when everybody in the sector had been in on it. What had the Dead Centers said to them—the blandishments of things you've never seen, have only wondered about, moving in their secret ways in the great darkness at the building's core and in your bad dreams. The whispering voices that had come through the thick, sealed walls way far inside; maybe a signal override on any Wire Syndicate transmissions coming in, just a crawl of words across the bottom of their terminals; maybe little rolled notes floating up in their toilet bowls, spidery handwriting, smeared sticky ink . . .

You're so wise and good, dear people. The whispers through the wall. *So clever and smart. Yet oppressed by those old lies, slanders against those who would befriend you. Let us come to you, and we'll give you . . . everything . . . everything . . .*

Everything, thought Axxter, looking down to where the scorched walls merged with the dark. What would that include? Who knows . . . all sorts of elaborate pre-War high-tech, no doubt. The Dead Centers were supposed to have inherited all of that stuff. Wonders upon wonders, hidden away in the building's core. Maybe it had even been watching that old Opt Cooder tape, of the dead gas angel tangled in the exterior transit cable, that had worked away on the poor horizontal suckers' imaginations. Common belief that the angels were the remnant of some military genetic technology, bred for some now-unfathomable strategic use. Forgotten the same as everything else connected with that ancient event. Maybe the Dead Centers themselves were what was left of one of the warring factions. Maybe the War itself . . . some effect of the other guys' weapons, or their own . . . had *changed* them . . . left them crouching in the dark at the building's

42 ■ ■ ■

core . . . whispering to those who could still stand the light . . .

Just let us come to you. Why should you let those ones above you push you around, cheat you of all you so richly deserve? We'll help you . . . just let us come to you . . .

A shiver ran under Axxter's skin. Fuckin' spooked myself. The image came of the sector's inhabitants, when they'd had flesh over their grins, drawing back the heavy bolts, cutting through the heavy steel plates, boring a hole through whatever stood between them and the darkness at Cylinder's core . . . their minds made up after a unanimous vote at the sector meeting . . . or just made up, without a word spoken, silent greed flashing round from eye to eye—

They'd had a big surprise then. Wonder how long they had to think, *Not such a great idea, after all. Not too cool.*

At least they got to satisfy their curiosity. About what the Dead Centers even *looked* like. Toads with jewels in their foreheads, or nothing but shining rods of light, or small golden-haired children with dead eyes—the scary stories of childhood romped behind Axxter's eyes. At least I listened to those tales; these poor suckers must not've. And look what they got.

Axxter's gaze came back to the burnt zone, the smell in his nostrils. He turned toward the jagged edge of metal curling beside him, grasped it, and hoisted himself back out onto the vertical.

■
■

Deepshade to night. Axxter made camp as far away from the ruins zone as he could get before dark set in. Even at a distance of several kilometers, the torn metal remained visible, a rim of jagged teeth biting at the stars. Other than that, a peaceful scene, as he lay in the securely anchored bivouac, hands behind head, rehydrated food inching warm through his gut. The Norton grazed a few meters away, scraping up the wall's vegetation with its extruded proboscis. *My cup runneth over, or at least closer to the rim*—Axxter scratched his stomach in deep meditation. *Weird day; small profits, smaller than I deserved, but still—profits.* A section of his lower intestine gurgled assent, echoing the noises from the motorcycle's conversion tank.

Overhead, out from the wall, a circle of dark silver: the Small Moon rounding the building, catching only trace light from the toplevel and the thin ribbons of the Linear Fairs' perpetual activity. He'd kept the transceiver on, angling his head to catch the weak bounce of a free-access station. Ancient music—the Liebeslieder Waltzes, somebody (-thing?) called Tampa Red's "She Don't Know My Mind, Part Two"—seeped up the wire to his finger and then inside to his ear. Interspersed with commericals—enlistment bonuses from the Havoc Mass (made him think of Guyer's surprising faith), new stuff on-line to buy and watch (maybe the mating angels were already in the catalog)—all of which he ignored. Or tried to; the image of the figures in the bright sky kept seeping into his thoughts.

"Well, I looked in the window, and this is what I saw—"

Axxter ignored the barely human voice vibrating at the hinge of his jaw. He reached over and picked up the camera—after this morning's lucky break, he had kept it handy—and cradled it against his chest. As if the image-data locked inside his archive were real blood and flesh. Magnified close enough to touch.

"—a man, on his hands and knees, doing . . . doing the cootie . . . cootie-cootie kuh-rawl."

Well, shoot . . . *made money today, didn't I? Deserve some kind of treat for that. That's how you program yourself for more of that kind of thing.* That five-year-old kid

44 ■ ■ ■

at the center of your brain . . . Axxter didn't know if he believed that sort of thing or not. Willing to let it slide, in the process of cajoling himself. Already knowing what he wanted. He shifted uncomfortably, the sling's confines suddenly tight. Switched off the free-access, fearing something even worse than prehistoric Tampa Red.

The decision had been made by the raising of his bank account, intersected by the length of time he'd been out wandering on the wall. Two variables evoking a programmed response, his brain along for the ride. For a moment, the sheer predictability of his desires twinged disgust inside him. An idiot; he gazed at nothing, shaking his head. You're an idiot. Why do you ding yourself around with her, anyway?

Axxter brought his vision back to medium focus, looking at the territory surrounding the bivouac. Seemed safe enough for a little indulgence in hollow time; at least in a certain fatalistic way, he supposed. There was no safecage for rent in the vicinity, the usual, advisable amenity for a disembodied spree. But then there wasn't anyone else around in these sectors who might come across his body and do something weird with it. Unless Guyer had doubled back for some reason—an intriguing thought; he wondered what strange souvenir she might leave behind if she came across the sleeping, breathing meat part of him, his mind vacated elsewhere. Some pattern of bruises and muscles stretched into unusual postures, a trademark of hers written in the fatigue of tissues. Might be worth sticking around for, feigning being off in hollow time; I could dig it. If I knew it would happen that way. But it won't. Guyer's long gone, heading for toplevel inside rather than out of her own flesh. Pity.

Only the torn metal, black teeth against night, visible over the wall's curve, worried him. Not enough to change his mind, though. A faint radiation, heat ebbing from inside the ruin zone, tinged the jagged limits. Whatever had done *that* wouldn't be much fazed by a safecage with the tempting Axxter-morsel locked inside; it, or they would eat the whole goddamn thing, fry me up like a wienie on a spit. Of course, if *they*—the other two words had gone back down inside himself, not to be spoken—were going to come romping out, through the devastated stretch of their previous fun, to swarm out over the wall just to get him, it wouldn't matter much if he was off in hollow time, or sitting up all night, eyes wide and gun on knee, waiting for the sun to break over the cloud barrier. So his reasoning, what was left of it after his internal cajoling, dissolved, fatalism giving the desired result. Might as well do what I want, without worrying about it.

He blinked on his terminal, the glowing words bright against the night sky.

YES?

"Get me HoloDays."

YOU ARE THE VICTIM OF IGNOBLE PASSIONS.

"Jesus. Just do it, all right?" Fucker who programmed *that* . . . Shaking his head, Axxter leaned back against the building's wall. The transceiver bounced a signal off the Small Moon's metallic sheen, right to the toplevel.

The center of his vision brightened with the hollow-time agency's logo. In one corner, the Small Moon Consortium nibbled away at his bank account, the call charges a shade less than the Wire Syndicate's—for which Axxter was grateful.

A woman's voice came, incongruous, from the smiling clock face. "What may we do for you?" One of the clock's cartoon eyes winked cheerfully.

"Um . . ." The clock's manic stare unnerved him, almost as much as the female voice. They always know what you want; otherwise you wouldn't have called them in the first place. Ignoble passions. "I guess I need . . . about an hour. That's all."

"The second hour comes cheaper. By the time you get to the tenth hour, we're practically giving it away."

I bet. Axxter shook his head, the motion translating as simple no over the terminal. Listening to voices like the clock's was how you wound up with a zipped-out bank account. "Just an hour, please."

The voice stiffened, sensing cheapskate. "I don't suppose you want full sensory, then."

Another shake. "Just the minimum . . . gravity orientation, optic, midband aural . . . you know."

"Right. Like your last order." The person behind the clock face had pulled his number. "If that's how you like it . . ."

. . . *how much fun can it be.* Axxter weathered the sneer. "That's how I like it."

"Guarded line?"

He could tell what answer the voice expected. "No; bare line." Screw it; didn't have any trouble with it last time. Why would ghosts be interested in his comings and goings over the building's wires? When the voice asked, he gave the horizontal sector he wanted.

Another programmed wink from the clock face as his order went through.

"Transmission set." (Inside his head, he heard the bored voice say *There you go, sport. Enjoy yourself, Diamond Jim.*) "Signal when ready. Your hour starts at the other end."

The last bit was another comment on his spending habits. Axxter ignored it, settling into a comfortable position in the bivouac sling. Where, after lying for an hour without moving, he wouldn't come back with a stiff spine and a tingling-numb leg. With a wadded-up shirt for a pillow

■ ■ ■ 47

under his head, he looked up; past the clock face, the Small Moon glowed silver. From the corner of his eye, he glanced over to the ruin zone's jagged outline. What the fuck—too late to worry about it now. "Go," he told the clock.

Walking, and he didn't feel cold. The exterior's winds no longer seeped through his clothing. On his skin, no warmth or chill; he supposed, as he had in his other hollow times, that he'd have to hold flame or ice to his arm to feel any temperature at all. At this low-resolution, he couldn't even feel his boots' impact, hear the ring of each step on the familiar corridor's floor. Back here on the horizontal; outside, somewhere far downwall on Cylinder's stark vertical, his vacated body rocked in the bivouac sling. *Waiting for me to finish all my little business.* He—or the carrier-image HoloDays had given him—scanned the numbers on each door he passed. Optic input not too bad, fairly crisp with only a little filtered stair-stepping at the edges of shadows and where the walls met. *At least they got me on the right level. Be there in a minute or two;* he wondered what she'd say. The same as last time—more of the same, actually, just continued; he remembered now how he'd pulled the plug and zipped back to his real body out on the cold vertical, scourged there by the whip of her tongue. *Maybe it'll be different this time; Christ, I hope so.* The numbers on the doors were mounting up to the one for which he was heading. *She's not always like that. Thank God.*

"You stupid shit."

"Christ, and ugly, too. Look at him."

The two voices, and the barking laughter that followed, sounded right at his ear, loud enough for him to flinch in reflex. The corridor bounced and wavered until the optic feed settled. Then he saw the grinning faces, edges sharper than the walls shimmering behind them.

48 ■ ■ ■

They looked like depraved children. As if—Axxter's heart sank under their leering gaze—as if they'd gotten an early start on every adult vice and sin. And their baby faces had never grown up, but stayed vapid, silly, and knowing.

"Boo-gitty boo." One of the faces grinned wider, floating toward him. A wispy shadow, dwindled torso and arms, trailed behind. "Whereya going? Whatcha doing?"

Shit. Axxter batted at the face. Should've asked for a guarded line. Pushing my luck—just because I got away without picking up any ghosts the last time . . . "Beat it." The back of his hand sailed into the idiot smile. "Get out of here."

"Awww . . . don't wanna play?" The ghost face, leprous freckles spattering the pug nose, had enveloped Axxter's hand. A wet-flannel tongue rolled up his wrist. "Come on. Play with us."

"Jee-*zuss*." He couldn't shake the face off his carrier-image. He waved it back and forth, the round eyes rolling. "Get the fuck away from me."

"Your ass. Ass, ass, ass." The other line-ghost, a face still on the wall, crossed its eyes and sneered. "Come on, let's go. He's no fun." The image flickered, bands of nothing running across the fat cheeks.

"No." The smile gummed around Axxter's wrist. "Not done." Looking up delightedly at him: "Play. Play, play, *play*."

The corridor wall was blank, the second ghost having gone to look for other amusements elsewhere on the building's wires. Axxter started walking again. "I'm not playing with you. I'm ignoring you." That was all he could do, short of terminating the call. And I've already paid for the hollow time.

"Yaah, sucks." His hand reemerged as the ghost slithered upward. It wrapped into a cylinder around his fore-

■ ■ ■ 49

arm, substituting itself for that portion of the carrier-image. The elongated mouth opened, revealing the inside of his arm to be now full of glistening teeth. I should just unplug and go back out on the wall—foreboding seized him as to how the rest of the call would go.

"Eeee!" shrilled the ghost face when he raised his hand to the door. Axxter hastily lowered the afflicted arm and knocked with his other hand.

Maybe she's not at home—then what's the point, ass-hole? You jerk. He couldn't help hoping, though. His heart sank as he heard steps approaching on the other side of the door.

"Hello, Ree." Forcing a smile. "It's me."

The door opened wider. She leaned forward, peering at the carrier-image until the low-resolution came into focus for her. "Oh, Christ." A sigh dragged her shoulders down. "Ny—what the hell are you doing here?"

"Hey. I just came by to see you. That's all." He real-ized that he had spread his arms out, slack crucifix, and that the ghost was leering and rolling its eyes at Ree. "Sorry." He tucked the arm and face back behind him-self. "It glommed onto me on my way here."

"What did?" Her squint became even more pain-filled, his mere presence, even in this diminished form, the cause. "Christ, I hate it when you show up all fuzzy like this. You were bad enough before."

The ghost's sawtooth voice came up his spine. "She can't see me, turkey. I'm on your sensory feedback loop, not the output to real. Hee hee."

"Ny—look at me." Ree leaned against the doorway, her broad shoulders blocking any possible entry by the carrier-image. "Where . . . are . . . you. Okay? Just tell me that. Where are you right now?"

He had to think about it for a moment, to recall the exact coordinates. The ghost face goggled down at him as

50 ■ ■ ■

he ran his fingers through his indistinct hair, dimly sensed. "Uh—remember where I called from the last time? There's that big exit site about fifty kilometers from the lefthand Linear Fair? You know? Anyway, first I was traveling straight downwall from there, then—"

"Shut up, Ny. Jesus Christ." Her coarse bronze hair tangled against the doorway as she shook her head, eyes closed. They opened to follow her hands rooting through the dangly pockets caught on the shelves of her hips, coming up with nothing but an empty cigarette pack, which she disgustedly threw into the corridor. It passed through Axxter's midsection and landed behind. "You're still out there on the fucking wall. That's where you are."

"Well . . . sure. Where else?" From the angle of his arm, the ghost regarded him, its smile gone, interest caught.

"Yeah, right. Where else." The bitter voice tugged down the corners of her mouth. "That's the whole problem with you, isn't it?"

"Hey! Tell this bitch where to go! Eat it, ya stupid broad!"

Axxter clamped a hand over his forearm, the goggling eyes leaking around his knuckles. "Come on, Ree . . . you *know*—"

"Damn straight I *know*." She turned straight toward him, her expanding anger filling the doorway's frame. If the carrier-image had a tissue's mass, Axxter knew, it would've been blown down the corridor by the pressure wave of her wrath. "We went through it all the *last* time you showed up like this."

He could hear, pitched over her voice, the line-ghost's shrill *Fuck you! Fuck you!,* his own hand glowing mottled red as the face's infantile passion seeped through. "Ree . . . please. Come on—"

Then it struck him. His head filled with light. The insubstantial body grafted onto his thoughts seemed to float equidistant from every corridor surface. "Fuck this," said Axxter. "And fuck you." (*Yeah! Yeah!* shouted the ghost.) For a moment the corridor, the door with Ree standing in it, all became insubstantial; he felt the narrow confines of the bivouac sling against his shoulders, his cramped muscles swelling with the pulse of his anger. Ree gaped at him as he continued to shout. "I spend all this money to come see you, and this is the crap you lay on me? Forget it. Just forget it. You—and all your goddamn fucking horizontal thought processes—you can just go fuck yourself." *(Eeee! Yeah!)* He swung his gaze away from the door, a dizzying sweep across the square-edged vectors. Even before the perspective sightlines settled down, he was striding away, the impact of his boots now loud enough to cross the hearing threshold. "See you in the funny pages, bitch." He shouted it ahead of himself, ahead of the carrier-image, and was gratified to see doorways all along the hallway snap fearfully shut.

"Way to go, ace! Yah! Yah!" The line ghost babbled happily.

"Shut up." He gritted his teeth—or tried to; the carrier-image fed back no corresponding pressure inside the skull.

The face swung in a short arc as Axxter strode on. "You really *told* her! It was great!" The rolling eyes filled with delight and admiration.

"Yeah—great." Never again. He shook the image's head. Absolutely promise yourself—no more of *this* shit.

"I can *get* her for you! Fix her little red wagon but *good!*" The face on Axxter's arm glowed, feverish in its excitement. "Come on—you and me—it'll be a gas!"

"Goddamn it. Get off me." He scrabbled at the face with the fingernails of his other hand. A pain signal traveled up the carrier-image's arm, triggered by the self-in-flicted violation.

"You're no fun." The face, sulky now, slid off and wavered in space. The grating voice called from behind him: "You stink, and your edges are all blurry . . . and . . . and . . ."

Alone with his own thoughts at last, and the anger still simmering in his guts. Or whatever's in that place when you're on hollow time; nothing, I guess. Nothing at all. Here or back in the flesh.

He looked up and saw himself.

A mirror, he thought at first. Right in the middle of the goddamn corridor. But different, he realized; as if it were made of some finer glass that had drawn the fuzzy low-resolution image into sharper focus, the outline razor-edged where it stood facing him. As he stared at it, the image turned its head, leaning a three-quarter profile toward him. Smiling; the centers of its eyes dark, nothing behind.

Ny— It lifted its hand toward him.

I— He heard the echo at his ear. The corridor filled with cold, and he felt afraid. "Okay! HoloDays!" He tilted his face up to the ceiling and shouted, all the while aware of the mirror-image's hand reaching on a line level with his chest. The odd notion struck him that the more solid image might be able to reach right inside his insub-stantial one, to pluck out some luminous fiber that was his heart. "That's it—terminate the call."

Don't go—

O— "Did you hear me?" An edge of panic filtered into his voice.

The corridor disappeared. On his back, lying in the sling out on the wall, he looked up at the agency's smiling

■ ■ ■ 53

clock centered in the terminal. He pulled himself upright, his spine unkinking with little stabs at each vertebra.

The clock face swam ahead of him, hanging in the dark night. A woman's voice, a different one, sounded. "We hope you enjoyed your time with us. And that we may again be of service to you in meeting all your recreational needs. Remember: absence may make hearts grow fonder, but with HoloDays—"

"Cut it." Axxter rubbed his brow; the time spent walking around in the carrier-image had left him hung over, as it had the last time and every time before.

Stiffly: "Will there be anything else?"

He gazed at the totaled charges in the corner of the terminal, and beyond them to the Small Moon in the distance off the building, relaying the signal from the transceiver. Away from the spooky mirror-image—whatever the hell *that* had been; more line-ghost shit, he supposed; but genuinely spookier—and back out here in his cheerless bivouac, the fear had dissipated. But not the anger; that remained, a dull rock under his breastbone.

That's a fuck of a lot to pay for no fun at all. As he watched, the total went up another few cents, for keeping the HoloDays agency waiting on the line. A lot, just to have walked into more of that stupid Ree's shit.

He brooded a moment longer before speaking. "Yeah, there's something more." He rubbed his hands across his knees. "First off, I want a guarded line this time . . ."

■
■

Guyer looked up from the book in her hands when he appeared. "That's sweet." Smiling. "You came all this way."

HoloDays had put his image floating in space, a meter away from the wall. He reached out and grasped the edge of her sling. Somewhere farther away on the vertical

54 ■ ■ ■

metal, the gentle snuffling sounds of her grazing motorcycle came sharp and distinct to his synthed ear.

"I just wanted to see you again."

She kept her finger in the book to mark her place.
"Must've cost you."

He let the carrier-image shrug for him. "They put on a
surcharge for having Ask & Receive figure out your location. That's all."

The smile saddened. "I don't usually do anything except real flesh, Ny. Just one of my little preferences. If
that's what you came here for." She laid the book down
on a pillow at the sling's narrow end. "You know there's
places you could go for that; I could give you some recom-
mendations."

He shook his head. "No; it's not important. But . . . if
you wanted to give it a try . . . I paid for the complete
sensory package. With on-line enhancements. I could re-
spond very well."

Her eyes widened a bit. "Really? You must be feeling
pretty flush."

Tilting the image's head back, he looked up the dark
height of the building, all the way to the distant top, the
same black as the surrounding night. "No—" He looked
back at her. "No, I just don't give a shit."

"Well . . . in that case . . ." Guyer reached out and
brushed aside his shirt, a film of smoke over his skin. "It'll
cost you a little bit more still. Just on principle, you
know."

"Sure." He closed his eyes. Her hand felt like fire as it
moved down his ribs. "I understand everything."

■
■

He laid his head on her breast. Lying together in the
sling; she held him in her arms, a circle carefully held

■ ■ ■ 55

around the image. "I saw myself." He tilted his face to look up at her. "Before. Before I came here."

She made a motion to stroke his hair, the dark strands unreachable beneath her fingertips. "Really?"

"It was like a mirror. Only it moved when I didn't."

He could almost feel her stiffen against him. "Ny—" Her gaze was level and no longer playful. "If you see something like that again—and if it says anything to you—don't listen. Okay? Just don't. I know about these things."

The carrier-image lifted up onto its elbows. "What would it say to me? It's just a ghost on the line."

With one hand, she reached and pulled a blanket over herself. "Some ghosts are different from others." She smoothed the blanket across her legs. "They all want to *play*." A sour word when she spoke it. "Just in different ways sometimes."

He said nothing, watching her brush her tangled hair back from the side of her face.

"You'd better go, Ny. This is costing you money."

He nodded. "What do I owe you?"

"Forget it. I'll put it on your account; settle up the next time." She lay back against the pillow and shut her eyes.

Back in his own flesh, he called up his bank account. The night's little excursions had wiped out his small profits from selling the tapes to Ask & Receive, the angels and the spooky ruins. Under the silver glow of the Small Moon, he looked across Cylinder's wall to the jagged silhouettes of the ruin zone's torn metal. Solid black against black now, all the heat had died away.

4

A dead angel. Another, different dead angel; for a moment Axxter thought that the old Opt Cooder tape, the one he'd watched so often as a kid on the horizontal, had somehow slid from some interior archive and across his vision. He brought the Norton to a halt, and gazed down over the handlebars at the sight below. The confused overlay between taped past and bleeding present faded as the delicate corpse lay tangled against the transit cable on which his motorcycle's wheel had locked.

She—female; he saw one small breast distorted against the steel wall—lay unmoving, cradled by the deflated membrane behind her shoulders. The thin tissue no longer spheroid with the lifting gases, but now a gray shroud, with a tattered fringe sifted by the wind. Blackened: as Axxter watched, one ashy streamer tore free from the membrane's charred edges and fluttered twisting into the atmosphere. Different from Cooder's celebrated tape, where the corpse had been undamaged, the membrane limp due to the stilled blood no longer replenishing its contents. And that one, long ago, had been blond, the hair pale, almost translucent. This one was dark; he gazed down at the black tangle over her shoulder and along her arm, high contrast against the white skin.

The wind caught a fold of the membrane, billowing it behind the angel's head. Her face turned from its kiss against the wall, the rise of the chin stretching the slender throat. The face returned his gaze, the unseeing eyes half-shaded by the dark lashes. His chest hollowed as he recognized the dead angel.

It's her. He knew it, the memory sharp; no need to call the tape file out of the camera's archive. I'll be goddamned; he reached down and shut off the Norton's engine, the murmuring idle an intrusion on the scene and his thoughts. The face he had last seen, the lashes trembling, mouth opening in a small cry; head thrown back, dark hair a pennant in open air; her hands straining against the male's chest, the taut spheres behind their shoulders filled with dawn light . . . he had seen the face then, in the camera's viewfinder, lens tracking the mating angels as they had turned far from Cylinder's steel wall. Now the same face lay below him, beyond the motorcycle's wheel, the torn membrane a pillow for a longer sleep.

He knew why the hollow in his chest. Irrational: I shouldn't have taped her. *Them.* Stole all their life, right when they weren't watching, busy at those other things. Way to go, champ; stole it and sold it, and the obliging world snared the husk and left it here for him to find. Just to make me feel like a shit.

Disgust stifled the mercenary notion of taking out the camera again, and taping the corpse. Fuck 'em; the hungry eyes stacked up inside the building already had one dead angel to look at.

Axxter swung his legs off the Norton and let his boot pithons snap onto the wall. With one hand grasping the transit cable, he awkwardly clambered down to where the angel hung. The silklike tissue of the deflated membrane wrapped around his arm as he reached down toward her. He wanted to pull her loose from the angle of cable that had snagged the light body, and let her fall free of the building, down through the cloud layer to whatever place all other dead angels went. His hand strayed for a moment, a centimeter from her face. In the cup of his palm he felt a faint motion of air, warmer than the wind curling over his back. It disappeared, then came again, a breath shallower than the one he'd felt a moment before.

"Christ!" His hand slid to the side of her throat. A feeble pulse touched his fingertips. The angel's head lolled to one side as he pulled his hand back.

Alive, barely—whatever had torn and burned the spherical membrane (a memory, *the dark place behind the ripped metal the smell of burnt things,* moved behind his thoughts) had left a small living thread inside the fragile body. But not for long, obviously. The flesh that had glowed with its own heat when he'd taped it two mornings ago now grayed with the dull tint of the silklike stuff fluttering around her limbs. He guessed shock, maybe some internal injury that he hadn't discerned yet. The loss of blood seemed minimal, with no break that he could see in the naked skin. The burn damage had mercifully cauterized most of the blood vessels feeding into the torn membrane.

"Shit." The word slid around one gnawed thumbnail. Dead had been one thing, bad enough; a dying angel was even worse. What are you supposed to do with something like that? That nobody—not out here, at least—would know what you'd done made it no easier. Can't just push her off into the clouds now . . . so then what? Watch and wait until she *is* dead? "Goddamn—" Gotta do *something* for her. And how easy would that be? Or likely to do any good? His medical skills, rudimentary by even freelancer standards . . . and were gas angels even human? They looked like it, if perhaps a bit on the childlike, ethereal side, bird bones thin and light enough to be carried through the air . . . Shit, maybe they *are* birds, featherless ones. Or something entirely different, cooked up by the endlessly clever people who lived before the War. Axxter shook his head, worrying the thumbnail farther down.

"Well—" The wind carried away his voice. Can't kill her any deader, can you? He tightened his grip on the cable and lowered himself closer to the angel.

The wind had picked up in the span of minutes since he had spotted her. A rapid flutter came from the blackened edges of the tattered membrane, the wind's force tearing off the longer ribbons. The angel sagged lower in the shroudlike cradle formed by her own dead tissue, one thin arm dangling down toward the clouds far below. Her slight weight tugged at the point where the membrane had become entangled with the transit cable, the twisted silk fraying into strings.

Axxter drew a pithon from his belt, letting its triangular head seek out an anchor point on the building's rough surface. He kept one hand on the taut line, sliding it through his fingers, an inelegant, squatting rappel, his free hand reaching down to gather up the angel. Her bare shoulders fit into the crook of his arm, her head lolling back against the point of his shoulder. Almost weightless, like picking up someone from hollow time, it seemed to him, a figure only perceptible by the eyes. That impression lasted only a second: his lifting the fragile body loosed a fold of the

60 ■ ■ ■

membrane that had been trapped against the wall. The wind caught it, a cupped sail; the line burned through his fingers' crook as he was jerked away from the building.

For a moment, clutching the angel to his chest in a reflex spasm, he saw the massed clouds skirting the wall far below, the angel's dark hair a net over his face, the strands twisting on his tongue as he gasped for breath. Another gust of wind, the membrane flapping and billowing around them, and he felt his boots strain against the pithons' hold. His fist tightened, the safety line a knife-edge in his grip, but stopping him perpendicular to the wall, leaning back against the air.

"Fucking *A*." He looked into the angel's face. She seemed asleep, cheek cuddling against a lover's collarbone, in naked ease. Axxter felt the warmth from whatever life residual in her, seeping through his shirt, and . . . The old joke; the persistent flesh. Goddamn it; you're disgusting, he told himself. Ass hanging out over the big step, straight down to the clouds—and *that's* all you can think of? Jesus H. Christ. Wearily, he lifted his hand, a less offensive member, from the angel's spine and reached across her to the safety line. He began pulling himself up to the wall, his arms holding the angel against himself. The drag from the membrane's sail lessened as it compressed back against the building.

Once he'd regained the vertical, the angel was light enough for him to carry with one arm, hers dangling limp over his shoulders, as he climbed back up to the Norton. He placed her in the sidecar, secured with a bungee cord sash from hip to armpit. Leaning over her, he felt her breath against his palm—shallower? He couldn't tell. From behind her he pulled out his graffex gear and his collapsible work platform.

Wherever the platform was set up and anchored, it gave him space enough to go completely around whatever stretched-out warrior he was working on; the slender form of the angel barely took up half that much room. Axxter drew the curtains to shut out the wind, and bent over the unconscious figure.

In the half-light filtering through the fabric curving above his head, Axxter watched the slight rise and fall of the angel's shallow breathing. He could have slapped some vital-signs monitoring equipment on her—he had the stuff somewhere at the bottom of his med kit—but figured there was no use. *I wouldn't know what it meant, anyway, human or otherwise.* No injuries visible, except for a few bruises, the largest along the ribcage showing the imprint of the transit cable's twisted steel strands. He lifted each limb, checking methodically for broken bones, before turning her over.

Out of the wind now, he could lift up the flight membrane and see the extent of the damage. The translucent tissue had more resilience than he expected, a thin film stretching between his hands, the network of capillaries expanding like a net. Only where the membrane was charred black had the wind and the angel's weight been able to tear it. He lowered the membrane, a gauzy cape to the base of the angel's spine, and knelt down to rummage through his med kit.

With a half-dozen bungee cords snagged onto the overhead curtain struts, the other ends hooked into the handle loops of a brace of hemostats clamped to the angel's flight membrane, Axxter spread the tissue into a sagging tent. Now he could see the actual dimensions of the burn wound. Whatever tongue of fire had hit her—the acrid smell from the ruin zone, behind the smell of charred flesh, rose in his memory—who, or whatever, had aimed it, had vaporized an oval section of the membrane. Over a third of the total tissue area, Axxter estimated, peering at the draped skin. Leaving a black O slanting from the an-

62 ■ ■ ■

gel's left hip up to the nape of her neck. The band of burned tissue was widest toward the bottom curve, narrowing to a few centimeters at the top. Studying the wound, Axxter could visualize the shot that had zeroed the membrane section out to ash, a blowtorch to a paper balloon.

She must've been there. He poked at the burned edge; a black flake adhered to his fingertip. Floating around out in the air, with that silly sweet smile on her face, when the Dead Centers blew open that whole section of the wall. All that screaming and various other loud noises as those horizontal suckers got crisped; plus big bright explosions—must've looked just fascinating to her. Axxter shook his head, grimacing at more than the burned smell rendered on his tongue. And then those fuckers—he meant the Dead Centers, even without the name forming inside his head—they looked out past the blown-open wall, out into the sky, and there's some beautiful naked female apparition bobbing around out there, with her little smiling face looking in all curious to see what was going on, and a great big butterfly sphere filled with light behind her . . . So they just naturally lift their flame-spitting weapons at her—or just *look* at her with their dead eyes, all flint and steel. And just zap her out of the sky. *Bad* fuckers. An angel doesn't stand a chance in this bad world.

"That's what you get for being curious, sweetheart." Axxter looked down at the angel's sleeping face, turned to one side against the table, but there was no sign that she'd heard. It's what I'll probably get someday, too; remembering his little stroll around the ruin zone, the burn stench in his nostrils and the empty gazes of the horizontal dead on his back.

She was still breathing; inside the curtained-off space he could even hear the slight motion of air. Just getting her

■　■　■　**63**

off the wall and into a secure space had postponed her death. Axxter scratched the side of his face, wondering what to do next. Probably won't even die from the torn-open membrane, he supposed. But just kinda . . . *starve* to death, go into a moping decline or something, from not being able to float around in the air and do whatever it is angels do. Like a wing-clipped bird, a big one; what he imagined an eagle would be like. Have to hand-feed them for the rest of their lives, which wouldn't be long, but would be sad. Shit; kinder to just kill her—he could dig enough anaesthetic dermal patches out of the med kit to do the job. Just slather them on the naked body and watch the heartbeat flutter and go still, under the massed chemical weight.

Or—the mercenary consideration; always that—I could just call up ol' Ask & Receive. Tell them what I have here on the table; they'd have a pickup squad zooming down the wall in seconds, right to this spot. Take her right back to their toplevel research labs, and—

He shook his head. You get to go to hell—someplace down below the clouds, he imagined—for something like that. Being responsible for angel dissection. If there isn't a hell, then there should be one, just for cases like that.

For a couple of minutes he stood by the table, gazing at the angel. Then he pushed through the curtains and clambered up the wall to where he'd left the Norton. He returned with his graffex gear. Setting it on the floor, he began pulling out the things he'd need.

■
■

He had strapped himself into the Norton's sidecar, and even managed to fall asleep in that awkward position, legs angled out over the side. Not wanting to be there in the curtained-off work space when the angel awoke; there'd

64 ■ ■ ■

been enough bad shit happen to her, he'd figured, without her finding some gross, scary human being beside her.

An alarm beeped inside his ear, pulling him up from sleep. It took him a moment, blinking and running his tongue over sour-tasting teeth, before he realized what it was. "She's up?" He had left a mike pinned to the curtains, set to detect any small sound.

I SUPPOSE. The letters moved across his gaze. EITHER THAT OR SOMETHING ELSE IN THERE.

Axxter climbed down to the platform. When he parted the curtains, he saw the angel sitting on the edge of the table, feet dangling. Her dark hair fell across her shoulders, one ribbon of it curling over her breast.

She looked straight at him. "Hello." No fear in her face or voice.

He stood on the platform's edge, curtain in each hand. "Uh—" His own voice had gotten lost for a moment. "Hello."

A smile, radiant and heartbreaking. "Lahft's my name. Angel's my game."

That threw him. Physically: he held tighter to the curtains to keep from swaying back from the platform's edge. Who knew they could speak at all? Let alone anything you could understand. "Loft," he repeated, unable to think of anything else.

She shook her head, the dark hair lifting from her shoulders. "Lahft. Lah-ah-ah-*ahft*." Again the smile, waiting.

A fierce, dizzy joy swept across him, which he had to marvel at even as it passed. This was why he'd left the horizontal, gone vertical, stared down the wall and felt his guts rise in his throat, just to wake up and see that . . . all of that. To be standing, gazing at this female thing. But not that; that wasn't it at all. An *angel* smiling at him. For her to be there, to be here . . . in a little space, nothing but the curtains and the echoing platform between him and the great empty air. If it only happened once, that was enough. Then it would always be happening, somewhere. Out here.

"Laaahhft. How's that—okay?"

She nodded, then laughed when he told her his name. "Ny." She looked upward, considering the sound. "Nigh, near, nearest. No such word as *nearer*. In a way."

Her voice so bright, madly cheerful—considering what had happened to her, the condition he'd found her in—he wondered how much she actually understood of what she said, and how much was just parrot tape loops cycling around. Where'd she get it from, then? Eavesdropping—on whom? He let it slide, one of life's mysteries. He stepped farther onto the platform, letting the curtains fall behind him; something small and metallic clattered away from the edge of his shoe. Looking down, he saw one of the scalpels he'd used to cut away the burnt edges of the angel's flight membrane. All of the med kit's implements were on the platform, arranged in lines and starbursts; the empty kit lay tucked under the table. She'd done all that, carefully and silently, before some small inadvertent noise had triggered the alarm mike.

He stepped over the surgical tools and stood by the table. The black leather satchel with his graffex gear inside was stowed beneath; with a real freelancer's instinctive caution about the tools of his trade, he had put them out of harm's reach.

The angel didn't look at him, but went on gazing at the spoked curtains above her head. "The sky's so small here." She sounded puzzled.

"Oh—hang on." He reached over to the nearest panel of fabric, unsnapped the fastener, and drew the curtain rattling to one side. The angel watched his actions with

66 ■ ■ ■

interest, and gave a little delighted laugh when the open air was revealed.

"There you go." Axxter grasped the edge of the table, bracing himself against the wind that now coursed over the platform. She looked at him, the same sweet smile indicating her incomprehension. You beautiful idiot; a sad twinge inside himself. How would she know anything, about anything at all? "You see—that wasn't the sky. You were inside. You understand? Before I pulled the curtain back."

"Before . . ." Lahft's gaze wandered from his face. "Beee . . . fore." Looking placidly at the sky. "Forbear. Four bears."

Christ; maybe Guyer's spoiled all this for me. The angel sat on the edge of the table, her hands folded in her lap, the wind tracing her hair over her bare shoulders. Axxter watched her with diminishing lust. Impossible to keep up a carnal interest in anyone—anything—this dim. Like raping a puppy. Enough bad payback there to last you for the rest of your life.

Or—he considered another possibility—maybe she's smarter than you think. In the kinds of things that angels would know. And with just . . . a different sense of time. If any at all—he wondered how much it would be logical for angels to know about something like that.

She had caught sight of something over her shoulder, and had twisted her slender neck to look at it. The flight membrane—whole and spheroid again, not the tattered rag Axxter had found her wrapped in—reflected her distorted face in the shiny metallic surface.

"Uh—I did that." Axxter didn't know if he was apologizing or bragging. "I had to, 'cause it was such a mess. That's why it's different now."

"Different?"

No *different* without *before*. "This—" He reached

■ ■ ■ 67

above her shoulder and poked the flight membrane, his fingertip dimpling the biofoil he had implanted to replace the burnt-away tissue. "This isn't the way it was . . ." He stopped, seeing her smiling, uncomprehending gaze. *Was;* what good did that do? Like teaching higher mathematics to a cat. He didn't even know why he was trying to explain.

He tried again. "Look." She obediently followed his lifted finger. "The sky—right?" A nod from her. She understands *something,* at least. "Okay, that's the way it is *now.*" He reached for the curtain edge and drew it around, shutting off the view beyond the platform, enclosing them again in the protected space. The sunlight filtered dimly through the curtain fabric. "Now it's all small again. Like it *was.*" The last word desperate; I'm blowing it, he thought. Not even getting close. He flicked the curtain partway open again, revealing an angled wedge of the sky. "Is." Closed again, in half-light. "Was." Shaking his head, a sigh; forget it. Somebody, a professional semanticist maybe, might be able to bridge this gap; he couldn't.

She still smiled at him. Which only made him feel more frustrated. An amusing thing, in a world full of amusing things. A wonder that she hadn't just broken out laughing at him. Maybe that's the benefit of being an angel; all the sad things are in that other world, of *before* and *was.* She doesn't have to worry about any of that. If she worries about anything at all.

He wondered how much she remembered of whatever had happened to her. *Remembered*—that was a laugh. Probably dropped like a stone through the clouds below, to whatever oblivion lay beneath them. He bent down and picked up a small battery torch from the tools scattered across the platform floor. The glowing ball of flame danced in her eyes as he held the torch in front of her and flicked it on.

For a moment Lahft smiled at the tiny spark—pretty light—then her face clouded. She drew back, hands pushing against the edge of the table.

Well, well. There's something there after all—maybe right down in the cells, the organism's own deep memory. Axxter snapped the flame off—the distress in the angel's eyes made it seem uncomfortably like torture—and dropped the torch.

"Not . . . here." She sounded almost thoughtful, gazing away from him, tilting her head to look up the expanse of wall above the platform. "A bright place. Like that." She pointed to where the torch's flame had been.

No time, no difference between *then* and *now* . . . She thinks it's still happening somewhere. Always happening, without end, in that bright place. "Up there?" He indicated the wall sector from which he himself had been traveling.

"Yes." Lahft nodded, the smile gone for a moment, brow creased with an effort at comprehension. "All bright . . . and *loud*."

"Loud?"

Her head tilted back again, this time with her eyes closed. She screamed.

It sounded as if every death in the ruin zone, all the charred faces gaping against the blackened walls, had been taped, dubbed into one stack, and dubbed into a loop feeding back into itself. If God were a parrot . . . the hell of his lungs, tongue, broken spine. The platform's curtains flapped as if they could rub into sympathetic fire.

The scream battered against Axxter. It didn't stop; the cords in the angel's neck tightened, vibrating. He stepped backward, the sonic wave pushing him away. His foot caught the torch he'd discarded, and he went down, landing on hip and elbow. He scrabbled to get away from the scream at his back, and found himself gazing over the platform's edge. Beyond his fingertips clenching into space, he saw the clouds massing against the building's curve. Even falling, hands outstretched, he wouldn't escape the noise raking up his spine.

It stopped. Just the wind sliding past his ears; Axxter rolled onto his side and looked back at the angel on the table. The smile returned to her face, but different. A tilt of her brows, the gaze no longer wide-open. *Not as dumb as you think, turkey.* Unsteady, he managed to get onto his knees, then his feet. Two parallel lines of medical tools marked his flight across the platform.

"You saw it, then? What happened?" Axxter stood beside the table again. She must've seen it just hanging out there in the air, the way angels do, when the Dead Centers blew open the wall, in the process of reaming out the foolish horizontal collaborators. Saw it, and watched: more amusing things, doing amusing things. Bright, fiery light and an interesting noise. Curiosity had its inevitable price, though.

She paid no attention to him. Looking over her shoulder, she was again absorbed in examining the mended flight membrane. The silvery biofoil reflected her intent expression.

All right, toots. He reached under the table, past the dangling bare legs, and fetched out his graffex gear. Now a little surprise for *you.*

A starburst blossomed on the taut biofoil, swirling and dancing, blotting out the angel's reflected face. She gasped, pulling her head away from her own shoulder and, behind it, the thin metal that had replaced her own skin. The startled face snapped around, staring at Axxter.

He tapped the side of his head; in his own vision, the graffex programming display overlaid her face. "Sharp, huh?" He didn't care if she understood how it worked or not. She could still see what he did. He blinked CANCEL

70 ∎ ∎ ∎

and the simple test sequence disappeared. "Look at it now," he told her.

Her suspicious gaze slowly left his face, turning back over her shoulder. The grafted biofoil, blank again, mirrored her face, unadorned. She looked at him, at the box in his hands, the smile replaced by the signal of further thought.

"You liked that?" He enjoyed this small power his skill gave him. Little bit of graffex magic; not often you found an audience this unsophisticated to spring it on. "Pretty great, don't you think?"

Lahft tilted her head, regarding him. One corner of her smile returned. "Was," she said. "*Was* . . . impressive."

"Oh . . . I see." He nodded, returning the half-smile. "'Was,' huh. Check this out, then." He had a number of demos sequenced; he blinked one up. The signal went direct to the biofoil—he could've reached over her shoulder and touched it if he'd wanted—and was not bounced off the Small Moon to a distant location somewhere else on Cylinder's surface; thus, the pattern came up immediately on the angel's flight membrane.

As if she could feel the black dots forming another picture, she looked over her shoulder without any further command. A cartoon face, recognizably a man's, showed on the biofoil, its broad neck terminated in a ragged collar and tie. The face's big oval eyes grew larger, as if in astonishment; a speech balloon appeared above, its tail tapering to the flapping mouth.

WILMA! YOU . . . AND *BARNEY*?! WELL, I'LL BE DIPPED!

There was no way of telling if she could read the words emanating from the ancient, mythic face. Probably enough that angels can even talk—I might be the only person who ever knew that.

The flight membrane had grown larger, the gases dialyzed from Lahft's blood inflating it. The cartoon face grew larger, more pattern dots filling in to keep the image sharp and black. Axxter looked over the angel's shoulder with a professional, critical eye. The flesh-to-biofoil seams were all holding against the increased tension; he took pride in the thoroughness he could apply to the mechanics of his craft. The foil itself had greater elastic strength than the thin flesh it had replaced—no danger of it tearing or bursting.

He put the face into REPEAT cycle. She looked around at him, smiling with pure pleasure. Entertained; all the amusing things in her world. He had become one of them.

"You did." She reached over her shoulder and touched the membrane, her hand muffling the cartoon face. "*You* made it be." She gazed admiringly at him.

"Yeah . . . I did." He'd figured out something else about her, or angels in general. It wasn't that they didn't have any *concept* of time—easy to catch the past tense *did* and *made,* on top of all the other little verbal clues—but maybe they just didn't care about it. For them, it was a disposable dimension. She was playing around with me. With that dumb act. "Did you like it?"

"Funny. But pretty—*beee-fore.*"

"Oh. I gotcha." CANCEL the face; then he brought back the starburst test pattern. Her laugh chimed over the clap of her hands.

She looked at him again, cocking her head to one side. "Why?"

"Huh? Why what?"

Again: "Why?"

He scratched the side of his face. "You mean . . . why . . . I can do this? That it?" He got the same wide-eyed, smiling gaze in reply. "Well, you see, it's my job; it's my trade, it's what I do."

"You do?"

72 ■ ■ ■

Maybe not a dumb act; who could tell? Might as well run with it. "You see, I'm a graffex. That's what I do to earn a living." What would angels know about that?—they live on sex and air, apparently.

She looked from him to the starburst looping on the flight membrane, then back to him. "Graffex . . . is?"

He wasn't sure how to explain it, or at least not from scratch. "Well . . . there're certain types of people who live out here on the building—you know the ones I mean? The military tribes?" No response. "People, uh . . . big bunches of them. Or little bunches. You've seen them. Anyway, they fight each other. *Fight*—you know what I mean?" Of course she doesn't, idiot. "Anyway, they like to scare each other when they, uh, fight. You know, like making . . . scary faces. Shit." Might as well be whistling and barking, for all I'm getting through. Desperate, he crooked his forefingers in the corners of his mouth and stuck out his tongue. "Yarrgh. Li' tha'."

Her laugh was even louder than before; deflated, he gave up on that front.

"So they hire me—people like me—to make scary faces for them. And other scary pictures. That's what a graffex does." Somewhat humbling to think of it like that, even if accurate. "And we use that stuff—that shiny stuff, there." He pointed to the thin metal he had implanted in her flight membrane. "That's what we call biofoil."

"Pretty."

"Yes, very pretty. But it's like skin—that's why I was able to use it to patch you up. Where you were hurt." Maybe she'd already forgotten that as well. "And I can graft it—put it into real skin—of warriors . . . you know, the people who like to fight and make scary faces at each other. But it's not really skin; it's metal . . . well, it's mostly metal, but with a polymer substrate that's got a pattern-mimesis capability on a molecular level. So it can

■ ■ ■ 73

form itself into blood-vessel and nerve pseudo-tissue; plus a narrow-band immuno-suppressant adapt, so it doesn't just fall off the host tissue . . ." He became aware again of her uncomprehending gaze. "Hey. That's all right; I don't understand it, either." Maybe nobody did; small comfort there. Just ancient technology, from those long-ago days before the War.

"You make the pictures?"

He nodded, lifting the programmer box. "I can shift the refraction index of the biofoil, on a molecule-by-molecule basis—you must just like hearing me rattle on. Is that it? You like the sound of my voice? Okay. That's how I make the pictures. But the people I make them for—the scary-face people—they might not pay me—give me *money;* forget it—if the pictures were there, like permanently, right there in the biofoil. Because they're supposed to go on paying for the service. If they could get away with it, they'd just kill the graffex and keep the work he'd done for them." Unfortunately true. You couldn't always trust warrior types, with their innate contempt for all other forms of life. The system-protecting graffices, and anybody else servicing the military tribes, had evolved to compensate for that characteristic. "So the signal that makes the pictures appear on the foil has to be zapped out on a regular basis and picked up by the foil, or else there's no picture, just dots scrambling around. I encode the signal and send it to the Small Moon Consortium—they're the ones who operate the little one, not the real moon, but the one that's smaller and closer to us. And as long as the tribe that I made the scary faces for pays me the money they should, then I pay the consortium the fee to send out the signal, and the signal makes the pictures appear. *That's* how it works."

He hadn't expected her to understand. At least she had sat patiently—more or less, her gaze sliding toward the open sky—through it. He knew he had worn through whatever odd charm his babbling voice had held for her. A lecture of no meaning, uncomprehended.

She slid off the table; on tiptoe, she held onto the edge, against the lift of the membrane and the wind catching its curved surface. "'Bye," she chirped. "Adios. See you around."

That's it. The thought made him sad. Her attention covered only a moment, with nothing before or after it. I saw it, had it, this brief visitation of grace . . . she'll exist for me, but I'm already forgotten.

The sun passed over the top of the building, the platform falling into shade. He watched her step into air; he went on watching until she was a small, humanlike figure a long ways out from the building.

A last ray of sunlight, passing through some notch at the toplevel, struck the metal skin, the new piece of the angel, and sent a bright flamelike spark back to his eye.

5

"For*get* about those assholes! They're dead
meat! Who needs 'em?"

He had never seen Brevis this worked up before. Axxter regarded the overexcited features of his agent, bright
in his vision. "I thought *we* needed them. That's why I'm
looking for them."

"Small potatoes, man—don't you get what I'm saying?"
Brevis's hand chopped the air beside his face. "*It came
through.* What I been tellin' ya would. A really big deal.
You don't have to go scrabbling after some penny-ante
start-up buncha clowns. This is the *big* one, Ny—I told
you I'd come through for ya."

Sitting cross-legged in the bivouac sling, Axxter rubbed
sleep from the corners of his eyes. Hell of a way to be
woken up, with Brevis—at least the agent had used his
own nickel to put the call through, a small comfort—yam-
mering away at him. Something about knocking off the

search for the Rowdiness bunch that he'd spent solid days on already. Right when I'm about to catch up with them, too—can feel 'em, somewhere close by. "So what's this big deal?"

Brevis's face grew, as though he could lean closer and dive right through the building's wires and out of the display. *"Havoc wants you."*

A moment to sink in. "What?" He tapped at his ear; the voice inside must've been garbled. "Did you say Havoc? As in Havoc Mass?"

"Yeah, yeah—come on, who the hell else?" Brevis bounced up and down, his excitement increasing. "I *told* you it was a big deal."

"Jeez." Well, I'll be dipped, as someone else had recently said. The numero two-o military tribe on the whole friggin' building—soon to be number one, right at the toplevel, if Guyer and a whole bunch of other usually-know-what-they're-talking-about people are correct. And even if they didn't wind up swarming over the Grievous Amalgam's gates, rowdy barbarians that they were, and just stayed locked in that tight balance of power, the mutual chokehold situation that endured on Cylinder for the last couple of decades; still—Axxter felt the digits of his heart's greediest sector ticking over and mounting up—still, to be in with the Havoc Mass, with its massive bank accounts, controlled turf, overlapping stock ownership and directorate memberships with other, lesser—but still heavyweight—tribes; all the alliances, fidelities, intermarriages, tributes, outright extortion, all mirroring the Amalgam's own Byzantine arrangements propping up its long-held power . . . Fuck it; Axxter had gotten dizzy just thinking about it. Who cares who wins? If anyone ever does. Just to get that close to all that sweet at the top, the heavy money, right at the source—instead of scrabbling around this far down on Cylinder's surface, where precious fuck-all of the honey comes trickling past all the other greedy mouths open to lap it in. I wouldn't be a dumb-shit freelancer, scrambling around looking for the big break. I'd have a *major contract;* major money for providing a service to a major tribe, like the other major contractors—

A darker thought struck him, pulling him back from the few seconds of pleasant reverie. "Hey." Staring suspiciously at Brevis's image. "What about DeathPix? What happened to them? I thought they did graffex for Havoc Mass."

Brevis's vibrating enthusiasm ebbed, replaced by a more familiar expression. The uplifted hand cautiously stroked the air. "Uh . . . you don't have to worry about them, Ny. This doesn't really have anything to do with DeathPix. You know?"

"Yeah, I know." Thanks a lot. You asshole. The grand estimate of the Havoc Mass wealth, and his tiny but juicy sliver of it, dwindled away. This is your *big deal?* Cutting in on DeathPix's action? He shook his head. "Great—you really earn your commission on this one, all right. When DeathPix sends over some of their pet thugs to cut off my nuts, I'll tell 'em to just do it ninety percent, and the other ten percent's for you. Okay?"

"Ny . . . come on." The voice displayed its wounds. "You're my *client.* Would I set you up for something like that?"

"No, I don't think you'd set me up. You're just a stupid dumb fucker who doesn't *know* what he's doing. Jesus." He couldn't believe this. Everybody knew what a stupid idea—stupid to the point of merrily embraced self-destruction—cutting in on DeathPix's business was. It was common knowledge among freelance graffices, one of those little bits of info that the oldtimers were happy to pass along to the new guys. Complete with grisly accounts

78 ■ ■ ■

of what had happened to those foolish enough to have succumbed to that temptation. Accounts that, even shorn of the embroidery years of retelling had given them, still contained a hard stone of truth: that DeathPix was nothing to screw around with. It had the true arrogance of power, blithely servicing the Havoc Mass *and* the Grievous Amalgam, and any other tribe that could afford its fees. DeathPix was an organization big and powerful enough, with more revenue than most B-list tribes, to be considered a tribe itself. Except not as much fun; its gray hierarchy had put Axxter off the idea of accepting the job he'd been offered with them. It wouldn't have seemed like going vertical at all; just one dud prison in exchange for the other. Grubbing away in some little cubicle and maybe three whole steps up the corporate ladder before he died, or got pensioned off good as dead. When he'd turned down the job, handing the contract back to the DeathPix recruiter, he'd thought it'd be better to starve out on some wastewall sector than to sign up for a life like that. He'd had occasion to think about that decision since; not quite so sure, now.

"Ny, believe me—I know what you're thinking, and it's not like that." Brevis patiently worked his line. "I'm not trying to get you to go up there just to cut in on Death-Pix's business, and get your butt kicked. It's something different. And it's something you're gonna have to keep your mouth shut about, too, okay? You got me?"

Secrets, no less. "This better be good."

"I promise you." Brevis's voice went lower, confidential. "There's some big changes coming up. I mean *really* big. The Havoc Mass is thinking of dumping Death-Pix altogether. I mean, boot them right out the flippin' window." He leaned back, eyeing Axxter's reaction.

Genuinely impressed—Axxter bit his lip and drew in a hissing breath. Sweet Jesus—maybe Guyer is right, with

■ ■ ■ 79

all her talk of revolution in the air. Big changes, indeed. If not a complete inversion of Cylinder's top power rankings—what Guyer's messianic faith was given over to—it was still a fundamental change in the organizational fabric binding Mass and Amalgam. As if one of them had decided to switch over to some other atmospheric constituent for respiratory purposes; about on that level. Big changes; Axxter rolled them over in his mind. And big money. A great big wad of it, no longer handed over by the Mass straight to DeathPix's accounts. It loomed in Axxter's imagination, a great big, spinning golden sphere, shedding a warm radiance over the whole building's uplifted faces, like some new, unsetting sun. When something that big came loose from the hands that had grasped it so tight, all sorts of little pieces came shooting off, to be snatched up by smaller, faster ones. That's what *big changes* meant.

Still. You had to be careful. Nobody lets go that easy. "Why would the Havoc Mass want to dump DeathPix?" The logical question; DP had graffex resources unmatched by anyone else—designers, techs, terrorist shrinks up the butt. And all those years of accumulated expertise; hard to get that same level of service elsewhere. There were reasons why DeathPix charged so much.

Brevis shrugged. "You want my guess?"

"No, I don't want your fucking guess. I want what you *know*."

"Okay, Ny; but if you spill *any* of this, neither one of us will be worrying about our nuts, or anything else. Got me?"

"Yeah, yeah." He shifted position in the sling. All this mysterioso talk had eaten up enough time to have given him cramps in his legs. "Just lay it on me."

All the pitch machinery faded from Brevis's voice. "This is the deal, Ny. *The Havoc Mass is making its move.*
80 ■ ■ ■

Finally. They've been building up to it for a long time, and now they're finally gonna do it. Not today, not tomorrow; not next week or next month. Not this year, and probably not next year, either. But the gears are in motion, Ny. The process has been started; they think the time has come for them to go straight for the top. They've got the numbers; they've got the alliances—man, they've go *secret* alliances that nobody's gonna be-*lieve,* until they see it all come down. Maybe they're gonna be able to knock the Grievous Amalgam off the toplevel, or maybe they'll go bust trying for it. But the time's come. Simple as that."

The time has come. That goddamned Guyer. Axxter had to shake his head in admiration. She *knew*. Something in the air that she could taste with all of her finely honed senses. She could just stick out her tongue and lick the insurrectionary molecules off the wind coursing down the building's surface. Plus all the little rumors and whispers, the intimacies to which a person in her trade is privy. One way or another, she'd known something was up, and had told him so. Still—

"Well . . . that's all fine. More power to 'em, I guess." Axxter studied the other's image for any further clues. "But what's all this got to do with me?"

"Coming to that, man. This is the deal: the Mass wants to do two things in getting ready for the big push. They want to completely revamp their visuals—rank insignia, trophy decs, psych-outs, ikons—the whole schmazzola. Head-to-toe redesign. And they want to plug any possible leak of their plans to the Grievous Amalgam. When they roll, they want all their military imagery to take the Amalgam and any of its allies by surprise. Get the picture?"

Axxter scratched his face. "I don't know . . . I don't see why the Mass would want to dump DeathPix. I mean, if that's what they want. DeathPix can do a complete re-

■ ■ ■ **81**

design for them; Christ, they've done it three or four times already." When he'd been working and saving up to go freelance, boning up on notable graffex achievements had been part of his preparation. You had to know what had gone down before, in order to come up with your own originals; plus it'd been cheap research, with nothing to pay but the Wire Syndicate access time to the toplevel copyright office. Some of the DeathPix redesigns for the Havoc Mass were considered classics, big conceptual advances in the graffex art—ten years ago, the "Bleeder/ Eater" ikon set had been the first to use optic phase-shift subliminals; that alone had been credited with bringing the pivotal Knives of God tribe into the Mass fold; the Grievous Amalgam had had to order up whole new graffex work to avoid any more defections. DeathPix had been the real winner of that little image skirmish, with big fees raked in from both sides and an even more solidly cemented reputation. So why would any tribe who could afford it want to bump a contractor like that? The absolute *best*—he couldn't figure it.

Brevis shook his head. "They've gotten stale, Ny. What have they done lately? Nothing but the same old shit. The Havoc Mass wants *fresh blood*. They want something nobody's ever seen before."

"Yeah, well . . . maybe." In spite of himself, he felt a little trickle of excitement wend past his skeptical defenses. It would be a wild thing . . . Some of the stuff he had in his design archives, the off-the-wall things he worked and reworked, getting every line and effect perfect, just waiting for the day . . . Some crazy things in there. Maybe the time *had* come. In more ways than one. "But what was that other bit? About the Havoc Mass not wanting any of this leaked to the Amalgam?"

"That's right." Brevis's voice went up in pitch, feeding

82 ■ ■ ■

on the small interest detected in his client. "Top secret, Ny. Clamped down to the *max*."

That was the part that tasted sour—and false—in his mouth. Producing unease. "I think somebody's fed you one, Brev. That just doesn't make sense. The Havoc Mass thinks that DeathPix has been playing doubles on them? Selling confidential info to the Amalgam? I don't believe it. Why the hell would DP risk losing that big a contract? Let alone all the other shit the Mass could pay them back with. Those people *love* to make examples of people who screw with them. Plus, if they survived whatever payback came round, their big-money markets would be cut in half; without the Mass bidding against them, the Amalgam would be able to pick up DeathPix's stuff for pennies. And they could scratch off any chance of lining up new clients, after getting caught out like that." He shook his head. "I just don't see it, man. DeathPix has got it set up too sweet to risk blowing it all with leak action."

Brevis smiled, replete with craftiness and self-satisfaction. "True, true; DeathPix wouldn't *want* to blow a nice, cozy setup like they got. But you're forgetting something—*DeathPix is a publicly traded company*. They're listed on the big board up here; Christ, I've got a few shares in 'em. They're a solid blue-chip, though they might not be for long, once the shit starts to fly. But they've got to file quarterly reports with the trading commission, and anybody can read those; you just have to call up the commission and ask for a copy. They're not secret info. And those reports include corporate *earnings*, Ny— there's the giveaway. DeathPix may have done complete redesigns for the Havoc Mass in the past, but never the whole thing in one shot. And never in conjunction with the kind of big push they're planning. If the money they'd have to pay DeathPix for a graffex project of this magnitude were to show up in those reports, then the Amalgam would flash on what was up, sure as shit. And that'd be the end of any surprise factor for the Mass. Get the picture, Ny?"

Got the picture. He looked away from the wall and the deadfilm, letting the bright morning light wash his agent's image to a ghost. Out in the distance, a darker speck floated, as though it were an intangible particle of dirt caught against his eye; he blinked, and it was still there. He gave it no more thought, his brain filled with Brevis's words. *Get the picture?* He supposed he did. *Some crazy things in there . . .* Just waiting for the opportunity to dig them out of his design archives and slap them into place, right onto the skin and armor of—the Havoc Mass? That'd be fine; my graffex for the Big Push, charging up and over the Amalgam. That'd be all right, indeed. *Time has come.* Maybe it has.

Brevis's voice broke in, revved up to an even more excited pitch. "You see, that's why the Havoc Mass wants to go with somebody *small* for this redesign project—they want a sole-proprietor operation, somebody who hasn't issued stock that's being traded on the board up here. *Somebody who doesn't have to file any reports with the trading commission.* They need a freelancer."

"Hmf." The scary part was that it was all starting to make sense. That's what the Mass *would* want. "Why me, though?"

"Je-zuss, Ny." Brevis's hands spread beside his face, as if to keep his head from exploding. "You drive me fuckin' nuts. You got no goddamn confidence in yourself, man. They want you 'cause you're *hot.* You got the kinda stuff they want."

"What stuff of mine did they ever see?"

"Remember those insignia you did last year, for that little buncha thugs, they called themselves—what, uh . . .

84 ■ ■ ■

Gnash Boy Squad, something like that. Remember them?"

Vividly, and with some regret. He'd really uncorked one for those guys; time *and* effort. There had been twelve of them in all, each wanting some distinct and grandiose rank, all meaningless given their slobbering berserker operational methods. But he'd been happy to oblige, on a standard cut-of-swag royalties rate: they'd gone wild for the corny taloned eagles and fanged serpents he did for them, not noticing the subtler matte black against glossy, details of teeth inside corneas . . . tiny pinpoints sliding a millimeter in and out of the glistening sockets at a tempo tagged to the bearer's pulse. He'd had to run sensor nodes from the biofoil implantations to the jugular vein, and set up feedback loops to modify the animating signals. That had been fine work; he could call the images up from his own archive, plain as ink. Too good for those slobs. Pearls before swine. Plus he'd never seen any more goddamn money from them. "Whatever happened to those guys, anyway?" He'd finally had to cancel the relay order with the Small Moon Consortium, killing the coded signals that brought the images up and into motion.

Brevis shrugged. "Yeah, well . . . they started out strong, but they didn't pan out. They got absorbed by the Havoc Mass, and—"

"Yeah? Where's my cut of the recruitment bonus? That was in the contract!"

Neck tendons made a harp as Brevis grimaced. "It wasn't like that, Ny. It was more like they got . . . *eaten* by the Mass. You know?"

He sighed, rolling his eyes upward. He knew. Goddamn wimps.

"Anyway," Brevis went on, "that's how the Havoc Mass saw your stuff. And they liked what they saw—I'm not sure, but they might even have . . . you know . . . *peeled it off* and kept it, at least until the animating signal was canceled. Your signature and copyright mark were right there; so they found out I was your agent, and they called me up. *Strictly* on the hush-hush. If we don't pick up on this deal—and I hope you're not going to be that big an idiot, Ny—it's going to behoove us to keep our lips zipped about it. Know what I'm saying?"

"Yeah . . . yeah; sure." Axxter nodded, lost in thought. If all this were true, it would be a big change, on the order of the difference between horizontal and vertical. Inside or out. Or, more accurately, between having money and not having it. And a lot of other changes would follow from that one. A snap memory of a door slamming in the face of his hollow-time image; *that* would be different, for one thing. Money does that.

"Ny . . . Ny, what's it gonna be?"

The voice pleaded in his ear. From far away; easy to ignore. Other things louder: *Time has come.*

"All right." He pulled in his breath, spine against the curve of the sling. "You got it; let's do it. Just tell me where I'm supposed to go for all this." He flicked on transcript mode with a quick glance to one corner of his vision—just to make sure he had a record of whatever instructions his agent would give him. His brain was still too full of everything that had been said to trust it with any more.

"I knew I could count on ya, Ny. Believe me, you're not gonna regret this." Brevis smiled and winked. "Here's the deal. The Havoc Mass wants to see what you can come up with, on a commission specifically for them. Just a little taste, to make sure they've made the right decision, before they give you the whole job. 'Cause the job's gonna be so *big,* total redesign for the whole tribe, all the alliances, everything, they're probably gonna have to pull

86 ■ ■ ■

in several more freelancers, set up a team. But you'll be the guy at the top, calling the shots, farming out the designs. That cool with you?"

Axxter nodded, letting the voice slide past his awareness. Until Brevis signed off, with an even more radiant smile and cheerleader jazz. The terminal went blank; he gazed at the empty deadfilm for another minute before he shifted position.

The Norton had stationed itself next to the bivouac sling; its nightly grazing over, its fuel conversion tank now gurgled with mechanical contentment. The sling's anchoring pithons creaked as Axxter stood up and began loading the wadded-up blankets and other gear into the sidecar.

Good-bye to all this; thank Christ for that. With everything stowed away, he straddled the Norton's seat, pushing himself up and back from the handlebars to look around. No more scrabbling around these friggin' wastewall sectors looking for business; that's something I won't miss. Even if this last little expedition had been something of a season of wonders, both grim and bright. The ruin zone, the black twisted metal of the torn wall, and the smell of burned things inside—all that came sliding out of memory with no effort on his part. And another burned thing . . . more pleasant to think of that. If you had to go out into the wilderness to encounter angels, then maybe it was worth it. For a little while, at least.

He looked out across the sky, and saw the little speck again. Larger this time; he could almost recognize it. He dug the camera out of the sidecar and zoomed the object into close focus.

The angel Lahft drifted in the sky. He knew it was her even before he tilted the camera up to see her face; the biofoil with which he'd healed her flight membrane flashed silver into the lens, brighter than even her radiant skin.

He stowed the camera away and gunned the Norton's engine. Turned the machine around in a tight circle, the wheels' pithons snapping from hold to hold, and headed upwall. Making the effort not to look anywhere but toward his destination.

6

"hat's with the fuckin' training wheels?"

"Wheels?" Axxter looked into the other's grizzled face, as if some addendum were hidden in the network of scars.

"These suckers." The Havoc Mass warrior reached down and twanged one of the pithon lines running from Axxter's belt. It sounded a high rubber-band note, resonating in the wall where the pithon had taken grip, and in Axxter's clenched teeth.

"Oh . . . those. Uh, well—" He shrugged and smiled, instantly regretting it. "You know . . . old habits die hard."

The warrior grunted and shook his head, his grease-shiny braids dangling parallel to his shoulders. With no more anchor than what his boot-pithons gave him, he strode perpendicular across the wall toward the encampment's banners and tents. Axxter lifted his bag from the sidecar's bullet nose and hurried after him, slowed by the spidering pithons.

It had taken two solid days of traveling—including an over-nighter, drifting in and out of half-sleep while strapped into the Norton's seat, wheels locked onto a vertical transit cable—to reach the camp. The directions Brevis had given him hadn't brought him to the main Havoc Mass headquarters; that would've been even more days travel upwall. And more of a city than an encampment, a sprawling military base and political center within sight of the hated Grievous Amalgam's patrolled borders. He'd passed by the Havoc Mass HDQS once, when he'd first set out as a freelancer, and had received a jocular warning shot, a tracer bullet over the Norton's front wheel. The thug's raucous laughter had seemed to follow him for kilometers down the wall.

This camp smaller, but still impressive enough. A division of the Mass, two thousand or so warriors—Axxter had developed a quick eye for estimating a tribe's numbers, both military and financial—with the necessary support staff, contractors, camp-followers, and other hangers-on all swelling the total to ten thousand. The gaudy tents, crested with fluttering pennants, had been set up in random profusion, creating a chaos of intertwining pathways, dangling catwalks, rope ladders, and nets. The division had been stationed in this one spot long enough for a second and third layer of tents and platforms to have grown out from the first, like overlapping limpets protruding from the building's wall.

A wave of noise battered at Axxter as he followed his warrior guide into the encampment. A trophy ring, the circle of stakes that marked the camp's original boundaries, sagged under the weight of vanquished enemies' armor; some of the breastplates and helmets, obviously the most recently captured, still shimmered with the embed-

90 ■ ■ ■

ded graffex. The grislier trophies twisted and flapped in the wind, no effort having been made to tan or otherwise preserve the peeled skins. Swarming flies gave a pseudo-life to the rotting tissue; underneath them the implanted biofoil was either dead gray or pulsing, like the corresponding armor, with the graffex remnants. Axxter supposed his former clients, the luckless Gnash Squad Boys, were somewhere in the display. Or at least part of them were; a hollow face, bloody scalp attached, gave him a lipless smile as he passed. He shuddered and hurried to catch up with his guide.

The noise came from the camp's machine shops and the voices trying to shout over clatter of metal against metal. Crouching figures in welders' masks sent sparks dazzling down the building's blackened side, past the charred remains of tents that had been set up too close to the furious torches. Blades honed, dented shields pounded into rough circles with sledgehammer blows; underneath layers of grease and scar tissue the broad faces looked over at Axxter, then went back to the tasks beneath their hands and tools.

"Hey—" The close lanes of the camp had slowed the Havoc Mass warrior enough for Axxter to pull next to him. He shouted at the calloused ear: "Where exactly are we going?"

The warrior had been waiting for him in the clear space at the camp's downwall perimeter. Squatting on his haunches, squinty eyes scanning for anything that might come up the transit cables. With the ashes of a fire built on a small shelf stuck to the wall, and various gnawed bones and garbage remnants caught in the cables' extrusions and loops below him, it was obvious that he had been there some time, stationed by his superior officers to await the arrival of the summoned graffex. The eyes looked to Axxter like razor slits cut into creased leather.

An old vet, the braids gray ropes; swirls of a tattooed tiger-mask—*ink* actually needled into the skin—traced out of the wrinkles. The guy should be in a museum, Axxter had thought. Even if grim and bulky enough to put a shiver up any normal person's spine.

A brace of camp-followers—younger than Guyer, and with more avarice in their glittering eyes—lazily regarded him from their perch upon a cable loop. Their gaze dismissed him as unprofitable; they went back to their monotone chatter.

"CO's tent." The old warrior's thumb pointed into the heart of the encampment. "The general wants to see ya."

"General—"

"Them's my orders." The warrior swung himself ape-like through a tangle of ropes, then strode on without a backward glance.

Axxter worked his way through the ropes, then caught up with him again. "General who?"

A grunt, amazement at civilian stupidity. "Cripplemaker."

He didn't recognize the name. The exertions of their progress into the camp had sapped the oxygen from his brain; he couldn't decide whether the unfamiliar name was a good or bad sign. A number of Havoc Mass commanders figured prominently in the tribe's PR releases, complete with gruesome accounts of their military prowess. This one could be some nonentity, an also-ran in the blood-and-gore sweepstakes, not worth making publicity out of. Or—what he hoped wasn't the case—somebody so goddamn horrible, flat-out bloodthirsty, that the Havoc Mass didn't *need* to publicize him with a twenty-part hack-slash-&-parade miniseries fed gratis into the Wire Syndicate's juvenile entertainment channels. Somebody they haul out like a secret weapon and ten seconds later, without any advance hype, you *know* you're in deep shit. Axx-

92 ■ ■ ■

ter resisted an impulse to stop, call up Ask & Receive on his terminal and get whatever info did exist on this *Cripplemaker*—at this point, what use would it be? He was already in too far to walk out on this deal.

They arrived at the camp's center. A tent larger than all those surrounding it, the center pole extending straight out from the building's wall, the ribbon pennant at its tip twisting snakelike above the other multicolored roofs. Two guards, looking like younger brothers of Axxter's guide, lounged at the curtained entrance, one asleep in a rope sling, the other picking at his black nails with the point of an ornamental knife. No ancient tattoos—Axxter noted only the minute segments of biofoil set into the warriors' cheekbones and brows, quiescent now, awaiting the sparking signal to bring the images into view. A nodded greeting for the old warrior, a bored visual scan of the stranger; the rough-skinned hand pulled the curtain aside for them.

A moment for his eyes to adjust. Gazing around the tent's interior, Axxter realized he'd expected more. More than empty space divided by ropes and nets. The patterns and hues of suspended carpets were dimmed with age; when he put his hand against one for balance a cloud of dust bloomed into his face. From the tent's central pole hung a large-scale map of Cylinder's surface, or at least the known morningside portion of it.

The old warrior left Axxter standing on a swaying catwalk. From some zone closer to the wall, a dim light filtered across the map. He could hear the muted tones of the old guy's voice mixed with a couple of others, but too distant to make out what they were saying.

Axxter looked up at the map beside him. Blank sections marked MURA INCOGNITA; from little spots close to the top of the building, growing larger farther down, finally merging into the great unknown below the cloud

■ ■ ■ 93

barrier. Someone had drawn little childish stick figures, with horns and pitchforks, dancing around at the map's bottom margin. The left and right sides were bounded by the two Linear Fairs, depicted as vertical ribbons of dollar signs. Obscenities, scrawled in a big looping hand across the top and over the faded red toplevel zone. The Grievous Amalgam's alliances, in red stripes, clustered underneath. Below that, solid blue for the Havoc Mass, stripes for their allies, and a motley selection of other colors for the various unaligned small-fry tribes moiling about in the lower territories of the building's exterior.

The map was woefully out of date. It didn't take much political expertise on Axxter's part to determine that. Some of the colored areas were labeled with names of military tribes that had disbanded, either voluntarily or by having their collective ass handed to them, years ago. Others, who'd come up from nowhere just recently, weren't indicated on the map at all. Where were the Gone-Bad TV Cops?—they'd come storming up and carved out a major strategic niche between the map's red and blue zones, and were currently receiving heavy recruitment bids from both sides. Just shows what can be done with a nasty enough attitude. That fuckin' Brevis should've hooked me up with that bunch; *I*'d've been able to tell they were hot go-getters. The freelancer who'd wound up doing their graffex—some punk with less time out here than me—had been able to cash in his stock options in the tribe for a *bundle.* The thought wheeled a stone of envy around in his guts.

The return of his guide interrupted his morose inspection of the map. "Over here." His broad thumb pointed to the farther reaches of the tent.

"This him?" A figure looked up from papers strewn across a desk; wet eyes, magnified by antique round spectacles, blinked. Rows of file cabinets, drawers ajar with

94 ■ ■ ■

overflow folders, formed an L-shaped boundary to the small platform. "You this Axxter?" A pen pointed toward him.

The old warrior shoved him forward. Someone in a black uniform with shiny leather and metal bits on it turned a herpetoid gaze around from one of the file drawers at the edge. The narrow face impassively regarded the small scene before him.

"Uh . . . yeah. Yes, that's right." He regained his balance and nodded. "Got here . . . soon as I could." He saw one of his hands fluttering nervously, grabbed it with the other, and secured them both behind his back. "When I got the call—you know, from my agent—I was way down near—"

"Have a seat." The pen indicated a chair by the desk. "Sorry to keep you waiting, but things are in their usual state of chaos around here." A smile, or a close imitation, as the hands went back to rummaging through the papers on the desk.

From where Axxter sat the papers looked like bills, long dangling printouts of invoices and expenditure receipts, the hard-copy clutter of a substantial business. The little guy behind the desk—he could look down at the bald circle of head bent over the shuffled mess—obviously a concrete type, who couldn't think without being able to grasp something solid. "When do I get to meet the general?"

The moist gaze swung up to his face again. "I *am* the general."

Without looking around, he could feel the black-uniformed man smiling at him. Unpleasantly; the face had been disagreeable enough to lodge in his memory.

"Oh. Sorry."

"Just hang on a little bit, and we'll—get down to business. All right?"

"Sure. No problem." He eased the strap of his bag off his shoulder and lowered it to the platform floor. "Take your time." Shut up, he ordered himself.

Black Uniform slid the file drawer shut. The hollow ring of his bootsteps circled behind Axxter. He heard the man's soft voice, interrupted by the old warrior's guffawing laughter, retreating down the catwalk. The tent's silence was broken by the scratching of the general's pen.

"There." The general shoveled a stack of papers into one of the metal bins on the desk. "What a fucking pain in the ass." The same ingratiating smile came up on the round pink face. "You cannot *believe* the amount of work that comes with a job like this."

Axxter made a little clicking noise at the corner of his mouth. "Yeah, must be tough." Who *is* this guy? Must've got sent to the Havoc Mass's pussy unit. Not gonna be easy working up hot graffex for somebody this mild.

"Care for one?" A bottle had emerged from the desk's bottom drawer. General Cripplemaker dangled two glasses in his other hand.

"Sure . . . thanks." He sipped cautiously. A gentle warmth slid down his gullet. A small sense of disappointment; he'd had more potent brew when he'd still been on the horizontal. Some hard-ass. He sipped again, and leaned back in the chair.

"Yeah, screw it . . . kick-back time." Cripplemaker leaned back in his chair and balanced his own glass on the round curve of his stomach. "You know, Axxter . . . Ny, is it?—fine . . . you know, Ny, I want you to approach this job in a . . . *relaxed* fashion. You know what I'm saying?" He knocked back half the drink and gestured with the glass, slopping the remainder over his hand. "I know sometimes people get a little . . . nervous when they get put in a situation like this."

Axxter shrugged. "Yeah, well . . ."

96 ■ ■ ■

The general patted a folder on the desk. "I've had the complete scoop given to me. About *you*, Ny." Magnified damp wink above his smile. "This is a big step for you, isn't it? I mean, from those diddly-ass little gangs you've had to work with in the past."

The warmth had spread to his stomach, and went about unlocking doors along his spine. "Oh . . . some of 'em weren't so bad." Sipping again. The general extended the bottle and splashed in more.

"Well, we all have to start out small, don't we? I remember . . . I go back a long way with the Mass, you know." The damp gaze focused beyond Axxter, lost in reflection. "All they way back to the ol' Romp & Stomp days . . . I was personally recruited by one of the original Tin Can brothers—old Bobo himself . . . what a character he was." The wetness in the general's eyes brimmed over. He dabbed at their corners with a single knuckle.

Shit. Embarrassed, Axxter looked into the bottom of his empty glass. He had noted, for the first time, the fine network of wrinkles on the round, pink face, the gray film behind the glasses. This poor old duffer . . . what kind of old folks home did Brevis get me into? Romp & Stomp . . . good ol' Bobo Tin Can . . . ancient history . . . fat chance of getting anything juicy enough to work up a decent design set.

"I'm probably boring you." Cripplemaker refilled his own glass. "The impetuosities of youth." The chair creaked as he swiveled back around to look at Axxter. "Enough of this. Let's get down to business." He leaned forward, planting his elbows in the muddle of papers on the desk. "You know why we wanted you to come here. We've seen some of your stuff; we think you may have what we're looking for."

"Well . . . I'll give it my best shot."

"No, no; you'll do better than that, Ny. We want you to deliver the goods. We want the real thing."

Looney old fuck. Pep talks, I gotta hear. "What the fuck *is* this shit?" He realized that he was drunk. Incredible—not *how* drunk he was, but that it had happened fueled by so little drink. As if it had unlocked some deeper, darker reservoir inside him, a more volatile substance ready to be ignited. And, incredibly, that he had let it happen to him at a time and place like this, *mucho* dangerous territory. These military tribes were nobody to fuck with, at any time. You had to keep your guard up, not get shit-faced and likely to cause trouble. But he'd conspired with himself to get into exactly that position. Because I just don't give a fuck sometimes. That was the real intoxication of danger. A bad position to be in. *There's* incredible for you—you can know that, and *still* not give a shit. "I mean, what is it you *want?*"

"Now, now. Simmer down. I just wanted to get everything started out on a nice, friendly, personal level. But I can see that you're a man who doesn't like to waste time. I admire that." Cripplemaker brought his pink face closer to Axxter's. "We're gonna start you right out on something important. See how you do. We need a new ikon."

"Yeah? What kind? I mean, if you want a new corporate logo—I mean, for like the whole Havoc Mass . . . or do you mean, just for your division here?" Axxter rolled the empty glass back and forth in his palms. Half of his brain kept his mouth moving; the other half searched through the mental archive of the stuff in his working files, for something he could plug into this situation. "And are we talking about a battle ensign? Formal parade regalia? Um . . . real blood-and-guts working stuff, or just for PR use? It makes a difference."

Cripplemaker folded his arms on top of the desk,

98 ■ ■ ■

breath close enough for Axxter to feel. "Ny . . . we want the big one. We want you to do a new *death ikon* for us."

Bingo fucking *City.* Axxter closed his eyes and leaned back in the chair. Previous anger dissolving in elation. Right on the money. That, I *got.* Somewhere in the camp outside, muffled by the intervening layers of the tent, came the sound of a military band, all thumping drums and skirling horns. He took it for his personal, synchronic fanfare. Smiling: I can deliver, Jack. You came to the right man.

"We're retiring our old megassassin." Cripplemaker spread his hands wide. "He's up at the main encampment right now, getting de-opped; takes a long time to slice off all that armor, and those prosthetics . . . Hah. Always thought it'd be funny if they peeled away all the fighting gear and found nothing inside at all. Like the gear had been walking around and raising hell all by itself for the last twenty years. That's how long he's been the tribe's hitman. He was a good one, too; just a *scary* mother-fucker." The general rummaged around on his desk, then handed some photos to Axxter. "Here, take a look at these. Since he's been decommissioned, there's no harm in you seeing them now."

He took the photos and looked at them. Something big and black, squatting down, as wide as it was high, with little red dots for eyes; a megassassin. He'd seen one be-fore—on tape, that had been bad enough—but this one was different. Its chest panels were open, revealing the death ikon inside. A corny but effective design, typical of DeathPix, all daggers and teeth. But then again, it didn't have to be the world's most memorable design; it was meant to be the last thing you saw before you got your head ripped off. To see the ikon was to have the last few seconds of your life snuffed by grim inevitability; that was the whole psychology of it. Fear of the image being somehow greater than the fear of what would follow.

But this one's history now. "I think . . . I'll be able to give you what you want. Something really . . . special."

"Well, good. I'm glad to hear it." The general patted the desktop, catching the tempo of the distant music. "'Cause the new megassassin is also going to be something special. I've seen the designs for the battle gear; the grafting surgery's supposed to start any day now. He's going to be a a hundred percent bad-ass piece of fighting hardware. And we want *your* ikon on him." A wobbling finger jabbed toward Axxter's chest. "*Your* design is going to be the last thing a whole *bunch* of people ever see."

"Yeah . . . great. Can't wait to get started." He found himself rising from the chair. Looking down, he saw a grizzled hand cupping his elbow. The old warrior had returned, summoned to guide him back out. The audience with the general had ended.

"That's the ticket." Cripplemaker rocked back in his own chair, hands clasped behind his head. "I'll be talking to you. There'll be more jobs than just this one. That's a promise."

■

■

They gave him a pass to go in and out of the camp. The noise level outside the muffling layers of the generalissimo's tent had swelled to the deafening point; in the sprawling compound of the machine shop, the clatter and snarl of engines crescendoed over the hammers' ostinatic beat. The lounging off-duty warriors compensated by increasing the ferocity of their revels. Heading for the camp's exit, Axxter squeezed past a mock battle, scarred, sweating forms stripped down to ribbons of chiming bells, all thwacking each other over the head with aluminum poles and laughing in demented glee. One of the watching camp-followers snaked a hand around his thigh and tugged him toward the rope sling she sat on, meanwhile barking an invitation drowned in the general hubbub. The woman pantomimed her intent; startled, Axxter pulled his arm free and quickly scrambled down to a point where he could regain his pithon-assisted stance on the building. The uproar, on top of Cripplemaker's booze, had his head throbbing in sync with his crawling pulse.

The guards at the exit took a bored glance at his pass, then waved him on through. "Comin' back in later?" The sun had already passed over the top of the building, setting the wall into shade.

He shook his head, immediately wincing and regretting it. "No—I got some stuff to do. Things to get. I'll be back in the morning." Really just needed some place he could hear his own thoughts. "That okay?"

A shrug as the big hands looped the chains back over the gate's bar. "Suit yourself."

He found the Norton grazing a half-kilometer from where he'd left it. Climbed into the sidecar, doused a rag with water from a canteen, and plastered it to his forehead. What a bunch of fuckin' *animals*. The feeling he always got when he left the lonesome purity of wandering—and going broke and starving; that had to be admitted—out on Cylinder's emptier wall sectors, and had to get down to the actual business of his trade. Maybe after this job all those wandering and starving days would be over. A depressing thought, in some ways.

Leaning his head back against the sidecar's rim, he looked up into the dimming sky. The speck he'd seen before was there again, floating in the air.

"Aw, Christ." He knew; no zoom lens necessary. By now some invisible link had been set up between them, a kite string by which he could detect her presence on the other end. She followed me here. The stupid thing. This being no territory for angels . . . especially one who'd already been winged once, by *somebody*. Or something.

He stood up in the sidecar, holding onto its windshield for balance. "Get out of here!" The shout smeared in the wind; he knew she couldn't hear him. But shouted again, waving his arms. "Go away!"

The angel, the little speck, hung at the limit of his vision. And didn't go away.

7

"So we had these guys, see, all rounded up, and we were all still pretty revved up from the battle—you know how you get?—and we were sitting around wondering, well, you know, what could we do with 'em? What could we do with 'em that'd be *fun,* I mean. So we had the engineers bring over this spool of cable, see, this real heavy-duty stuff, and we—"

"Excuse me." Axxter held up his hand in front of him, trying to stop the old warrior's monologue. "Hey . . . I'm just going to go outside for a minute." He had to wave his fingers in front of the rheumy yellow eyes to get the man's attention. "Okay?"

"—and we put it through the first guy's *neck,* but that didn't work, you see, 'cause it just ripped right through when we lifted it up, so we—" The old warrior's gaze focused on Axxter's hand as he came back up from memory time. "Huh? Where ya going?"

"I just, uh, need to get some fresh air." Axxter pointed with his thumb over his shoulder to the tent flap. "We been going at it for a couple of hours now; I just need to clear my head a bit. That all right?" He didn't like the way the warrior was looking at him.

"Don'tcha want to hear the rest?"

The warrior's jaw poked forward far enough to hook the points of his bottom teeth over his straggling gray mustache. His eyes burrowed under his lowered brow, leaving just two glints of red.

Axxter reached out and patted the recorder hanging on one of the tent ropes. "No problem. Getting it all right here." The little box swayed on its knotted strap. "Great stuff—just great." He felt his stomach rising into his throat again; it had been threatening all the time he'd been listening to the war stories. "You just keep right on talking; I'll listen to it later." He turned away and ducked under the tent flap before he got any more argument.

Outside, he climbed over to the closet transit cable and anchored his hip belt to it. He glanced down to make sure he had a clear shot downward, in case he lost it completely; all he needed now was to upchuck on some Havoc Mass sentry posted at the camp's downwall boundary. Even if he did have privileged artisan status with General Cripplemaker—these bastards were all touchy as hell. Affronts to honor could get you drilled, with no thought given to what brig time they might pull for it. Drilled, or given the big step—or something even worse, along the lines of what that old bastard back in the tent was still gassing on about. Axxter shook his head as he relaxed against the cable, as though he could shake the veteran's grinning words right back out. Judging from his anecdotes, the guy must have risen in the Mass's ranks not from any military prowess, but from his bent imagination regarding what to do with any unlucky POWs after a skir-

104 ■ ■ ■

mish. *What a sick sonuvabitch*—Axxter gazed down at the clouds; at the atmosphere's bonding edge, they roiled up into guts and skulls, tangling around each other. He closed his eyes for a moment, but could still see them, and hear the old warrior's voice, leering with fond violent memories.

Still, a paying job; the thought soothed his own gut, a warm glow easing outward along his limbs. He gathered the sour taste that had seeped under his tongue, and spat; it looped silver, and was gone. Paying job, and not just that: the second one from these good folk. Which meant he'd pulled it off.

I did it. In solid with a major tribe. *The* major tribe, if you left out the Grievous Amalgam, which had been locked in up at the toplevel for so long it was like air or the vertical wall behind your back, part of the nature of things. But to have cracked the Havoc Mass . . . to have slid right under the nose of DeathPix, and *done it* . . . because he was good, his stuff was just so fucking good . . . That meant his scrabbling-around days were over. That was worth listening to gruesome after-battle stories, any number of them.

The first commission that he'd gotten from the general—the new death ikon for the megassassin—had just about burnt him out. And his portfolio; he'd been saving up ideas for years, all the time he'd been out on the wall, good bits just waiting for a job worthy of them. Stuff you couldn't waste on some scrub-ass little gang of hooligans, the kind of gigs he'd been getting up until this had fallen in his lap. But some had leaked out, naturally enough; you couldn't hold back all the time, if only to keep your skills up. He still wondered what he'd done that had caught the Mass's eye; maybe one of the deep subliminals for the Gnash Boy Squad, the black teeth hidden in blackness, the rotating and replicating mirror-images in a throat

■ ■ ■ **105**

that could swallow you down to your ankles if you looked at the biofoil image long enough. But that had been subtle stuff; those Gnash wankers hadn't even known what they were getting, just groused about how long it was taking him—a lot more work than they were paying him for. He'd really been doing it just to see if he could pull it off. But somebody here with the Mass had spotted it, or some other neat piece he'd done, and realized its worth; that must mean there was some real aficionado of the art up in the top brass. Cripplemaker himself?—Axxter doubted it; the man was strictly blood-and-guts, bluster and politics. It must've been some behind-the-scenes type, a secret string puller, the kind with a wire running to every little detail, like a spider with a web so fine you didn't even know you were caught in it. Not that he minded being caught; it was what he'd been hoping for all along. He just wished he could trace out who it was in the Havoc Mass that was responsible, so he could wrap himself up even tighter in the web.

He rubbed his eyes, still fried from the round-the-clock sessions on the death ikon for the megassassin. Fried, but worth it. No tricky sublims on that job; he'd wanted something that would zap Cripplemaker right off, impressive on the percept surface. Repeat-fold macro-to-miniatures were best for that; a cheap trick, as long as you were willing to work the details down to those levels, but still a trick that always went over big with the rubes. You could watch them reverting to children—or as much of a childhood as somebody born into a military tribe ever got—as they went staring down into all that mandelbrot jazz-and-dragons. And then when it moved, when you sent the prearranged code up to the Small Moon and they came bouncing back with the animating signal—spasms of pleasure. Grizzled old murderers wriggling like puppies. Got 'em where you wanted 'em.

Fuzzy stars pulsed into the salt rim under his eyelids as he pressed harder with his thumb and fingertips. Now wasn't the time to crap out; bear down, and be set for life. He pulled his hand away, one finger smearing tear leakage across his cheek. Blinking, he scanned out over the clouds. She wasn't there, this time at least. Maybe she'd finally gotten tired of hanging around, making her own moon out of her wordless crush, or else, more likely, she'd just drifted away with the other angels, off on one of their slow random errands. She'd disappeared from the sky before—the vacuum draining his heart with both a sense of relief and an odd sadness—only to show up again, a distant sphere and figure laced with sun. Smart enough to dangle out there, beyond easy sniping range of one of the Mass warriors lounging around bored. They didn't like firing and not hitting anything.

His stomach had settled down. You could get used to anything, as long as you were getting paid for it. He unhooked himself from the transit cable and swung back up toward the tent.

He heard the snoring, deep, gelatinous, even before he lifted the flap. Inside, in the cozy filtered light, the old warrior's hands fumbled at his belly hair, the black-crescented nails tracking some vague itch. The face behind the beard had gone soft, babyish, the pleasure of his dreams seeping out in a wet smile. Axxter didn't want to know what the old bastard was unwinding inside his head; something disgusting, no doubt.

A chemical smell, the same as always on the old warrior's breath, but stronger now, filled the tent. An empty bottle rolled in a clattering circle, dislodged by Axxter's knee as he squatted down. A centimeter of clear pink fluid rolled around the bottom as he picked it up. He was about to sling the bottle out through the tent flap when he realized, looking over his shoulder, that there was someone standing behind him, head bent low against the ridgepole.

"What a grand old fellow." General Cripplemaker gazed down at the sleeping warrior. He squatted beside Axxter, balancing himself with one hand against the tent's springy mesh floor. The knuckles of his other hand stroked the warrior's beard, evoking snuffling noises and one of the dirty paws rising up to brush at an invisible fly.

Cripplemaker nodded. "This old sonuvabitch," still gazing at the warrior, "he was the one who ran me through my first basic training. Scared the shit out of me, he did." A glance at Axxter, almost shy, embarrassed at revealing the tender lining of his soul. "End of the course, he'd rape the bottom ten percent of the class. The bottom one percent, he'd rape and eat." The general's eyes locked fervently on Axxter's. "You can't believe what a desire to excel that instills in you."

"Yeah . . . well . . . I guess it would." Cripplemaker's hand had grasped Axxter's wrist, squeezing hard enough to rub the bones together. He wondered uneasily what that was supposed to mean. The general was dressed all in black, he saw now, an outfit suitable for spies or assassins skulking around in the dark. Every time he'd seen the general before, there had been a double rank of medals dangling on his chest.

"Tradition—that's important, you know." The general looked again at the sleeping figure, his nostrils flared as though he could inhale the warrior entire. "There's nothing we can do without it. We'd *be* nothing without it—not warriors, just rabble driven by the wind, bellies wrapped against our spines, getting our asses kicked by every little pipsqueak on the wall. That's what we'd be." The general's voice had gone quieter and tighter, a vibrating wire. His eyes moved around to Axxter again, two little sparks inside narrow slits. "That's why this job we've given you is

108 ■ ■ ■

so important. This man—" He let go of Axxter's wrist and stroked the warrior's gray hair, tenderly. "This man represents the tribe's history; he *is* our history."

Axxter kept his mouth shut. He'd heard this whole spiel before, when Cripplemaker had given him the new commission—couldn't quite figure out why he was going through it all again.

"Do you understand me?"

"Well . . . sure." Axxter shrugged. "I mean—that's why I've been down here listening to him so much." *I'm not listening to this shit 'cause I dig it*—he held that back behind his teeth. "All the campaigns and stuff, the big march, uh, the battles and . . . um . . . stuff . . ." Christ, what else had the grizzled old sadist gone rattling on about? He reached out for the recorder dangling beside their heads. Holding it against his chest, he sent the little glowing numbers dancing back to zero. "Great stuff . . . I mean—it's just great material for me to use. You want to hear some of it?" He held up the machine.

"No, no; that's all right." The general smiled and patted his knee. "I'm sure you've been working very hard."

"Well . . . always like to do a good job." Axxter felt the recorder's metal grow slick with the sweat from his palms. The general had eaten up all the space in the tent somehow, except for the little bit between them. And that he could gulp down in one swallow.

"A good job . . . yes . . ." The general's face drew tight, skin becoming angles of chiseled stone. Eyes deep in the sun-wrinkled crevices. "But more than that. A, a *great* job. I know—you can do it."

Axxter shrugged, as though the skin around his shoulders had gotten uncomfortably tight. "Well . . . thanks. Give it my best." He pulled back—slowly—from the other, his spine pushing against the tent fabric.

The two little points followed him. "The whole history

of the tribe—that's what you have to catch." The general nodded, sinking deeper into his brooding. "On one man." He stroked the broad curve of the old warrior's breast-plate. "The living embodiment of . . . of a *saga!*" The points brightened into sparks.

The guy was sure getting worked up about this deal. Axxter couldn't figure what the big song-and-dance was for. These historical friezes were a regular cliché in the graffex industry. *Every* tribe had one, right down to the couple of louts who had nothing more to brag about than a successful shoplifting expedition in the stalls over in Linear Fair. Saga, my ass. He didn't say it out loud—not with the general in front of him, all worked up—but this was the kind of job that really got on a graffex's tits. Lots of busy little details to get down, you had to listen—Christ knows—to one grisly war story after another, you usually had about fifty different top brass sticking their noses in, each of them wanting some particularly flattering exploit embroidered into the friggin' *saga* . . . Though Cripplemaker had saved him from that last hassle; it seemed to be a one-man project with him.

Maybe that was why the big leaning-over-my-shoulder number, the pep-talk rerun. The man's an enthusiast—I can deal with that. Better that than starving out on the wall.

Axxter felt the tent rubbing against the back of his head. "I think . . . you'll like it."

The general smiled. "I'm looking forward to it. At the banquet—are you going to have it done in time?"

The usual push. The customer is always antsy. "No sweat." If the senile old bastard snoring away between them could be woken up, and the last few good bits tapped out of him. And that was just for color, the little personal bits, frosting on the cake. He'd rung up Ask & Receive days ago, when Cripplemaker had first given him the frieze assignment, and gotten a full historical rundown on the Havoc Mass. On the sly; clients usually didn't want you going outside and getting a losses-and-all account, and working from that. Their own PR line was all ups. "It'll be ready. You don't have a thing to worry about." He patted the sleeping warrior's breastplate, sounding a dull heartbeat from the blank biofoil. No worries at all: he'd have to push it to get it all implanted, but he'd already sketched out the major panels, programmed the routines.

The general straightened up from his crouch, reaching behind himself for the tent flap. "Keep it up." Smile wider, and a wink that crinkled his face like a finger poked in an eye-socket. The black skulking getup slid out and looped away on the nearest hold.

Whatever that was all about—Axxter rubbed the side of his face, wondering. But not much. He was too tired, the grit under his eyelids getting sharper edges, to worry about it.

The old warrior was still snoring, scratching with one of his grizzled paws at his breastplate. He'd managed to peel up the edge of the biofoil; a hairline trickle of red oozed out from beneath. Axxter had stripped off the old foil from the armor, implanted in all fresh; you could recycle old foil, often did if you had a standing contract, blanking out the old stuff or just coding up new animation signals if the basic patterns were close enough to what you wanted to do. Not for a job like this, though. It smacked of working on the cheap, and the fine details tended to come out blurry. Plus—the big trouble—the coding for the warrior's old foil was still being carried by the Small Moon Consortium as a DeathPix account, keyed to this locus. They might not know that the old foil had been stripped off, wadded up, and tossed downwall—but if he'd been stupid enough to try and contract for an override signal,

■ ■ ■ 111

that would've been a dead tip-off that he was horning in on one of their clients. At this stage, he couldn't be sure of the Mass protecting him from DeathPix retaliating for that kind of action. But what they didn't know . . . Beyond that, overrides just cost too damn much money; the Small Moon Consortium threw on a prohibitive fee schedule for that sort of thing, to discourage graffices from sabotaging each other's work and generally giving the industry a bad name.

The old warrior snuffled as Axxter prodded him in the shoulder. The aged baby's-face contorted against the intrusion of the world outside its delicious remembering. "Hey. Come on. Wake up." Realizing how tired he was had made Axxter nerveless. The aged bear didn't scare him now; he just wanted to get the job done.

The warrior's fingers had smeared the blood across his leather-sheathed ribs. He'd complained—fussily, like a child—that the new foil "tickled"; Axxter knew that whatever nerve endings the old boy had left were buried so far down under armor and scar tissue that he couldn't feel a thing.

Have to reimplant it. Put a bandage or something over it so the old fool couldn't go picking at it again. He reached into the corner of the tent for his toolkit. As long as the subject was relatively still, sleeping away . . .

As Axxter bent over his work, the warrior opened his yellow-and-red eyes, beard splaying over his chest as he lifted his head to watch.

"So that's what happened." The warrior nodded. "Just like that. I was there, so you can believe it."

"You bet." He watched the tip of the soldering gun tracing the edge of the foil. *Great; one less stupid anecdote to listen to.* The old guy must have been dreaming, and talking inside the walls of his head. "That was great."

112 ■ ■ ■

He worked on as the warrior closed his eyes and smiled.

■
■

When he called up the Small Moon Consortium and blinked on GRAFFEX SERVICES, then ACCOUNTS (NEW) (CONTINUING), he got his favorite order desk. Somewhere up on the toplevel, where the Consortium had its offices across a thoroughfare from their Wire Syndicate competition, somewhere a body housed that coarse-sand, laughing voice. Axxter took it as a sign of the high tide his luck was running at to hear it now.

"Ny—how ya been?" She coughed, the rasp right in his ear. "Haven't heard from you in ages. Not since, um . . ." She was looking up his account, he knew. "Jeez, it's been a coupla months."

"Had a slack period." He shrugged, though she couldn't see him. "You know how it goes."

"You poor saps." Her mother routine; it killed him. "You oughta give up this bullshit, get into something that's worth money." Every freelancer on the wall, male and female, had the hots for her, the voice alone.

He didn't even know her name, though he'd experimented in his head with *Lauren* for fit, on a historical/cultural association basis. "Don't worry about me. I got a big payday lined up."

"Yeah?" Sad and laughing at the same time. She'd heard that one before, from all of them. "I really hope you do. You could use it."

The uploading of the animation coding took a couple of minutes. "My," she said when it ended. "That's a big one."

He had to laugh—she knew all the old lines. "All of mine are big, sweetheart. That's the kind of guy I am."

Laugh in return. "Seriously—big job?"

"I told you." He'd been up for the last twenty-four hours straight, just doing the code. And there'd only been maybe four hours sleep between that and the long stretch working the patterns into the old warrior's armor and skin foil. Which followed the hours of listening to war stories and then doing the final designs for the frieze. His eyes had now filled with sand, with black stick figures jeering and contorting through rubbery dances at the corners where he could just barely see them. During the last pull, he'd developed the notion that if he'd rubbed his eyes, his fingers would've come away with blood. "This one's a real break for me."

"Mmm—guess so." The rasp moved down an octave. "Who ya working for?"

A little warning bell drilled through his fatigue. "Oh . . . uh, just a start-up outfit. But, uh, they got some heavy financing. Venture capital from up your way." Best to be careful. He didn't think she'd finger him—it would've broken his heart—but still . . . Things had a way of getting around if you didn't keep a lid on them.

The advance from General Cripplemaker had raised his operating account to the highest level it'd ever been. He watched the numbers slide back down at the corner of his vision as he transferred a hefty whack of it over to the Consortium. Enough for the setup costs for the code and a locked/following narrowcast for a six-month period. That still left a nice fat little wad in the bank.

"You want this started up immediately?"

Axxter shook his head. "No—I got a kickoff time for it." Cripplemaker had already gone over the details of the banquet with him, right down to the presentation ceremony when they'd bring out the old warrior. Ostensibly to hang some concocted veteran's medal on him—good conduct, low absenteeism, something or other—but really to

114 ■ ■ ■

show off the new frieze. Hit with a pinlight a second before the animation comes to life: oohs and ahhs from all the tables. With these military tribes, you always knew the timing would be dead on. Axxter dug a slip of paper from his jacket pocket and read it off. "Exactly then. On the dot."

"You got it." The voice from the order desk swooped down, almost a kiss. "Hey . . . Good luck."

"Yeah, thanks." She was already gone, replaced by the charges for the call. One bill for the Wire Syndicate connect at the start, then the rest switched over to the Consortium when the Small Moon itself had rounded the building and come into transceiving angle. He turned his head and saw its metallic glow, bright against the first of the evening stars.

Should get some sleep. He knew that; it was six hours or so until the banquet. They were already setting up the ceremonial tents when he'd slid out of the encampment, rolling his Norton and Watsonian rig downwall for a bit of privacy. Cripplemaker wanted him there for the shindig, honored-guest status. Or at least the bottom rungs of it; there was a limit to how far you could advance in tribal eyes without killing people. A certain respect for artisans, that was about the top.

Absentmindedly, he rubbed the corners of his eyes, then jerked his hand away, seeing with relief the unstained tips of his fingers. He wished he hadn't cut it so close, finishing up the code and sending it off. A lot of the last few hours had been just fussing, fine-tuning shit you couldn't see without a scanning microscope. Way beyond the percept level of an audience like this. Just carried away; and afraid to let it go. The big one, the big break.

Sleep. He could just curl up in the sidecar, set the terminal to blast a rouser down his optic nerve in about five hours or so. Plenty of time.

He knew he wouldn't be able to. Keyed-up the way he was. Heavier than the fatigue.

Hollow time—money in the account; he debated a quick visit to his girlfriend. And decided against it. He didn't want the fine edge of his mood destroyed by her lacing into him, as he knew she would.

Or he could look up Guyer, wherever she was out on the wall. That'd be nice. You pay, but you get something . . . nice.

Thinking, dragging the point of his focus across the options laid out at the top of his sight, triggered a spark.

Dreams to none are so fearful . . .

One of those weird bits the previous owner had programmed in.

. . . as to those whose accusing private guilt expects mischief every hour for their merit.

Christ, what was that supposed to mean? He let it run on.

Wonderful superstitious are such persons in observing every accident that befalls them; and that their superstition is as good as a hundred furies to torment them. Never in this world shall he enjoy one quiet day that once hath given himself over to be her slave. His ears cannot glow, his nose itch, or his eyes smart, but his destiny stands upon her trial, and till she be acquitted or condemned he is miserable.

The words drizzled away, into silence. *Well, fuck*—it had left him befuddled.

Crouched down beside the motorcycle, strapped to a transit cable, he let his gaze wander out across the darkening sky. She was there, the angel; he could see her out in the distance. Sparkling with the last of the sun creeping to the other side of the world, a smaller moon whose face he could remember.

8

The General nabbed him just as he worked free of the crowd and got inside the ceremonial tent. General Cripplemaker shouted into his ear against the din of ragged fanfares and drum paroxysms.

"Where the hell you been!" Axxter felt a spit fleck hit his earlobe. "You got ten minutes! Till it goes!"

"I had to go back out to—"

"What!" The general's face was red, laced with straining blood vessels. "Speak up!"

A conga line of warriors almost pulled him away; he had to peel a hairy arm from around his waist. The line stamped and writhed through the crowd, fists pummeling into laughing faces.

Axxter leaned closer to the general. "I had to go out to my rig." The general nodded; a section of the bandstand had collapsed, spilling the hornplayers into the crowd and taking the screeching top edge off the din inside the tent.

Axxter fluttered the cardboard square he held. "To get my invitation. Security—uhff—security wouldn't let me in without it." He rubbed the small of his back, where something round and hard, like a human head, had jarred his spine. A serious fight, with glints of steel in fists, had broken out; he stepped around to the general's side to get out of the widening shockwave.

Fetching the invite wouldn't have taken so long if he hadn't had to go all the way out of the encampment to get it. When he'd woken up, in the dark, his heart had gone racing into a panic before he blinked on the clock and saw that he just had time to scramble into a clean outfit and make it to the banquet. Looking upwall, he'd seen the crowd around the guards at the entrance, besieging the great striped bulk of tent on its platform cantilevered out into space. He'd figured it would be easier to leave the motorcycle and sidecar where it was, and just swing on up the transit cable on his own. A good decision, he'd realized when he'd seen the ranks of vehicles, scooter fleets to half-track howdah pavilions, piled up around the tent; the Havoc Mass had sent out invitations to all its allied tribes and several grudging but nonthreatening rivals. There wouldn't have been room for the Norton in the tangle of wheels and cables.

Even though the sentry at the tent's entrance recognized him, he still couldn't get in without the little rectangle—gilt lettering on black: *Nunc est bibendum, nunc pede libero mura pulsanda*—in his hand. So another whole trip outside the camp, keeping his head low to avoid fists and missiles, weaseling between sweating backs and legs. He was just now getting his wind back, his good jacket torn, a suspicious-looking beige stain clotting on his boots.

Cripplemaker wrapped an arm around his shoulders and pulled him toward the center of the tent. "But you

118 ▪ ▪ ▪

made it! Great!" Axxter flinched against the general's roar.

There was a seat waiting for him near the central dais. Junior ranks and a few hereditary dignitaries on either side of him, the closest on the left facedown in a pool of wine dribbling off the edge of the table, one hand still locked on the handle of the jug. "You're who?" demanded the bleary face on his right.

In the corner of the tent, the horns had climbed back onto the bandstand and were duking it out with the percussion. "Just a hired hand," said Axxter. Pacific smile, as he lifted his elbow from the wine spill. "Little graffex work here and there."

"Yeah, yeah; great." The other looked away, down the length of the table, and snagged another pitcher. He drank and stared heavy-lidded in front of himself, ignoring everyone else.

Axxter craned his neck, looking up toward the dais. Pretty sure he'd missed out on the food; the waiters were clearing away greasy plates with gnawed bones on them. He had no appetite, anyway: his stomach was bouncing up and down in expectation.

He could see Cripplemaker in the center of the dignitaries' table, reseated and talking—laughing, shoulder-clapping—with the men on either side of him. They weren't in Havoc Mass formal dress; some high muckety-mucks from the major allied tribes, Axxter figured. *The big guns*—old, grizzled bastards with that same narrow, gunslit gaze the general had, the long stare of command and slaughter. When they laughed, it was like steel-jawed traps creaking apart to show the hair-trigger mechanisms within. Cripplemaker leaned back in his chair, drawing on a torpedo-size cigar; his gaze intercepted Axxter's. The general's thumbs-up sign showed through an exhaled barrage of smoke.

The alarm clock Axxter had set in the terminal trilled inside his ear, a little red dial ticking at the corner of his vision. Three minutes to showtime, and counting. The band left off their internecine combat and segued into a major-key ostinato, growing less ragged with each *da capo*. Waiters with cattle prods began clearing the floor in front of the dais.

A corridor formed through the crowd, bodies held back by the Havoc Mass sentries linking arms, digging into the platform surface with their heels. Behind them, the party mob, compressed into a smaller space, frothed and howled, worked up by the band modulating through minor seconds. Axxter could see one of them chewing a sentry's ear into red gristle; an elbow to his throat sent him tumbling back under the feet of his comrades.

The horns held and vamped a half-step short of resolving the octave; the drums kicked into a double-time accelerando. The tentlights dropped except for a single spot lancing through the dark, picking out a figure at the far end of the tunnels of faces.

They oiled him good—Axxter barely recognized the old warrior as he strode toward the center of the tent. The medestheticians, the Mass's own or some freelancers brought in for the occasion, had pumped the old boy full of something that had straightened his spine and put a fierce glitter in his deep-set eyes. Beard washed and combed, then braided and tied with black ribbons, some of them long enough to flutter over his shoulders as he walked, planting a silver-headed staff tall as himself with each step, a contact mike at its tip to snap a bullet report over the mounting din. An embroidered cape hung to the tops of his glistening boots, concealing the armor beneath.

The band's chord resolved as the old warrior hit the middle of the space cleared for him. He stopped and threw back his head, arm locked to thrust forward the

120 ■ ■ ■

head of the staff. He surveyed the crowd, his yellow teeth showing as he relished the collective gaze fastened on him.

The horns and drums cut; miraculously, there was silence. Axxter felt his head vibrating from the battering noise, now ended. The crowd had shut up, right on cue. They were all straining to get a better view, raising themselves on tiptoe behind the armlocked fence holding them back.

00:00:30 flashed the clock at the corner of Axxter's eye; *00:00:29, 00:00:28* . . . His heart moved up to sync with the red light.

He looked up to the dais just as General Cripplemaker raised his hand and let it fall like a hatchet. A signal to the old warrior: Axxter swung his gaze around and saw that the bearded-and-beribboned figure had already shrugged the cloak from his shoulders, the bright cloth lying in a puddle around his boots. The air inside the tent thinned as the crowd sucked in its breath.

The warrior's armor, the great curves of the breastplate, the wide band of the stomacher, the domes of shoulder pads and knee protectors, the brassards and jambeaus—all were blank. Shining foil, mirroring the goggling faces on all sides. An empty canvas, grafted onto the calloused flesh beneath, warmed with the blood pulsing under the skin. Waiting to come to life.

00:00:01 and—*00:00:00*. The red clock exploded at the corner of Axxter's eye.

For a second, he had the feeling that the biofoil would just stay blank. Nothing would happen. *They screwed it up.* The voice inside him rose, gibbering in panic. *Those Small Moon assholes, they screwed it up, they didn't send out the animation signal—*

A black dot formed in the center of the old warrior's breastplate, metastasized into a Fibonacci swirl. The

■ ■ ■   121

crowd went *aaahhh*. Axxter slumped back down in his chair, his spine suddenly liquid with relief.

The dots swarmed, merged; the armor went obsidian, a black mirror. Then gray mist, banks of fog rolling back to reveal a skull-strewn battlefield. Above the landscape, the old warrior looked down at himself in childish wonderment.

Figures on the battlefield, backlighting stretching their shadows out before them. A murmur went up from the crowd as they pointed out to each other old dead heroes, grizzled veterans bearing their squadron colors, the current chiefs of staff looking sage and decisive as they gazed over the crushed limbs of their adversaries and toward a distant horizon full of future glories. Behind them all stood the mythic figures of the Tin Can Brothers, the founders of the tribe, radiant in the manner of immortals.

The crowd was cheering, scrabbling against the backs of the sentries to get a better look. The old warrior grinned, raising his hands wide to gather in the appreciative noise.

Axxter looked around to the dais. The top brass, the ambassadors from the allied tribes, all were watching the graffex show unfold. He tried to catch Cripplemaker's eye, but the general's gaze was also locked onto the figure in the floor's open space.

Then Cripplemaker's expression changed. The cigar dropped from his open mouth, scattering spark and ash over the table. His face drained to gray, then blossomed with red, a blue vein jumping at his temple. On either side of him, the faces registered shock; at the far end of the dignitaries' table, one burly emissary burst into guffawing laughter.

The crowd's applause died, trickling into silence.

What the—Axxter rose up in his chair, looking around the tent. All eyes were fastened onto the old warrior. *Something*—He turned and looked in front of him.

The warrior's glee had melted away; he gazed down at himself in bafflement. Across his breastplate, and in the smaller panels on his armored limbs, the heroes of the tribe were engaged in maniacal buggery. The stern, chiseled faces that a moment before had been looking into the future with the scalpel gaze of eagles, were now rolling their eyes and comically smacking their lips, savoring their own and each other's shit.

The old warrior looked up, scanning across the rows of faces staring back at him. He looked as if he was about to burst into tears, just an old man now, a fool, the joke played so everyone would know.

Across the biofoil, the Tin Can Brothers' images rolled like a hoop, their heads wedged between each other's thighs.

Axxter felt his own head go light and vacant, the space inside the tent tilting and starting to swim around him. *That's all wrong*—he wanted to stand up and shout it to the watching faces, but his legs had disconnected from his body. *It's all wrong, I didn't do that; that's not my stuff.* He opened his mouth, but the words didn't come out.

And at the same time, a red light blinked at the center of his vision. A priority call, INTERRUPT status plastered all over it: somebody somewhere was paying all the premiums to talk to him *right now*. Without even thinking, he blinked to receive.

The red light danced apart into words, no voice.

THAT'S WHAT YOU GET. And a little symbol, a servicemark, one that he could recognize right off. The skull-pallete-and-brushes emblem of DeathPix.

The words stayed superimposed over the warrior and the crowd behind him for a few seconds, then faded away.

That's what I get—he wondered about the message for a second, as if it had been delivered in some unknown language, the tongue of the Dead Centers or somewhere

■ ■ ■ **123**

beyond that, the building's eveningside maybe. Then it all became clear.

His brain wasn't frozen still now—everything outside of him was, though: Cripplemaker and the dais full of tribal dignitaries and ambassadors, the other tables, the crowd and the fence of sentries, the old warrior, even the coprophiliac figures on the decorated armor. They were all in stopped time, or swimming through air thick as syrup, the mob climbing over the backs of the sentries a centimeter an hour, their shouts rumbling down into the infrasonic, too low to hear at all. While his brain went skittering ahead, so high and fast that it saw everything.

They knew. All along. DeathPix had; he saw that now. That he'd been horning in on their action; they'd found out—from whom? Maybe Lauren of the Small Moon order desk had scoped it out, turned him over for a bonus or maybe a little money on the side. Or someone on Cripplemaker's staff, working off a retainer from DeathPix to keep an eye on things for them.

Then all they'd have to do is just cook up a different animating signal and lock it onto the track he'd paid for. A nice fat fee to the Consortium to grease the way, and then there'd it be. Full of nice little surprises, for him and the Havoc Mass. Something to pump their blood up, homo references being a heavy taboo among these brawny warrior types. Hitting a nerve, a lot of times—either way, it was enough to get Axxter's head ripped off.

Dimly, through the congealed vista around him, he saw the sentries break ranks, dissolving into the mob they'd been holding back, their faces contorting with the same anger.

Shit, it could've been anybody, anywhere up and down the line. A corporation as big as DeathPix had its feelers everywhere, like a spider sitting at the center of its web, waiting for a twitch down the silk. He'd been a fool, ex-

124 ■ ■ ■

posing himself to a risk he couldn't have even begun to calculate. Believed in luck, and how much he deserved it. That his time had come round at last. When you start thinking like that, you can convince yourself that you're immune, you don't have to worry.

Might not even have been turned over at all. His thoughts bounced around inside that one. Maybe it'd been a DeathPix setup from the beginning. It'd been awhile since they'd had to fuck somebody over for cutting in on them. Good management style to send a little object lesson out over the bush telegraph, remind any and all uppity freelancers of what the consequences were for client infringement. Keep 'em all on their busy little rat-runs, chasing after their two-bit hooligan accounts, and out of DeathPix's hair. Arrange to have some fool smeared over the wall like cake frosting, word gets around.

Cripplemaker in on it? Point man for the setup? Could be, could be. A wall of faces contorted with rage moved at a glacier's pace toward him, as he glanced round to the dais. The general was on his feet, standing on his chair in fact, his features boiling over, the blood about to spurt in twin jets from the throbbing blue snakes at his forehead. He was shouting something too, but Axxter couldn't hear it through the bass roar filling the tent. He admired the possibility of the general's acting ability: Cripplemaker looked genuinely outraged, jabbing a trembling finger toward him, urging on the crowd's revenge.

All so clear now. Just how he'd been screwed over. If not in every detail, the hand behind the knife, still the glittering point of the blade sent sparks all around him. His thoughts floated above himself and the whole scene below, bobbing up against the top of the tent. He felt a laugh, a crazy bray, spreading open his jaws and battering at his teeth.

■ ■ ■ 125

The poor fuck—the old warrior, weeping, had been bowled over by the mob's slow tide. The angry figures nearest him were diverted, an eddy in the middle of the advancing wave, by the task of stripping the offensive armor off the old man. Foil and skin ripped, red seeping from broad patches of raw skin. Axxter felt bad about that: it wasn't the old man's fault. Much less so than his own. The old guy had been a pawn used to spear another pawn. He'd wind up spending a lot of time in the Mass hospital, getting new armor grafted on. Not that there would be any remedy for his senile broken heart.

The human wave hit, snapping Axxter back into real time. He toppled back in his chair as the edge of the table slammed into his stomach. The table itself rose, turning on its long axis, as the front of the mob surged against it. Axxter, knocked breathless, looked up in time to see the table come crashing down on him.

Or almost. The top edge caught against the tent fabric behind him, forming a triangular space with the platform underneath. Axxter uncurled from his knees-drawn-up egg, unlacing his fingers from the top of his head. He could hear the outraged Havoc Mass warriors foaming and scrabbling at the underside of the table, as though their black fingernails could scrape right through to him.

Jesuschristfuckingshit—the lofty, time-dilated perspective snapped away from him. On hands and knees, he listened to the shouts coming from the other side of the capsized table. The sonsabitches were going to kill him. *If I'm lucky*—once they got their hands on him, they had all sorts of ingenious ways to salve their wounded pride, at the expense of his flesh and nervous system. And that prickly emotion had been revved flat-out inside their breasts—being made mock of, like *that,* in front of the ambassadors and hangers-on from all their allied tribes—

and by some little outside freelancer punk like him—they all had major payback to deal out.

The table shivered with the blows raining against it. The angle between it, the platform, and the tent wall formed a narrow tunnel; none of the crazed mob had thought yet of going around to either end, crawling in, and pulling him out. There were probably only a few more seconds before the crowd backed up enough to let the table be pulled away, exposing him.

One chance—the thought, of all those whirling through Axxter's head, stood out—of saving his life, or at least enough little spark of it to get through the beating-plus that was going to come crashing down on him. If he could scoot down the triangular tunnel, pop out at the open end a few meters away, and make a dash up to the dignitaries' table, get there before any of the mob spotted him and collared him with a hairy forearm around his neck . . . throw his arms around General Cripplemaker's knees— then he could make a chattel declaration to the tribe. And then he'd be under their protection, or at least a little bit, enough; they couldn't kill him, by the usual rules, though he knew they'd come as close as they could.

The plan, and the consequences—of becoming an owned thing, no longer human, an object—zipped through his mind without words.

He looked down the tunnel; he had a clear shot to the dais. Everyone on the floor seemed to have come around to join in the assault on the overturned table. What looked like the bottom half of Cripplemaker's dress uniform, shining black trouser legs striped with red, appeared in the distance, a chair knocked over behind the standing figure.

Go— He started crawling, the heel of his hand crunching on a broken glass. *Just go, for Christ's sake*—

■ ■ ■ **127**

"Uhff—" The muffled sound of blows came through the table. "Get back, ya asshole—" Somebody out there was finally taking charge. "Come on, move it back, goddammit!"

Axxter froze, staring down to the triangular opening ahead of him. And beyond; he didn't see the chaos of tables and chairs, and the general's legs. Something else, like looking down the wall at night, into dark without bottom.

"Get back, get back; come on, come on, move it—" The commanding voice barked, and the table creaked in response, relieved of the weight pressed against it.

The narrow tunnel lengthened and spiraled as Axxter gazed down into its depths.

Fingers appeared around the edge of the table. "Ya got it? No, over there, come on—get outta the way—okay, pull—"

The table crashed over, its legs sticking up in the air.

General Cripplemaker had climbed on top of a chair on the dais, to get a better view of the operations. The little graffex bastard was going to pay; he'd make sure of that. For making a fool out of him . . . "Well?" The general shouted down to the men swarming over the table. "You got him?"

The sergeant who'd been directing the operation pulled a pair of men back by their shoulders. Down the length of the upside-down table, the rest stood back.

"Where is he?" The sergeant looked to either side, and got shrugs and upraised palms in reply. "Where'd he go?" A couple of the Havoc Mass warriors pried the edge of the table up from the platform, as though the graffex might have been squashed flat underneath. The baffled sergeant looked up at the general.

Axxter could hear them, swearing and stomping around, through the platform. He swayed in open air, the

128 ■ ■ ■

big step down the wall gaping below him; he kept a white-knuckled grip on the ropes slung beneath the ceremonial tent. He'd have to move fast now, or his one slick move would have been in vain. A glance down to the cloud barrier far below brought his stomach up in his throat. He gripped the rope tighter, his ankles locked around its length farther along, and started inching himself toward the wall.

In the expanded seconds just before the Mass warriors had pulled the table back over, he'd had a vision. A peek down the line into the future. *His* future. After he'd made his chattel declaration to the general, and after that, when he was finally out of whatever medical facility was deemed appropriate for someone—something—who'd made himself into the tribe's disposable property. His human status being the traditional price for hanging onto his life, breath and heartbeat being the only things his new owners wouldn't pry out of him. In that dismal future line, once he was put back together—mostly—the tribe would've sold him off on a long-term, open-ended—meaning endless—labor contract to some horizontal production plant, way deep inside Cylinder's metal skin. A long way from the rotation of sun and night, and into the perpetual glare of jittering fluorescents, the tiny slice of the visible spectrum that made everybody walking around in it look like corpses. An accurate perception, that: to get locked into one of those interior factories, with the proverbial key thrown away, was to be dead, your life over, the fun parts of it at any rate. Sleeping next to some plastics extrusion machine for four hours—or what you'd be told was four hours; no way to tell, since objects don't own other objects, like watches or terminals—and then punching out widgets for the next twenty, over and over, until there was nothing left in your head except the platonic ideal of a

■ ■ ■ 129

widget. You might as well *be* a widget then; the transformation into object would be complete.

That so bad? You'd be alive, at least. And not so different from any other poor bastard pulling some gig on the horizontal, high-paying or slave labor; it was all a life where you knew that every day was going to be exactly like the one before. That was the nature of horizontal existence. It was what he'd come from, his polyethylene roots; only fitting, the closing of the arc, to go back to it.

Back to it . . . Those had been the only words going through his head, in the seconds when he'd been crouching on his hands and knees, staring down the dark tunnel stretching ahead of him, the hands of the Havoc Mass warriors prying back the table over his spine. Everything else, down at the bottom of that tunnel, just pictures and the sense of dead time. *Back to it* . . .

Until he'd turned his head, a bright flash catching the corner of his eye, and he'd seen a thin sliver of sky, down by his left hand. He'd seen what had happened: when the table had gone flying and its edge had hit the tent behind where he'd been sitting, it had torn the stiff fabric loose from the rivets binding it to the platform. A little gap, flapping in the wind this far out from the building's wall; he'd caught the cold air in his teeth and nostrils. Air, and a section of distant cloud, far off in space.

Air or the tunnel. The table had started to topple back, pulled by the hands on the other side.

And when it fell back, he was gone. Stuck his head out through the gap and wriggled through, the snapped rivets raking his shoulders. Not even caring what was on the other side, a handhold or not, the edge of the platform or the big step below.

There was a rope, one of the tension lines for the big tent. Luckily, as grabbing it had been all that had kept him from plunging headfirst off the platform as he came

130 ■ ■ ■

wriggling out through the gap. For a dizzy second, he goggled at the fleecy ranks of clouds far downwall, one leg dangling over the edge, his other hand gripping the sharp corner of the platform. Behind him, he heard the voices of the mob booming against the fabric. A quick glance over his shoulder, then he let the pithons out from his belt; they snapped onto the rope, sliding along its length as he rolled himself over the edge. He'd held on for a moment, then had followed the loop down underneath the platform.

A crisscross metal forest of support struts and other dangling ropes, shadows forming an abstract grid against the building's wall. Axxter was still catching his breath— as much of it as he could force past the fright and nausea in his throat—and sorting out the thoughts whirling inside his head, when he heard a voice shouting above him.

"Hey! There he is!"

He looked up and saw a face, upside down, greasy braided mustache dangling past a warrior's forehead. Just that, meters away, the warrior's body hidden by the platform. The warrior grinned nastily, then lifted his head, shouting back to his comrades. "He's down here!"

Shit— Axxter let go of the rope as he grabbed another one with his free hand. The pithons whipped around and fastened on.

More shouting from above, several joining in the cry of pursuit. He stretched for and caught one of the struts running into the wall at a forty-five-degree angle. He wrapped his legs around it and inched down.

"Ya little fucker! Your ass is grass!"

Tilting back his head, he could see the warriors clambering over the edge of the platform. Their rage had simmered down to calculation and the expection of more fun to come. He was giving them more enjoyment than they'd expected; a little spirit to this one.

■ ■ ■ 131

Sonsabitches. A glance over his shoulder, to try to work out where he was heading, had loosed his brain inside his skull, spinning sickeningly. The hinge of his tongue thickened, choking him. *Bastards*—fear brought out his own anger, his vision blurring with salt. He'd never been this far out before, with nothing around him, neither horizontal floor nor the building's wall to grab onto.

A loud metallic clang jarred his ears, the noise buzzing up through his fingers where they gripped the strut. From the corner of his eye, Axxter saw one of the warriors, arm swooping around in a follow-through. The knife had zipped past his head, hit the strut, and fastened on. A black wire slid lengthening out of its haft, danced snake-like in the air for a second, then spotted the nearest of Axxter's pithons.

The knife's wire sliced through the pithon; Axxter felt himself fall backward until the other lines caught the slack, redistributing his weight among them. A surge of panic, his fingers clutching tighter on the strut; he opened his eyes and saw the black wire weaving back and forth, the sensor at the tip searching for another target.

It struck, darting toward another of the pithons. Axxter forgot his hold, and grabbed for it. The wire wrapped around his hand, burning across his knuckles. The sudden pain jerked his hand back, and the knife popped loose from the metal where it had lodged. A red welt striped his palm as the wire slid away, the knife's own weight sending it flying from him, then dropping into empty space below.

He remembered where he was—the view of the knife spinning down to the clouds snapped him around, wrapping both arms around the strut, his heart pounding against the metal.

"That's right, sweetheart." A leering voice from above. "You just hang on tight, right there, and we'll be down to get ya. And then—then we can all have a little party. Won't that be fun?"

Axxter looked up to the platform's edge. A pair of warriors had already clambered onto the first joint of the struts. The sight pushed away his acrophobia, a bigger fear supplanting that. Palms wet, he loosened his grip enough to slide down to the wall.

The pithons had the right skills built in, overriding his own clumsiness; the boot lines let go of the strut and struck holds on the wall when he was still a meter away. They dug in and contracted, pulling him within range for the belt lines—all but the one clipped by the knife, the stub now waving futilely about—to join them, anchoring him safely to the building. He could hear the warrior's heavy boots clanging against metal above his head, and their laughter and shouts to each other, as he let go of the strut. His dead weight, palms flat against the wall, triggered the pithons' abseil mode, the lines whipping down-wall in rotation. He picked up speed in the controlled fall, friction burning the side of his face.

A break: the sentries at the encampment's main gate had deserted their posts. Probably when the ruckus had broken out up in the big tent, Axxter figured. *Didn't want to miss the fun.* He slowed the pithons' furious motion, braking himself against the wall; he'd already spotted the Norton where he'd left it before. A sigh of relief—the motorcycle could have been off grazing, scraping up lichen for its conversion tanks. The Mass warriors would've been on his ass in the few minutes it would've taken to whistle the machine back here.

He scrambled over the sidecar and onto the Norton's seat, the belt pithons locking him into place. Already praying, harder than usual, as he fumbled the key into the lock and hit the ignition. The engine coughed, sput-

■ ■ ■ **133**

tered—agonizingly; the shouts of the warriors rang in the distance above—then caught, roaring into life. He hit the gears and punched it.

Falling straight down, faster than falling; Axxter rolled the throttle, pouring on more. The wind pulled his face back into a rigid mask, lips bloodless against his teeth. He leaned low over the handlebars, chest pressing on the gauges. Staring downwall, to the clouds far below. The speed made him giddy, the hammer of air down his throat pumping blood into his roar-filled ears. Never this fast before; he'd always been too scared before. But now—*I just never got scared enough.* The flash of realization banged through his skull and was gone, swirling behind him.

He looked over his shoulder, sighting across his bowed spine and the Norton's rear fender. He saw them, upwall: the Havoc Mass warriors, a posse in hot pursuit. It had probably taken them a half-minute or so to sort themselves out, leader and crew, rough strategy shouted to each other, then wheel out their fastest vehicles, then get on and dive toward the target, the throat they wanted to tear out, the limbs they wanted to spread and dance upon. Too far away to see their faces, but Axxter knew they'd be grinning.

All right, all right; just think. Think—he clamped his teeth against the battering wind, commanding his brain into gear. *Figure it out . . .*

A shudder ran through the Norton's frame, jarring his hands. The grappling lines spun in a blur from the front wheel's hub, locking onto the transit cable, then snapping loose. Axxter turned his head toward the Watsonian. The sidecar had lifted free of the wall, airborne by a few centimeters. Its single wheel struck the metal surface every few meters, spinning through a burst of sparks.

He blinked and got a readout of velocity. The numbers in the upper left quadrant were still advancing, the final

134 ■ ■ ■

digit a dancing flicker. APPROACHING ADHESION LIMIT flashed red in the middle of his vision.

That was the least of his worries. Feedback from the grappling lines would kick in the Norton's governor circuits before the machine could tear itself from the wall by sheer speed. As long as he could stay fast enough to outrun the machines behind him . . .

What did they have? He closed his eyes, letting the Norton accelerate on its own, the cable guiding its faster-than-a-fall, as he tried to remember what vehicles he'd seen in the Mass encampment. Mostly attack trikes, big armored cruisers; he could outdistance those easily—they were built for combat, not racing. Big lumbering transports, personnel carriers—no problem.

And scouts. *Shit*—he'd almost forgotten those little whippets, Guzzis stripped down and hot-rodded. Those would be leading the pack, cutting away the distance between them and the outgunned Norton.

If they'd had them ready to go . . . if they'd rigged one up with a snareline or some kind of weapon . . . Their military value was in sheer speed, zipping into enemy terrain for a quick peek, then out again; not even any armor on them, just light and fast.

He'd have to find out what was back there, upwall from him. If he knew that—he could get a strategy worked out, an escape route. *And territory—gotta know, gotta know.* His thoughts whirred up toward their own limit of acceleration.

And what was in front of him—that, too. He couldn't just go shooting down the wall forever, even if they never caught up with him. The clouds, when he hit them, would mean nothing; the big Nothing, the place that swallows up the ones who took the big step, just let go and fell. You got there soon enough that way; nobody was so wildly stupid as to pour on the gas to get there even faster.

■ ■ ■ **135**

The wind had sliced inside his jacket, chilling the skin over his ribs. He tried to remember, squeezing tight his watering eyes, pulling a fuzzy map together inside his head. Downwall from the Havoc Mass encampment . . . anybody . . . some tribe not allied with the Mass, with enough balls or a mutual-aid treaty with the Grievous Amalgam . . . whatever it would take to pull the posse bearing down on his ass up short . . . if he could just get there . . .

That'd be perfect, if the cable the Norton was locked on led straight into something like that. Some bunch with a real gripe against the Havoc Mass, where they'd get a big laugh out of what had happened at the banquet, shelter him until he'd figured out what to do, where to go next. The wind-forced tears ran in razor-straight lines to his jaw as he gritted his teeth and wished.

Can't fucking remember— He knew it would've been no good even if he had been able to; he'd been there in the Mass camp long enough that everything could have changed in this sector of the wall, tribes moved out, new ones taking their place. He'd kept his head down, working, paying no attention to the usual flow of reports and rumors that freelancers based their itineraries on. Anything left in his head from before then would be old news, useless.

He'd have to call up Ask & Receive, pay the info agency for a current-time map, the extra bite for a high-reliability depth. Even with a band of murderers riding hard behind him for his blood, the thought of shelling out that kind of request fee made him hesitate. If there was any other way—

Shit. So much for that major segment of his bank account. It'd gotten so nice and fat when General Cripplemaker had paid him his advance . . . *Back to reality.*

He looked off to the right and saw the Small Moon

136 ■ ■ ■

hanging in the sky, bright silver and waiting. *Those fuckers. Thanks a lot.* But at least it was there for him to bounce his call up to Ask & Receive on the toplevel. If it hadn't been there, if it had been hidden around on the Cylinder's other side, he'd have been screwed. No way could he have stopped the Norton, climbed off, and gone looking for a contact point to route his call through the Wire Syndicate network; not with major ugly ass-kicking bearing down on him from upwall.

Even as he blinked on Ask & Receive's number from the directory, the digits supered over the clouds below, the thought nicked him, whether he could trust his call going through the Small Moon relay. They'd already screwed him over once, in league with DeathPix. *But they probably think I"m already dead.* That was a comfort. *They'd figure I got my lights stomped out back at the banquet.* The Small Moon Consortium wouldn't be expecting him to be making priority calls from this far out from the Mass camp. He could slip in, get the info he needed, and out before they could dink with the relay. He blinked on the last digit and listened to it go bouncing off the reflecting satellite.

YOU WANT IT, WE GOT IT. The info agency's face spelled the words across his vision.

"Give me audible." That cost more, too, but there was no time to read dialogue.

"You want it, we—"

"Yeah, yeah; forget that." Axxter leaned closer to the Norton's gauges, hunching his shoulders to his ears, blocking out the rushing of the wind. "I need a map, a, uh, whatchacallit, a rolling trace, center of projection this caller. Got it?"

FEATURES? *"Sorry; features?"*

"Blank everything except operable transit cables and military tribes in map area. And on the latter, give me

■ ■ ■ 137

size of forces, estimated field strength, and political affiliations. I'm going to need at least eighty percent reliability depth on all that. Make it ninety."

"It's going to cost you."

He authorized the dip into his account. "Just do it. Fast, okay?" The Ask & Receive face zipped away; he glanced at the bank balance in the corner of the field. It had already been slipping away from the call fee; suddenly it dipped, the digit at the front end disappearing completely. The sight hit him like a knife to the heart.

Come on, come on—Jesus H. Christ— Another look over his shoulder. In the distance upwall, the face of the pack's lead man was just barely visible, at least in the high definition of his imagination. And the warrior's smirking grin.

Then the map he'd paid for came up, straight snakes and a few scattered patches blotting out the pursuers. Axxter turned around and leaned into the map, studying it.

Worse than he'd thought. His already-knifed heart sank, rolling along his spine. The snakes were scarce in this piece of map: they represented the transit cables, and there were hardly enough to form a square, let alone a grid of any kind. The pulsing circle that was him, the Norton and the Watsonian, hung motionless in the center of his vision, a bisecting line scrolling upward; right at the top, the Havoc Mass posse—black dots along the single cable—edged a centimeter closer as he watched. The blotches, different colors—the Amalgam and its allies always got shades of red, the Mass's tribes in blues and greens—just a couple of each. And too far away—he was rolling away from the nearest blue, in fact, upwall and leftaround, disappearing in the map's top right corner.

He scrolled down the map, the pulsing circle and the black dots rolling out of sight at the top. Kept scrolling, seeing nothing but the vertical line of the cable down the

138 ▪ ▪ ▪

middle—until words flashed over: INSUFFICIENT DATA TO MAINTAIN RELIABILITY DEPTH. He gritted his teeth; he'd scrolled so far down the map that it was into unknown sectors of the wall. "Go to fifty percent." The map scrolled for several more seconds, then went blank, even the cable line gone.

"Save your money. That's a long way past the cloud barrier, man."

Nothing. Just blank wall between here and the clouds. And nothing beyond that; everyone knew that. No bottom to Cylinder. Just nothing, the Nothing that he was accelerating toward.

And no perpendicular cable to switch off to, no way of working himself even a few degrees around the circumference of the building. To where he could find a hiding place, a tribe that'd take him in. If he tried going off cable, letting the Norton hunt out holds for the pithons—the slow grunt work of the devices—the Mass warriors would be on his ass in no time. He wouldn't be more than a couple meters away from the cable before they showed up: easy firing range.

Goddamn—the whole world had shrunk to one line, a string with him on one end and everything that wanted to kill him on the other. *For this I went vertical?* He felt like both laughing and crying.

Might as well just stop the Norton, turn around and stand on the pegs, exposing his belly to the coming knives. Get it over with—

The Ask & Receive face waited for another request. "Get me Strategies." He didn't bother loading the map into his own files. What good was a blank page?

His vision went clear except for the bank-account figures at the lower right quadrant. The numbers flickered; that meant they were checking him out.

"Sorry." The face again. *"You don't have the cash for that service. And we don't work on credit."*

"Uh—wait a minute . . ."

"Nope." The face was already dimming away. *"You can't afford us at all now, fella. Hasta la vista."* Gone.

Fuck 'em; there were others. He didn't want to look down at his bank account—how far *had* it sunk on this call?—but let the line search for a match between his funds and any of the various strategy agencies in the directory.

The search was taking too long, whole seconds ticking away. The line must've gone down into the far reaches of the strategy listings, down into the smallest of the various annlanders, the ones that charged hardly anything. For good reason.

A low-rez sign came up in his vision. ASK BENNY PERU—HE'S FAST, HE'S CHEAP, AND SOMETIMES HE'S RIGHT. That faded to a still picture of a fat man sitting behind an antique wooden desk. What had been left of Axxter's heart, clinging by adrenaline to his ribcage, fell with the rest.

"Got a problem?" No animation, just the audio laid over the still.

Nothing to lose—he was already zipping downwall, the Norton's throttle rolled full-on, Nothing ahead and everything to avoid behind him. He told the fat man's picture all about it.

A drain of seconds—both the clouds and the warriors were closer, too close, eating up the line racing under him. He realized that the person on the other end of the call—Benny himself, he supposed—was actually thinking it all over.

The bank account numbers hiccuped, a flat fee bite taken out of them. *"Well, young fella, there's a simple solution to everything. Isn't there?"*

140 ■ ■ ■

That sounded suspiciously like a prelude to religious counseling. Not what he needed at the moment. "Yeah? Like what?"

"Simple." The tone almost shrugged the picture's shoulders. *"Just—cut the cable."*

"What?" He didn't believe that; the signal bouncing off the Small Moon must have gotten screwed up. "Give me that again."

"I said, cut the cable. You know, the transit cable you're on. That's all."

The fat man, or whatever was behind the picture, had really said it. "Are you crazy—"

"You want a full explanation, it costs you extra." Bland, unperturbed, as though people had called him worse. *"Save your money—what you got left—and go with it."*

It hit him then: the guy was right. One hundred percent.

"That it? Got any more problems? I do all kinds. How's your love life—"

Axxter blinked to disconnect. He had all he needed.

Cut the cable—of course; if the world had shrunk to one line, you just had to get rid of the other end of it, the end with the bad business on it. The penalties for sabotaging any part of the building's exterior transit network were huge—the Public Works Department up on toplevel was a law unto itself, more enduring than the ruling tribes like the Grievous Amalgam, which came and went; there were stories that Public Works went back to before the War, an entity reaching back into other, more obscuring clouds. Whatever—taking out the cable, especially in a sector with as few in place as this one, would draw him a fine that would wipe out the little bit left in his bank account and put him in the red for a long time to come. He'd be working for the Public Works Department, in effect, at least until he'd cleared off the debt. *Better that than the*

■ ■ ■ 141

other—there being no alternative that left him either moving around or breathing . . .

Come on, get moving. All this had eaten up too much time. He didn't need a current-scan map to see how much closer the Havoc Mass warriors were to his tail—he could look over his shoulder and see they'd eaten up whole kilometers of the gap, grinning and pushing their machines harder, their mouths watering for fun.

There was a welding torch in the Watsonian's toolkit. Every freelancer carried one, repairs out on some godforsaken section of wall being your lookout entirely. That'd slice through the cable easily enough, given a couple of minutes.

He loosened the belt pithons holding him into the Norton's seat, enough to lean over toward the sidecar's open hatch. Stretching to keep the throttle rolled on, as he reached for the toolkit—the wind caught him full in his raised chest, nearly toppling him. He had to grip the edge of the sidecar's opening, dragging himself close enough to pull the kit loose.

A set of socket wrenches spilled out onto his crotch when he straightened back behind the handlebars and opened the kit. With only one hand free, he almost lost the torch as well; he clamped the cylinder to his chest to keep the wind from tearing it out of his grasp. He switched off the torch's safety lock and thumbed the ignition. A blue flame spurted out of the nozzle, sputtering, then narrowing to a fierce, steady glow.

He let go of the Norton's throttle, and the machine started to coast to a halt. As it slowed, he turned and crouched on top of the seat, then flattened his chest against the rear fender. The lines from his belt tightened, securing him in position. Raising his head, he saw the Mass warriors roaring down toward him; the cable

142 ■ ■ ▫

hummed from their machinery as he brought the torch's flame against it.

The patch of cable behind the Norton's wheel glowed red, then orange, finally white. Driblets of molten steel trickled down the wall behind. Axxter squinted as he aimed the blue glare, the reflected heat searing his cheeks.

He could hear them whooping now, their prey in sight, the warriors' shouts cutting above the thunder of their engines. Looking up from the torch's flame, Axxter saw the leader raising an ornamented scimitar above his head, face contorted in a manic grin. In a line behind the leader's machine, the others yelled and brandished their weapons.

A minute away, or less—he felt like throwing down the torch, climbing back into the Norton's seat, and rolling the throttle on full. Anything, just to get away, to buy ten more seconds—the chase had hopped up the Mass warriors, made them blood crazy. *My blood*— He bit his lip and pressed the torch closer to the cable.

Suddenly, the white-hot section seemed to thin, growing narrower where the flame played on it. The tension on the line that kept it taut against the wall—that was it, he realized. *I did it.* Stretching thinner, from two hands' width, to one, then less, the metal and flame becoming one—

He heard it then, a high-pitched singing note from the cable itself. It drilled through his ears, into the center of the skull, so sharp that he could barely keep the torch in focus, pressing it against the melting steel.

Come on—come on, you bastard! His teeth buzzed against each other, the scream echoing inside his head.

And the other sound, the roaring of engines, the wall shimmering with the rolling impact. A shout, loud enough to cut through everything else, and he knew the scimitar

■ ■ ■ 143

was glittering in the light, raised higher, ready to strike, meters away, then less, and he couldn't look up, his eyes locked on the flame and the glowing metal—

It snapped.

He saw, in a frozen moment, the cable suddenly thinning to the width of his finger. Then nothing, just the wall underneath, scorched by the flame; the tension-loading had snapped the ends apart.

He saw it, the bright line etched in his vision, the image still there when the wall had vanished. For a fraction of a second he wondered about that, about the sudden wind that streamed across his chest and outflung arms, about the welding torch with its blue flame tearing from his grasp, then spiraling away, out of reach. His head filled with a sharp tide of blood, reddening his vision, then sluiced away again, leaving dizzying black spots across the rotating sky.

Turning in air, he saw the clouds roll below him, then— amazingly—they were above him. Two Havoc Mass warriors, arms and legs swimming against nothing, drifted upward, their mouths wide with curses he somehow couldn't hear.

The wind rolled him again. He saw the building now, the wall shrinking away from him. The transit cable, snapped in two, whipped free, flinging the rest of the warriors into the air, their machines and weapons spinning loose.

He realized then, in perfect immediate knowledge, what had happened. He looked down and saw himself suspended, nothing under him but sky. The other end of the cable, which the Norton's wheels had been clamped on, writhed snakelike, dragging the motorcycle and sidecar rig in a wide curving arc.

I should've got off—he had time for the one thought before he felt the lines at his belt snap tight, the impact squeezing the air up out of his lungs. *I should've got off and then cut the cable—you idiot—*

144 ■ ■ ■

The world sped up and became real again. Axxter twisted his neck, looking over his shoulder. The loose end of the cable was snapping back toward the wall; the Norton was still attached, the grappling lines from its wheels stretched to their limits. The last link, the end of the whip, was himself, hooked by the pithons to the Norton's seat.

He hit the wall at an angle, the glancing blow against his shoulder sending sparks across his vision. He felt his hands, outside the shuddering pain, scrabbling at the wall's metal, trying to find a handhold. Then the building tore away from him again, the snapped cable lashing back out into air.

He managed to open his eyes, and saw the Norton break loose from the cable, the grappling lines peeling away. The rig spun about, the sidecar, split from where it had struck the wall, spilling his gear in a slow constellation against the sky.

The pithons gave way, strained past their limit; he heard them snap like distant pistol fire. Everything vanished, even the building itself, as the wind filled his hands, spreading him into an X, back arched against nothing. He saw the clouds below, still for a moment, then rushing up bright toward him.

He hit, and was blind, in a white, featureless world. He could still feel himself falling, turning in the mist heavy against his face.

Suddenly he could see again, in a soft gray twilight. He turned his head and saw the dark underside of the clouds, above him now.

Then he heard the singing.

And saw them, in circles around himself, their faces smiling, marveling at his passage among them.

He saw the ranks of angels, the sky filled with them, singing in the gray light. Darker as his thoughts ended, his head filling with nothing, his fall pulling the last bit of himself away. But still he heard them singing.

■ ■ ■ 145

9

He tried to wake up, then tried harder not to, to go back under the thick woozy dark. But it was too late: he'd already met the pain, the bruised layers that seemed to be piled in wet razor slices from his spine to his breastbone.

"Jee . . . zuss . . . Christ." He heard himself say it, a distant whisper under the wobbling roar inside one ear. Something inside him, which had been part of him but had been shaken loose, wanted to throw up; he could feel it swelling against the root of his tongue. He'd have let the thing have its way, if he'd known which way he was. If upside down, it probably wasn't a good idea; he remembered distant warnings about aspirated stomach contents—you could die that route.

Already, he'd assumed he was still alive. The frayed connection between the aches throbbing in sync with his blood and the trembling flinch inside his head—that was what it must mean. Dead, he wouldn't feel this bad.

He opened his eyes. The right eyelid stuck, then peeled open like a stiff zipper. Sky, pinkish around the edges of distant clouds. Seen through a tangle of his own hair, matted black with sweat or blood. He shook his head, gingerly, little needles jabbing at the back of his skull. The dark lines swayed against the cloudscape. *Right side up.* He could work that much out.

His jacket and shirt had been torn open; looking down, chin against his chest, he saw raw bruises, his ribs stenciled in ink blue, a red abrasion at the edge of his hip bone for balance. He could see his chest rise with each breath, and match it with a particular rhythmic stab near his heart, unseen but felt like a knifepoint. Definitely alive; that confirmed, he almost regretted it. The throbs rolled their dull weight along his spine. He was amazed, under the numb protective wooze.

He remembered hitting the wall, at the end of the transit cable's snapping rubber band. And then falling, the big step. Either one of those should have done the job. He lifted his arm, elbow creaking, and rubbed his hand across his face, letting more light slide under the stiff red fringe. The palm of his hand was red, too, in zebra bands with black grease and dirt. Its sticky wetness smeared across his cheek.

Grease—that made him think. Of the other poor wayfarer, his traveling companion, which had also gone smack against the wall, the louder clanging of metal against metal. It was probably the Norton's grease on his hands— hadn't he grabbed after it as it'd gone spinning away, half to save himself, to grab anything solid and mother-familiar in the empty air curling under his head and feet, half to save *it,* poor thing?—he couldn't remember. He just

■ ■ ■ **147**

saw it rolling away again, in a flat arc toward the atmosphere's crumpled edge, the wheels bent into bowl-shaped ovals, the grappling lines writhing helplessly around the hubs, frame snapped broken-back and the engine leaking bolts and scraps. The sadness of the memory, the last sighting, bubbled up and broke inside his own leaking chest. *You idiot*—on the verge of tears, he realized that he'd yet to feel anything except pain and grief connected with his discovery of still being alive.

"Way to go." Axxter opened his eyes again. There were probably all kinds of shit to take care of, if he was to go on living. He knew he couldn't just stay nailed to the wall.

For the first time, he wondered what exactly was holding him up against the building. His familiar nausea—another sign of life—knotted in his throat as he looked down and saw the cloud barrier roiling against the building's curve, far below his feet. His boot pithons had snugged in tight, locking his heels and ankles against the metal, bootsoles otherwise treading on air. The same for his waist, the lines from his belt fanned out and contracted, his butt flattened against Cylinder; the steel's cold radiated down the backs of his thighs and into his coccyx.

But there was something else, not alive the way the pithons were. And thicker, a raggy thing of shredded canvas and plastic, knotted around with multicolored wires, their stripped brass ends poking out of the crude rope. He could see it now, looped up through his crotch and across his chest, the sharp bits tickling the raw bruises, a tangled knot sitting on his shoulder as if the wires were probing for a socket in his ear. Somebody had tied him up here, knitted the awkward rope as a thin saddle for his weight; somebody who didn't trust the skinny little pithons, who didn't know just how strong they were—if they'd given out, lost their hold on the wall, he doubted if this straggling mess would have kept him from pitching headfirst

148 ■ ■ ■

down to the clouds. He could feel it parting, the rags and wires slipping out of each other's clutches, just from his leaning forward to look at it.

The makeshift rope continued from the knot at his shoulder, to a loop around his wrist, his right hand lifted above his head. He looked up to see if there was enough slack to pull his hand free. He saw her then, watching him.

"Hello. Hi." Lahft smiled at him, her eyes sleepy, as though his fumbling around had roused her from a snoozing vigil. "Hi-Ny-hi." The angel's smile grew bigger.

Axxter rolled the back of his head against the wall to see her better. A triangular section of the wall's metal had peeled away from the girder beneath, making a shelf just large enough for her to perch on; her bare legs dangled on either side of the protruding steel tongue. "Hi there." He nodded and managed a weak imitation of her smile. Now he knew who had knotted the rope around him. To keep him from falling again.

His hand came loose, and he shook the blood back into it. He remembered more now. Falling, and the motorcycle and sidecar spinning away, the Havoc Mass warriors toppling on down toward the clouds . . .

The clouds. The angel's big smile disappeared for a moment; all he saw were the luminous gray-and-white banks, the slow ocean of hills and crevices, rushing up toward him.

There had been angels. He remembered that, too. Rows and rows of them, in all directions, in the twilight shade under the cloud barrier. The inflated spheres behind their shoulderblades like muted sunbursts, the traceries of veins all soft blue in the half-light, lace into ash. All around him, in every direction he turned, rolling on his back in air, arms spread wide as he fell, the wind along his ribs, breath solid in his mouth . . .

That was the last thing that he remembered. There wasn't any more after that. He saw Lahft again, leaning forward, her hands gripping the edges of the peeled metal, waiting patiently for him.

"Okay." Axxter nodded. "I get it. You . . . caught me. When I came falling through. Right?"

She looked away, considering the statement. The little wheels were almost visible inside her skull.

"Caught." She pursed her lips, staring out toward the edge of the atmosphere. "Falling . . ." Her eyes suddenly widened in alarm; she reached down and grabbed Axxter's wrist, locking it tight in her grip.

"No . . . no." He gently tugged his hand free. "I'm not falling *now*. I was falling *then*. Remember?"

"Then . . ." Her face clouded with effort. Bright joy broke through: "Catch! *Caught!*" She hugged herself, pressing some invisible body to her breast. "Caught you then!"

The angels' elastic sense of time, first a point too small to be seen, then a rubber ball that filled a hand, but never any more than that. Axxter reached down and tugged the makeshift rope away from his chest. "Yeah, well—" It explained a lot of things. She must've been hanging around, the way she had been, outside the Mass camp's firing distance, when all the shit had come literally down. Or else she'd been consorting with her buddies, all happy angels together, underneath the clouds. And it'd just been his good luck to come crashing through the soft roof of their world, right at the best of all possible spots. At any rate, she'd been there for him; had put the grab on him, a great big hug—he wished he could remember that part; battered as he was, the nude body perched above him, the bare pink feet dangling inches away from his face, still twinged the other living part of him. Incorrigible; he sighed and shook his head. The rope parted, and he

150 ■ ■ ■

dropped the two ends swinging away from him. He twisted about, boots freed for a moment until the pithons took hold in their new positions. Face and chest toward the wall now; he let out the lines from the belt, so that he could lean back in relative comfort and look up at Lahft.

"Caught me, right. Okay . . ." Bit by bit, pieces fitting together. "Christ, I must've hit you like a ton of bricks."

She tilted her head, the smile puzzled.

"When I hit you." He slammed one hand into the other to demonstrate. "When you caught me. Boom. Then what happened?" Wasting time, he knew. There was a bunch of shit he should be taking care of, rather than just poking into the exact mechanics of his continued existence. Like finding out where the hell he was, and if it was anywhere close to all those who wanted to kick his ass. That should've been priority one. Still—

"Boom." Lahft nodded sagely, arms still wrapped around herself. "Then. Falling—right?"

"Fell." He could imagine it, his deadweight dropping the hugging angel along with him.

"Long, long way." She pointed to the clouds, and whatever was below them. "So I go *big*." The translucent sphere behind her shoulders expanded in demonstration; she lifted a bit off the metal seat as the gases inside the membrane made her buoyant. "Then. Not falling." The smile again.

"Not falling—right. Then what? Uh—drifting?"

"Drifting." She nodded. "Big, and the wind—" She made a pushing gesture with the palm of one hand. "Drifting and drifting. A long way. Then. Here."

She wasn't going to be much help in getting his bearings. Location was probably as fuzzy a concept as time for the angels. No difference out there in the air. They could've gone drifting over whole sectors of wall, one angel with her flight membrane ballooned out to the max,

■ ■ ■ **151**

and her unconscious payload; until some favorable gust had brought her up against the building's wall, close enough for her to grab on. His pithons had latched on, triggered by the proximity of steel, and she had knotted together that rope from whatever scraps she'd found nearby. Then waited.

Axxter looked to either side, leaning back against the pithons' tension. Bleak, featureless wall stretched out. Gotta find a plug-in jack, he decided. There had to be one around here somewhere. So he could call his bank—before anything else, he had to do that. He had to know how bad his financial situation was. His bank account was probably wiped out by whatever fine he'd been hit with for cutting the transit cable. Maybe even in the absolute red right now; he'd be hustling for years to get it paid off. Still, if Public Works Department had left him with anything at all, he could make a start at finding out what he needed to know. Like where he was, and how many were out looking for him. Ask & Receive—he could place a shielded, anonymous call to the info agency; by the time the Havoc Mass had wangled a trace, he'd be long gone. *If* he had the money left to pay for the info. Axxter bit his lip, letting his thoughts spin along without brakes. Gotta find some place to hook up so I can make the call; that was the first thing—

He stopped, his string of thought suddenly broken. The light around him had turned red, the building's wall deepening with it. That puzzled him, and he couldn't tell why. Except that it had been all bright, well into the day, when he'd come to, found himself hanging here. The red light tinged darker as he stared about; he could see it on the backs of his hands. It was as though time had decided to run backward; it had become as loose and arbitrary for him as it was for the angels. The dawn following the daylight, coming after it rather than before—

152 ■ ■ ■

He knew Lahft was staring at him, puzzled at his sudden confusion. Staring at him, as he stared out into the sky, toward the far edge of the clouds. Out where he saw something he had never seen before.

The clouds were all molten gold and red, turning darker, even to black as he watched.

The sun was setting, vanishing below the rim of the cloud barrier.

Axxter went on staring, as the sun became a slice, then a red point. He had never seen the sun set before. Nobody had.

■
■

He had a long time to think about it. All through a long and cold night, waiting for even the gray shadowlight that would come from the sun rising on Cylinder's morningside.

By himself; Lahft got hungry, or bored, and went floating off. Axxter figured he'd see her again. In the vertical cradle of his pithons, he hung close to the wall, shivering in the dark winds, working things out inside his head.

He was on the other side. The eveningside—that much was clear. Where nobody—nobody he'd ever heard of, at least—had ever been. Just his luck—a whole new world stretching out in all directions, and he'd landed up in it with nothing but the clothes on his back. In one piece, at least; he had to admit that. The throbbing of his bruises had diminished, the blood ebbing back to his heart. One sharp pain remained in his side, which he'd prodded once with his finger, then promised himself he wouldn't touch again.

Must've been drifting out there for—what? A day, two days? How long would it take to get this far from everything? Axxter gazed out into the darkness, wondering. Unless *drifting* wasn't the exact word to be used—maybe

Lahft, with him in her arms and her flight membrane distended all the way, had got caught in a ripping current out near the atmosphere's edge. Out in the jet stream: that would've raced them along, right over all the sectors of the morningside, right over Linear Fair, the Right or the Left one. And then—*spang*—down here in unknown territory.

A new thought wormed its way in. Maybe she'd done it on purpose. Hanging out the way she'd been doing; she wasn't so stupid as not to have known that he was in major trouble. Time to split, before more of the Havoc Mass ass-kickers arrived on the scene. The farther away from the scene she could deliver him, the better. And there wasn't any farther than this.

"Christ almighty." A cramp had bit into his leg. "Shit." He reached down and massaged his thigh. Without his bivouac gear—all gone cloudward with everything else stowed in the Watsonian sidecar—the night cold became fully evident for the first time in his vertical career. You could freeze to death out here—he let the cramp be, and nestled his arms tight around himself again, drawing the edges of his torn jacket together. He'd be glad to see the first shadowlight filtering gray across the wall—meaning the sun had risen above the cloud barrier on Cylinder's other side—as then he'd be able to see where he was going, moving to pump up the warmth in his blood. Plus find a place to plug in and make his call to Ask & Receive. Dig up whatever files they had concerning the eveningside. Any scrap of knowledge might be useful. And food—what the hell was he going to do about that? His brain niggled on, each worry marching after the other in time to the grumbling ostinato from his empty stomach. As the pain from his bruises receded, it had revealed that deeper one, growing sharper with time instead.

Impossible to sleep; that had always been difficult

enough, even with a securely moored tent to cradle him, a nice cozy little womb to stretch out in. It had taken him a week of increasing red-eyed exhaustion, when he'd first gone out on the wall, to manage it. Now, strapped to the metal by nothing but his boots and belt, Christ only knew how far from anywhere anyone else had ever been, and his butt freezing . . . He scrunched his head down as far as he could. Got enough sleep, he supposed, when he'd been drifting along in the gas angel's arms.

His gut panged again. Should've eaten at Cripplemaker's banquet; he hadn't known that it was going to be his last chance for a while. He closed his eyes and waited for light.

■

■

He spotted it, a little dimple on the building's edge; a rush of joy blossomed inside his head, enough to squeeze tears stinging in his eyes. The straight line between Cylinder and the sky wavered for a moment.

Panting his thanks, Axxter hauled himself toward the plug-in jack. His arm and leg muscles trembled from the hours of spidering over the building's surface. Noon already, Cylinder's noon; the vertical landscape had gone from gray half-light to bright full as the sun had broken over the top far above him. That was a sight he had never seen before—a dawn you had to tilt your head back to see—but he'd been too tired to marvel at it. His slow progress, prodded by hunger and a carefully held-down panic, had come close to exhausting him. With his lost motorcycle-and-sidecar rig under him, Cylinder had seemed big enough to him. Now he'd had its immensity beat into the stiffening crooks of his hands.

"You sweet thing. Come on over here." In the slanting crab-scuttle the pithons at his waist and ankles afforded him, he slid toward the plug-in.

"Gotcha." There were concentric yellow rings painted around the spot, the plug-in the exact center of the target. Axxter knuckled the tears from his eyes, then probed the hole with his finger. Dust and cobwebby muck; he scraped it out with his nail. He stuck his finger back in, waggling it back and forth to make contact. "Come on, you sonuvabitch . . ."

An unnerving fear that he hadn't let himself think about during his search dried his mouth. Maybe the Wire Syndicate lines, the pre-War network it had inherited, maybe they didn't run all the way to this side of the building. Who knew? Maybe there was no connection to be made, his finger rattling inside a dead hole, no line to the far world of help and money . . . "Come on—" The dot of bright metal on his fingertip scraped against the side of the hole. He squeezed his eyes closed. "Please—"

Behind his eyelids, a word pulsed on, luminous.

NUMBER?

He could've wept. "I need to talk to my bank." He blinked on his display, his directory reeling across one side of his vision. "Right now."

NUMBER? The idiot word flashed, on-off, on-off.

Some ancient circuit, built-in at this end. You ran across them sometimes, out in the less-traveled sectors. Christ only knew when was the last time this plug-in had been used. Maybe back before the War. "God*damn*." Axxter stared at the word printed on the sky. What'd the thing want?

"My number?"

NUMBER? On-off.

There was a registration number for the vanished Norton, and his business license. He could dig those up, but he couldn't figure why the circuit wanted to know.

It dawned on him. The bank's number. He opened up

the entry on the comm list and let the digits dance in sequence across the center of the field.

DIALING. He let out his breath. PLEASE WAIT.

The Wire Syndicate's logo flashed by, then the bank's. Thank God they picked up the charges for inquiry calls. "Give me my balance." He wanted to know the worst.

It took longer than usual; that made him nervous. Maybe there was some funky lien already slapped on the account, a black hole to suck up anything that might come in. Christ, how big *was* the fine for cutting that cable? Sweat trickled into the corners of his mouth.

His vision filled with a blinking red square. He'd never seen *that* before, either. And didn't want to now. It spelled trouble.

ACCOUNT CLOSED. Red, black, red; the words stayed hanging there.

"What?" He'd expected zero; that would've made sense.

ACCOUNT CLOSED. CLIENT DECEASED.

Something cold, with ice teeth frozen to diamonds, seized his heart. "What—" His voice caught in his throat. "What do you mean?"

CLIENT AXXTER (NY) DECEASED. Red. Black. ACCOUNT CLOSED.

"But—that's *me;* I'm Ny Axx—"

DECEASED. INQUIRY TERMINATED.

Then it was just black.

.

Maybe his agent would front him some money. He had to. If Brevis wouldn't do that much for him, what with his being stuck out here starving in the ass-end of nowhere, then what the hell good was he? The sonuvabitch.

Axxter reversed the charges, praying that Brevis would accept a collect call. Just this once.

WHAT NAME (CALLING PARTY)? The Wire Syndicate logo waited for his reply.

"Uh—tell him it's Ny. Ny Axxter."

He listened to the distant ringing, a world away. The wire from the plug-in jack ran all the way through the building and up to the toplevel; his only link.

Then he heard Brevis's voice. "Yeah, I'll take it. Give him to me."

Sweet Jesus. "Brevis—" he blurted out.

The agent cut him off. "Listen, mac—whoever you

are—I don't appreciate little jokes like this. You got a sick sense of humor to try something like this. Now fuck off, and don't—"

"Brevis—hey, no, it's really me—"

"Yeah, right, very funny; now go get—"

All he could think of was the agent hanging up, breaking the connection. Desperate: "It's really me, for Christ's sake, this isn't a joke. I'm not dead. Brevis, you gotta believe me."

Silence. But at least not a click and a buzz.

"Ny?" Brevis's voice was half skeptical, half wondering. "That's you? How—"

Keep him on the line. "Brevis, I swear it." Don't let him get away. "I know what you probably heard, but it's not true. I'm not dead. This is really Ny Axxter talking to you."

Another beat of silence. "Prove it. I mean, prove it's you."

"For Christ's sake, what do you want me to do?" He studied his finger in the plug-in jack, as though it might be possible to squeeze himself through the hole and confront the agent. "I'm talking to you, aren't I?"

"Could be anybody." The skeptical tone hardened. "Sounds like it's Axxter—but that's easy enough to fake."

"Okay. Okay, just hold on a second." His thoughts sped up. "All right, how's this: the first thing I ever did, the first piece after I signed on with you. It was a commission from a little band, about a dozen guys, they're all dead now, they were called—um—" He snapped his fingers. "Abrasion Surtax. Right? And the piece I did, I went blank and I couldn't think of anything, so I ripped off a dragon spreadeagle from a collection of old tattoo flash that Howe Drafe lent me. Only the Abrasion guys found out about it, and they were all pissed off 'cause they'd paid for an original, so you had to give 'em their

■ ■ ■ 159

money back plus ten percent, which you deducted from my next job, only it wasn't true, they hadn't dinged you for any ten percent penalty at all—"

"Jeez—you still remember *that*? Christ, talk about carrying a grudge."

Axxter allowed himself a smile. "So is it me, or not?"

"Well, yeah; I suppose so." No skepticism now in Brevis's voice, just baffled wondering. "But how come you're not dead?"

"Just lucky, I guess."

"No, no; I mean it. What the hell's going on?"

He shrugged. "I'm still alive. That's all there is to it. Whatever you heard—"

"'Heard' ain't it. I *saw* it, man. There's a tape of you heading for the clouds. After getting all whammed to shit against the wall. The Havoc Mass—that bunch had a telephoto trained on the whole thing; they had one of their archives men right behind the thugs who were on your tail. He was sending the signal back on a tightbeam to the camp; that was the only way it got recorded, because he bit it along with the rest of them when the cable went boing. Whose bright idea was that, anyway?"

"I had help. All right? I didn't think of it all by myself." The agent's old-womanish hectoring got under his skin. He would've thought Brevis would be happy just to know he was alive.

"Yeah, well, that little number cost you, Jack. The Public Works Department was in here so fast, sucking out your account . . . They took the wad, buddy. That tape was *prima facie* evidence. When it got broadcast, and everybody from the toplevel on down saw it—"

"What? Who saw it—"

"Everybody; that's what I'm telling you." Brevis's voice went shrill. "The Havoc Mass sold the tape to Ask & Receive's entertainment division—it was on the air while you

160 ■ ■ ■

were supposedly still falling through the cloud barrier. A bunch like the Mass doesn't need the money they got for it; they just enjoy making people they don't like look like assholes."

"Jeez . . ." Everybody on or in Cylinder had seen him sawing away at the transit cable, like an idiot. The kind of thing you saw in an ancient kiddy cartoon, the cat cutting off the tree limb he's sitting on. His girlfriend had no doubt seen it, too. Her last memory of him, on the "Here's a cutie for you" segment of the evening news. Great.

"So how do you think I feel about it? You think it does an agent any good to have the whole world know you got clients with shit for brains? You ever try to do business with people, they gotta ring off and get back to you later, 'cause they're laughing too hard?"

That was the problem in dealing with Brevis: no one had ever suffered the way he had.

"Okay, okay; look, you don't have to tell *me* it wasn't a great idea." Axxter tried to get the call back on track. "I was under a lot of pressure at the time. Those guys were trying to kill me. All right?"

"Yeah, well, just don't do it again. Jesus Christ!" Brevis's voice broke into a yelp. "Do you know what this call is costing me? Where the hell are you calling me from?"

He must've seen the Wire Syndicate's charges piling up. "Look, Brevis, you're going to find this hard to believe, but I'm a long way away from you—"

"I'll bet—mother of God—"

"—I'm on the other side. Of the building. I'm on Cylinder's eveningside. You understand? *I'm on the other side.*"

Brevis was silent for a moment. "Jeez, Ny, you're full of surprises today. Am I supposed to believe that? Just because I believed you're alive?"

■ ■ ■ 161

"It's true, I swear it. Look, have the Wire Syndicate run a locate on this jack. You'll need to get the number anyway, so you can call me back."

"What the hell should I call you back for? You're broke, you're officially dead, and as a client you're a liability, not an asset. I should get the Havoc Mass looking to cut my nuts off, too?"

Axxter felt his palm sweating, his finger trembling in the plug-in. If Brevis should hang up . . . "You're gonna want to call me back. Because I can make money—big money—for you."

"Yeah?" Skeptical again. "How?"

"I'm talking *big* money now." He had to give himself time to think. "The biggest deal you've ever done; I mean, this is the one that'll put you right up in the front rank of agents—" Come on, come on, *think.* "Top dollar; top dollar, Brevis—" Blank, blank, blank.

Then it popped out, all in a piece. The words came spinning out, effortless.

"I may not be worth much as a graffex—not right now, at any rate—but we got something else to sell. *I'm on the other side.* Don't you see? I'm someplace no one else has ever been, at least no one who's ever talked about it. We got info-gathering here, tons of fresh data, stuff we can unload to Ask & Receive for whatever price we ask. Plus—there's the entertainment value. This is real-time adventure we got going here, Brevis. This isn't some little stroll around some diddly-shit morningside sector that everybody's seen a million times before. I'm going to hike all the way across some unknown wallscape—without even a rig to carry me—and encounter God knows what—there could be fuckin' anything out here, man—then cross over through whichever Linear Fair I come to—all that just to make it home. What more could you want? That's a goddamn odyssey, for Christ's sake."

162 ■ ■ ■

"Hm." Brevis, mulling it over, couldn't hide his interest. "Yeah, but . . . you'd have to make it all the way back. Like you said, you don't know what you're going to come across out there. Or what's going to come across *you.*"

"So? Even better. That's exactly why you'll have people getting hooked on the story, following my progress—the suspense factor. Half the audience will be hoping I *don't* make it. If I starve to death, or something worse happens, then it's a big tragedy for everybody else. Real sob stuff. Either way, you get your ten percent."

"Twenty percent. This is outside the usual range of what I handle. It'd fall under a special provision in your contract with the agency."

"Ten, twenty, who gives a fuck." Axxter knew he had him hooked. "It'll be tons of money for both of us."

"Mm—could be. I'd have to run it by some people, see what they think. But . . . it's not bad, Ny; not bad at all. It has some possibilities." Brevis's voice moved up a gear. "Yeah, I think we could get an offer on it."

Bingo. "We gotta have an advance on it, though; a good-sized one. There's stuff I gotta pay for, info to dig out. I'll need to get my location pinpointed, get whatever files or maps exist about this side, I don't care what shape; we'll have to get a search done for every fragment, no matter how small. I'm going to need all the help I can get, if I'm going to pull this off."

"All right; all right, let me work on it." Little tongue-clicking noises came over the line, the sound of the agent revving up. "It's going to take some time, though. Look, just sit tight where you are, okay—"

"Where the hell else am I going to go?"

"Just hang on. I think this is a genuine hot one. I'll get the locate on this call soon as you hang up, and then I'll get back to you soon as we've got an offer. Like I said, though, it'll take a little time."

Axxter's stomach had become a brass-lined vacuum. "How long?"

"You gotta give me twenty-four hours at least."

He sucked in his breath through his teeth. "All right. Just do it, okay? I really need you to come through on this one."

"Hey. Trust me."

After Brevis rang off and the line went dead, Axxter stood up to ease the cramp from his spider crouch by the plug-in jack. His belt pithons reeled out, bracing him in full extension against the wind. In all directions, this sector of eveningside wall looked as bare and empty as when he'd been slowly crawling over it.

A few more hours of sunlight, this side's real day, he calculated. He could go looking around—for what? A nice big cache of dehydrates that some other poor bastard had left behind? His mouth watered hard enough to sting under his tongue. The fantasy rolled in his head, unstoppable: some other poor bastard who'd been luckless enough to land over here somehow—no, he'd *planned* it, a wanderer, like Opt Cooder, that's why he had such nice big supplies of food with him. Then something happened to him—

He didn't like the way that was going. Whatever'd happened to the nice wanderer could happen to him, too. Better to just think about the food and the canned water and the other good things in life. He'd found some rainwater earlier in the half-morning collected in pockmarks a few inches deep in the building's surface; the water tasted like metal, but was better than nothing. It enabled him to salivate, running the fantasy's best moments over again.

Just as he was ready to pull himself back into a more comfortable position hanging close to the wall, he noticed two things. One was that his usual dizzy nausea at moving

164 ■ ■ ■

around in the vertical world, standing perpendicular and the like, was absent. The feeling had abated from his first long-ago days out on the wall, but had never completely vanished. Until now. *Shows how far gone I am. When you're this far out, even your body doesn't give a fuck anymore.* He wrapped his hand around the pithon lines, then saw the other thing.

There was something moving, out at the limit of his sight, silhouetted at the far edge of the wall.

Axxter felt his empty gut clench around itself. There had been no sign of any living thing all the time he'd been clambering around the wall, looking for a plug-in, but that didn't prove anything. All sorts of sectors over on the morningside were just as barren; you could be crossing some bleak territory, and the next thing you knew, be right in some amazing mess—the memory was still sharp of the ripped-open steel and the burned-out horizontal community underneath that he'd stumbled upon. The smell of charred flesh, and the stink of his own fear seeping from his sweat glands, haunted him. Something could always be hiding under the surface, ready to jump out, boogedy-shoop, and *get* you, like those poor bastards. Out of the dark, the Dead Centers. Maybe you never saw them because they spent all their time over on this side, frolicking around and sharpening their teeth.

He strained his sight toward the spot, but the thing, whatever it'd been, was gone. Nothing moving on the building's straight vertical line. It didn't make him feel better.

Could've been anything. He tucked himself back into the wall. *Or nothing.* That rope that Lahft had rummaged together from the bits of trash and wire—there had been rags in that big enough to have caught a stray wind, gone lifting and waving about. He thought he'd gone farther than that on his search; the spot where he'd woken up should've been well hidden by the building's curve. Still, something like that; just junk, scraps banging around. Nothing to worry about.

Nothing at all. He kept telling himself that, all through the rest of the daylight hours, until another sunset—it still astonished him, if not quite as much—and it was dark enough to catch some sleep. The dull ache of his bruises had him exhausted.

He couldn't even close his eyes. He went on staring into the dark, at the distant spot on the wall.

■
■

The gray seepage of the shadowlight woke him up with a start, his spine jerking tight and his forehead bouncing against one of the splayed-out pithons.

He rubbed a crust from the corner of his eye. It took awhile to work up enough spit to swallow the evil taste in his mouth. The sleep, however much he'd gotten—no memory of when he'd finally nodded off in his dangling sling—didn't seem to have done much good. His arms ached down into the sides of his fists, as though he'd been punching them into the wall all night long.

Another surprise, a new thing, when he'd finally managed to pry his eyes all the way open. A package wrapped up in gray paper and crisscrossed with twine. Somebody— something—had managed to sneak up on him while he'd been unconscious, and leave it, tied onto one of the pithons with the same rough cord.

He reached over and prodded it with a finger. Nothing happened; his fingertip poked into something soft under the paper.

"I'll be damned." Awake enough now to catch the faint smell, an aroma trace that jerked his stomach into a knot rattling against his spine. He pulled the package loose— the twine's knots slipped free with his tug—and held it against himself, tearing the paper loose.

Some kind of bread, two flat rounds; they wobbled up and down in his hands. Also a plastic pouch filled with water, or something equally clear. Axxter eyed everything with caution. Lahft wouldn't have come round and left him something like this—who'd ever seen angels carrying things? What other friends did he have over on this side?

"Well, shit—" He tore off a piece of the spongy bread and stuffed it in his mouth. He'd be just as dead, eventually, if he didn't eat it. He chewed and swallowed, then tore off the corner of the pouch and drank, tilting his head back.

He left half the water, knotting the top of the pouch to keep it from leaking, and a handful of the bread, rolled up and tucked inside his shirt. It might be awhile until more presents showed up. He supposed it was connected to whatever he'd seen before, moving around in the distance. *Fattening me up, probably.* A full gut only took the edge off his worrying.

When Brevis called, it jerked him awake; the happy working of his gut had lulled him out. He nearly pulled his finger out of the plug-in jack, breaking the connection.

"Ny—hey, man, how you doing?" Brevis's voice burbled in his ear. "How's things out there?"

Axxter's heart sank. He knew the range of his agent's tones by now. Rattling excitement meant he had a deal cooking; that bright chirpy hello meant shit.

"I'm fine. Couldn't be better." Axxter shaded his eyes. The sun had just come over the top of the building. "So. What's happening?"

Brevis's voice went soft and apologetic. "Well, it doesn't look too good right now, Ny. I wasn't able to sell the rights for you."

"Why not?" He jabbed his finger harder into the jack. "What the fuck do they want?"

"Hey—don't jump down *my* throat, man. I was on the phone for *hours*, right up to the top buyers at Ask & Receive. Both the research and the entertainment divisions came down against the package. They just weren't interested."

He couldn't believe it. "For Christ's sake, why? This is a hot idea—when would they ever have another opportunity for something like this again—"

"Ny—what it is, is that they just don't think you're gonna make it. If it was just that you were going to make it back around to the morningside, I could've worked the tragic odyssey angle harder, gone for the sob appeal. But they don't think you're going to make it very far at all; at least not enough to build up some kind of audience. They think your ass is grass, right where you're sitting."

He felt the sweat chill between his shoulderblades, a cold wind across the empty wall. "All right." Carefully, slowly. "What's the deal? What's happening that makes them so sure I won't make it?"

Brevis was silent for a moment. "It really doesn't look too good, Ny. You're really in the middle of nowhere; you're a long ways from either one of the Linear Fairs."

"So I got a hike in front of me. Big deal. No, I want to know what else there is. Come on, lay it on me."

"I didn't want to make it any rougher on you, Ny, but if you really gotta know—you're still in deep shit with the Havoc Mass. Somehow the word got around to them that you're still alive. I figure once I started negotiating with Ask & Receive, they contacted the Mass to see what they had to say about the whole thing. And it wasn't good. That Havoc bunch is still major pissed at you. They've already sent some hit teams out to the Linear Fairs, plus put an open bounty out on your head. You come waltzing into either Fair, trying to cross through it to the morningside—*if* you make it that far—and any little thug can just nail you and collect a nice bit of change. The Ask & Receive people didn't figure there was much entertain-

168 ■ ■ ■

ment value in seeing some fool walk into a slaughterhouse with his name on it. I mean, there's no *suspense.* Let's face it, Ny—you're a dead man right now."

"All right. Fine." Those fuckers—his anger purged every other emotion; he could feel the blood pumping up into his face, stinging across the bridge of his nose. "They think they got me nailed—fine. They think they can leave me hanging out here to dry? I got news for 'em." The words seethed through his teeth. "If I can't make it back by going around the building, I'll get there another way."

"Ny—" Sad. "There isn't any other way."

"Oh? Is that right? Well, how's this, then—I won't come around the building. I'll go *through* it."

Silence, the seconds ticking by, adding up to a full minute before Brevis replied. "What—what're you talking about?"

"You heard me." Axxter had heard himself, the words still turning and shining inside his head. Now that he'd cooled off a bit, he could admire the idea in all its simplicity. Why screw around? You just head in the straightest line possible to where you want to go. "I'll go through Cylinder, right through the middle. I won't have to dink around crawling all over the surface, and I won't have to worry about a bunch of hardcases waiting for me at Linear Fair. I'll just head straight from here over to the morningside; all I gotta do is find some entry around here, and get onto the horizontal levels inside. Hey, if nothing else, I'll save myself a lot of time and traveling. And screw the Havoc Mass—I can work it so I pop up on the other side in some sector controlled by the Grievous Amalgam. They'll think I'm a fucking hero for making the Mass look like a bunch of idiots. Those guys think that tape they sold to Ask & Receive was funny? Wait till this little stunt gets broadcast." That was a pleasant thought: *Har har har on you, turkeys.*

"Jeez, Ny—I gotta hand it to you." Brevis was probably shaking his head in amazement. "That's a hell of an idea you got there. It's not a very good idea, but you get points for the concept, you really do."

"What's not good about it?"

"Ny—you're *talking* about *going* through the *center* of the building. Not just right under the wall, in some cozy little horizontal sectors. We're talking right smack in the middle of Cylinder. You know, there are reasons why people don't just go for little Sunday strolls in there." Under the joking edge in Brevis's voice something darker showed through. "*Bad* reasons, Ny. I mean, good reasons, but bad shit. You know what I'm talking about?"

"I know." Words neither one of them wanted to say aloud, yet they sat there on the line between them like a lead weight. *The Dead Centers*. The thought of them screwed with his brain more than they ever could with Brevis's; he'd seen—in real time, not just off some tape replay—what the dark skulkers could do. He'd already walked around in their cold footsteps—if feet was what they had; the unbidden image of giant snail trails, smearing ashes and slobbered bones, crawled inside his head. The smell of the burned-out horizontal sector he'd stumbled on was always there, ready to come bubbling up at any spooky moment.

"Brevis—I know all that stuff." Voice level, down to the fundamental rock. "But I don't have any other choice. Do I? And what do I have to lose, anyway? Like you said, right where I'm sitting now, I'm a dead man."

The agent took a moment to think it over. "I suppose you're right. You know, it's wild enough, maybe they'd go for it. Let me run it past 'em. Can you hang tight for about an hour?"

"I'm not going anywhere."

It was half an hour. Brevis's voice jumped out over the wire.

170 ■ ■ ■

"They went for it, Ny. We got a deal. Ask & Receive is cutting the transfer of funds right now. They went apeshit for the bit about going straight through the building. I mean, the odds are even worse on your making it all the way, but they figure they'll recoup their upfront money to you and go into profits just on the research data you'll generate. The entertainment value of seeing just how far you go before you get snuffed, that's just gravy."

"How nice for them." Axxter's thoughts started ticking over again. All the stuff he'd need; whatever maps, data, unconfirmed rumors, old historical fragments, whatever already existed in Ask & Receive's files. He'd have to get it all dumped out, break it down, before he could even get started. One thing to say what you were going to do, another to actually get off your ass and do it.

"They're gonna want daily reports from you, Ny. Whatever happens to you, whatever you come across. You'll have to keep an eye out for phone lines in there—"

"Yeah, right; whatever." Ask & Receive would have to be happy with whatever they got. "Look, Brevis; thanks for setting it up, but I really gotta get cracking now."

"There's some other things about the deal you should know about, Ny—"

There were always other things. "I'll get back in touch with you. Okay? Talk to you later." He broke the connection to his agent. Time to check in with his bank.

ACCOUNT REACTIVATED. Blinking in a cheery green.

That made him feel better. Even more when his account balance came up, right in the middle of his vision. He looked out across the clouds, counting the zeroes superimposed on the sky.

11

There wasn't a lot to go on.
Axxter stared into the
darkness, the night sky beyond Cylinder,
going over the scraps he'd winnowed out of the Ask &
Receive files. He chewed the last of the bread, draining
the plastic pouch to wash it down.

Nobody had ever done it before, gone all the way
through the building; that much was established. Otherwise Ask & Receive wouldn't have paid over that nice fat
sum, which he'd already spent a good whack of rooting
around in their archives. *Should've asked for some kind of
discount*—since he was, in effect, working for them. *Next
time, ha ha.* He didn't feel like laughing. His eyes stung
from the luminous words that had been crawling across his
sight for hours.

The best piece of info he'd come across—UNCON-
FIRMED dancing all over it—was cross-compiled from the
few reports of those who'd gone even a little way past the

usually sealed barriers that kept the horizontal sectors nice and safe from the bad things further inside. Risky shit, that; little wonder that nobody had ever done much more than stick their heads past the barrier, take a quick peek, then jump back and seal up the hole.

The intriguing bit was the repeated speculation that there were tunnels running straight through the building. That the major access sites on the morningside, which allowed one to go back and forth from the building's horizontal sectors to the vertical world outside, were the former openings of the supposed tunnels. People on the horizontal weren't much interested in archaeology—from his own days there, Axxter didn't recall them as being interested in much of anything—but some research had been done, dating the barriers just inside the access sites, finding them to be of a later date than the surrounding walls. The conclusion that beckoned, if one was given to the whole notion of transbuilding tunnels, was sometime, back in those misty War days, somebody had sealed up the openings. *And they'd probably had good reason to—* Axxter stopped that thought from going any further.

Say the tunnels were still there, though, straight shots from *this* side to *that* side— That'd be cool; you could walk from where the sun went down to where it came up. Back home on the morningside. A pleasant little stroll, and a helluva lot easier than clambering hand-over-hand along the building's exterior without the Norton to make tracks on.

Axxter found a few crumbs in his jacket pocket, rolled them between his thumb and finger and popped it into his mouth. Maybe his phantom benefactor would tie another present to him while he slept—he could use the provisions for when he set out to find some means of access underneath the building's surface.

He knew where he was, at least. Not learned from Ask

& Receive, but the Wire Syndicate: they'd been able to give him a pinpoint on the location of the plug-in jack he'd been using.

So to find an entry point on this side . . .

Axxter worried a fingernail, nothing else left to chew on. Step by step; he'd already figured out the parameters he was working inside. Assume everything about the tunnels through the building was true, and the entry sites into the horizontal sectors on the morningside had been the mouths of the tunnels before they'd been blocked off inside; then just work back from there. He pulled up a large-scale map of the morningside, with the entry sites indicated by red circles. His drifting odyssey in the gas angel's arms had brought him almost exactly equidistant from either Linear Fair, the two dividing lines on either side of the building. And two-thirds of the distance down-wall from the toplevel to the cloud barrier below. So draw a line on the map, right down the middle from top to bottom, and another crossing it, then pick out the entry site mark closest to that X-point—

You idiot. Rubbing his eyes; he must've been getting tired. To think that was all he had to figure out. The morningside entry sites were where the tunnels used to open out onto Cylinder's surface; they were sealed up now, just inside the building. What was he going to do, make it all the way through the building and then wind up rapping his knuckles on some steel plug, trying to convince somebody on the horizontal sector on the other side that he wasn't some Dead Center paying a visit? If there was anybody on the other side to hear him—there were more uninhabited horizontal sectors than otherwise inside Cylinder, and not all of the occupied ones cozied right up to the inner wall that sealed off the building's spooky core. Even if he let Ask & Receive know ahead of time where he'd be showing up, it wouldn't be worth it to them

174 ▪ ▪ ▪

to piss off a heavyweight tribe like Mass by assisting him—Ask & Receive kept a strict hands-off policy regarding physical intervention, only recording events, not creating them, precisely to avoid conflicts of interest like that.

Nice going, smart guy. He started over, trying to work it out inside his head, going fuzzy around the edges from fatigue.

What he needed was some place where the seal had been broken, an entry site on the morningside where the tunnel—still assuming there was one—ran straight through to open air.

Where the seal had been broken . . . A bad memory, a memory of bad things, rose up and connected, socketing in tight to the analytical thought.

The burned-out sector.

His own little discovery, come back around. Some place you'd swear never to go back to; that one look was all you'd need for the rest of your life, every little sensory pulse, every crunch of ashy bone beneath your feet, every scent of blackened flesh, sealed under diamond crystal.

No problem with the seal having been broken between that brightly-lit horizontal world just under the building's surface and the dark stuff farther inside. And then some. He dug the coordinates for the burned-out sector from his archive, then scanned them across the map filling the center of his sight. A match: one of the little circles marking an entry site lined up.

"There you go—" He nodded to himself, not sure how pleased he should feel about this new discovery. If there were tunnels running through the building, then the end of that one was definitely open. Would've been handier if the spot was closer to the crossing of the two lines he'd drawn on the map. It'd take him days to get to the corresponding spot on this side, the other end of the line drawn straight to the building's center.

That was also assuming that the tunnel was open on this side. Also that the supposed tunnel did run through the center, instead of at some other angle through the building. And a few million other things.

He had the advantage of being up against it, with no other choice. You were absolved of the fear of making the wrong decision. In some ways, Axxter figured, dead men had it easy.

In the morning—morning on the other side, the disconcerting half-light on this—he'd start out for the spot where he'd calculated the tunnel opening should be. In the meantime, there was this night to get through.

You're a fool. Knowing already what he was going to do. With money in his account, and a phone line handy, he always did the same thing. He reached over and wriggled his finger inside the plug-in jack, made contact, and called up HoloDays.

■
■

He didn't expect her to be waiting for him. She never was.

He extended a forefinger of the image he was walking around in; the sensor at the side of the door picked up the presence of coherent light activity, and rang the bell inside her apartment. The sensor, at least, interpreted him as being human.

Maybe she wasn't home—whenever he got this close, he started hoping that. Though he couldn't imagine where else she'd be. Off work, she socked in tight into her cozy home space. The same as everyone else on the horizontal.

The door swung open. Axxter held up the image of his hand. "Hi. Just thought I'd drop by. And say hello."

Ree glared at him. There was a discrepancy, a jitter on the line: the image she perceived of him was displaced a few inches behind his sensory feedback. The effect was as

176 ■ ■ ■

though her narrow gaze was boring right into the back of his skull.

"What do *you* want?"

He made the image shrug. "Hey—like I said. I just wanted to see you. That's all. I mean, I don't even have tactile sensation. See?" He poked at the doorjamb, the image of his finger disappearing two inches into the panel. "So it's not like I'm here just to . . . fool around or anything."

A weary sigh from her. "Believe me; you wouldn't have, anyway." She leaned against the door, arms folded. "So now you're here, you've seen me—is that it? You're happy now?"

"Well, there were some things I wanted to tell you—"

"Tell *me*? I'll tell you a few things. I'll tell you that I don't appreciate having some idiot that everybody's seen is an idiot come round knocking on my door. I don't need my neighbors checking it out, that I got the biggest fool in or outside the building thinking that he's got something going with me—"

"I don't?" Axxter tilted the image's head, puzzled. "I mean—you and me—we're not—"

Her eyes, small to begin with, disappeared in the tight lines of her scowl. "Not after this latest bullshit. You don't care about yourself, you're happy to be some bum out on the wall, some . . . some glorified tattoo artist—fine. That's up to you. But you're not going to embarrass me with it anymore."

"That's what I came to talk to you about. What I came to tell you—I'm going to give it up." His image had stepped back, away from the freezing chill of her words; he could feel that with or without any sensory input. "Really. I'm not kidding you about this. I've thought about it a lot. And that's what I've decided. Soon as I get back, I mean back for real, I'm going to go back on the

■ ■ ■ 177

horizontal. Give up running around on the vertical. I'll have plenty of money, I'll be able to buy myself a commission, some nice junior executive job . . . the whole bit. And then . . . you and me . . . you know, we could work it out."

She shook her head. "Ny—I don't believe you. You've always been a lying sack of shit."

He was about to say something, some vow of intention, when another voice shouted, loud enough to rattle the image's optical feedback, setting the corridor and the open door shimmering in his sight.

"Hey! Who the fuck are you!" A female voice, but not hers; he could see her mouth, closed and tight-lipped. "Get off this line or I'll deck you so hard you won't know what's happening!"

He saw her staring at him now, eyes widening a bit, lips curling in disgust.

"You heard me!" The voice, attached to nothing, went louder. "You little shit! Just you wait!"

Then he wasn't standing outside his girlfriend's apartment, way over in the distant horizontal. The hookup with HoloDays had evaporated with a jarring suddenness. He was hanging in the dark again, over on the eveningside.

"I'm gonna kick your butt so hard—"

He pulled his finger from the plug-in jack, and the voice inside his head disappeared. Leaving silence.

What the hell was that? Some kind of a parasite on the line. He'd encountered line-ghosts before—the main hazard of being too cheap to shell out for shielded calls—but never any with that brand of death-threat hostility. Usually they just made nuisances out of themselves with their constant wheedling to come and play, to join in their little line-ghost games.

He stuck his finger back into the jack; an experiment. With immediate results.

"There you are, dickhead. I wasn't through with you."
The voice grated low. "You're in deep shit with me now."

"Hey, hold on a minute." The barrage was getting
tiresome. "Who is this? What's the problem?"

"You're gonna find out what the problem is, fella. And
you know damn well who this is. And you know this line
is part of *my* network, too. You're one of those cracker
defects guys, aren't you? I can tell."

"Who? What are you talking about—"

The words CRACKER D:FEX spelled out in his sight, one
red letter after another, then faded away.

"I've had just about enough shit from you D:Fex
clowns. This is *my* network, and it's off limits to you and
your jerkoff buddies. And now that you've been hanging
on the line long enough for me to get you pinpointed, I'm
gonna be over there in person to kick you off. See you
later, dipshit."

Silence again, then more red words. This time spelling
out FELONY M:PULSE. They took a lot longer to fade
away.

Jesus H. Christ. The cold hard tone in the woman's
voice had been more unnerving than her initial wrath. He
hadn't understood half of what she'd been rattling on
about.

Violence had been promised, though of what sort—
Screw it. At this point, what was there to worry about?
His dead-man status still insulated him.

Still with his finger in the jack; a legit call came
through.

"Ny—where the hell have you been?" Brevis's voice
was excited, but not in any way that indicated money.
Panic, instead. "I've been trying to get hold of you for
hours!"

"What's the matter?"

"You gotta get moving, Ny; I mean, like *right now*. You

don't have time to go figuring out routes and stuff. You gotta get off that spot immediately, man."

"Hold on. Come on, slow down." His agent's words had come swarming over him, almost too fast to understand. "What're you going on about?"

The sound of a big gulp of breath came over the line. "Heavy action, Ny. I didn't count on shit like this. It's the Havoc Mass—they've sent major weight out after you. A megassasin has been spotted crossing over Linear Fair Left; it's apparently making a beeline straight for you. I can't believe how pissed those people are at you; I mean, this is the first reported instance of any military tribe personnel entering eveningside territory. It's just unheard of. But the word's out, Ny—they're not going to stop until they've got you squashed like a bug."

He felt dazed. As if he weren't in enough shit already. *Don't these guys ever give up?* They'd already had their shot at him. Time to give the rest of the world a turn.

"How long ago? I mean, how long ago did it go through the Fair?"

"Don't know, exactly—might've been four, five, maybe six hours ago. And it was making tracks, by all reports. Those big megs can really move."

Axxter wondered if it was the same one that he'd done the graffex designs on; Cripplemaker's commission. It'd appeal to the warriors' sense of irony for him to get squashed by the megassassin bearing his own work. The last thing he'd see would be the emblem he'd designed himself. It'd be like getting killed by your own signature.

Brevis's voice rattled on. "That's what I mean, Ny— you gotta get moving. It's got you pinpointed by the location of the jack you've been using. The longer you hang around there, or anywhere nearby, the sooner it's going to be on your ass."

"Christ . . ."

180 ■ ■ ■

"Look, just get away from there. Any direction's fine; but just *go*. I'll do what I can from this end—maybe I can find out what direction the meg'll be coming in—but everything else you're going to have to figure out on the run. Okay? And give me a call when you find some place just as far from where you're at as you can make it."

When the first gray half-light oozed around him, the plug-in jack with its yellow marking rings was already beyond sighting, hidden by the curve of the building. His progress had been slow in the dark, clambering blind, his chest close to the wall, only the pithons sure about striking out for new holds.

He paused to catch his breath; his heart had been hammering in his throat the whole distance. Brevis's panic had infected him, locking into his spinal column. *Take it easy*—he could make it if he just kept a steady pace, kept traveling. Maybe he could. If he could reach the entry site to the interior, the tunnel opening he'd calculated . . . then he might have a chance.

His pulse had slowed with the light; trying to move in the dark had spooked him. Too much like running in nightmares, where there was no sign of motion at all. He filled his lungs, nostrils stinging with the chill air, and reached out for another handhold.

He heard the whistle of the cable reeling out before it hit him. Across the shoulderblades, knocking him flat up against the wall—then he was jerked back by an arm around his throat.

"Don't move, sucker." The voice snarled at his ear. A woman's voice; he'd heard it before. Something pointed dug through his jacket toward his ribs. The sensation ended, simultaneous with the appearance of a shining knifeblade close to his face. "Get the picture? Be smart."

The woman shifted her weight off his back. He turned his head to look at her.

She sat in a loop knotted in the cable, dangling alongside him. A kid, younger than he, with dark hair cropped short. She looked him over, her level gaze traveling from his boots upward.

"You're not a circuit rider." She used the point of the knife to scratch the side of her face. "I can tell. You should be over on the other side. What're you doing here?"

The voice that had broken in on his hollow-time call; now confronting him in the flesh. "You know, you don't need to wave that thing around." The blade annoyed him. "You want to know something, you can just ask."

She smiled and tucked the knife into her belt. "I thought you were one of that D:Fex bunch. I've got it in for 'em." She leaned back against the wall. "So what's the deal—you trying to get back over to the morningside? Is that it?"

"You've heard about me?"

The woman shook her head. "What you people do is no concern of mine. I've got other business to take care of. I wouldn't've come around here at all if you hadn't been using part of my network."

"Your network?" He remembered some of the things she'd said before, when she'd just been a voice on the line. "Was that that M something or other?"

"M:Pulse. Yeah, that's it."

"So you're, uh, Felonious."

"Felony. Sometimes; most of the time, actually. When I'm not something else."

Axxter glanced up the wall, along the length of the cable. He could see where it emerged from a peeled-back section of the wall, just large enough for someone to wriggle through. *Work on this one*—anybody who had working knowledge of things like that was worth cultivating.

"You're a line-ghost?"

"'Line-ghost'—give me a break." She looked at him disgustedly. "Line-ghosts are just phenomena, like static or something. They're just echoes on the wire. You should be able to tell the difference between a ghost and a circuit rider."

"Oh." He nodded. "So, uh, what's a circuit rider?"

A pitying smile. "Circuit riders are people like me, people who can do things. Do things with the wires, man. We're into the systems. People like you, you make a call, you go over the wire, through the grid, little dot-dot-dots moving along. But you're like a rat that's got its way through the maze memorized; all you see are the little walls in front of your rat nose. The trick is to get above the maze, get your hands on it, make it do what *you* want."

"I get you." He couldn't hide his disappointment. "You mean phone phreaking. Hacking and stuff."

"Hey, fuck you, man." Felony seemed genuinely offended. "Don't give me that. That's ancient stuff—people were doing that shit before the War. Those punks, that D:Fex bunch and the other network families, they can waste their time that way if they want to; gaming each other and breaking into restricted access files and kid shit like that. I've got more important business to take care of. I've got *territory*."

"What's that supposed to mean?" Keep her talking.

"I'll tell you what it means. It means I don't have to band together with a bunch of other circuit riders, just to have somebody to watch my ass while I'm out working the wires. M:Pulse is a lone-wolf network, fella; it's nobody but me." A broad smile accompanied the swagger in her voice. "I got circuits that nobody can get on except me. That was why I got so pissed when I found you on that line, making your call. I don't handle encroachment well, it just burns me up, man. Those wires are *mine*."

He figured she was referring to some part of the phone grid running through the building. Out here, in the middle of nowhere. "So what makes them yours? Just because nobody else uses them?"

Felony shook her head, still smiling. "No, man, it's more than that; a *lot* more. I've cracked the interface; I was born able to do it, I just had to learn how much I could do. And I can do anything on the wires. I mean, anybody can get into the wires—that's what having a terminal inside your head is all about. The trick is to get back out, and come up inside *somebody else's head.* When you can do that, there ain't shit that can stop you."

She really was just a kid, he realized. Easy enough to bait her into bragging about stuff like that. That was what living on "the wires," as she put it, spending your whole existence messing about inside a maze of electronic circuits, did to you. Nothing but games, a sealed Peter Pan existence. Everybody, on the vertical or the horizontal, knew of that little world just on the other side of the phone. You could dabble your toe in it easily enough— there was always a standing invitation to "come in and play," more kid mentality—with the accompanying risk of getting your whole head sucked in. And spending the rest of your life there, your body a vestigial organ in reality, the real you stripped down to the infantile wiggle on the circuits, looking for fun among the electrons.

"That's the trick, huh?" It sounded like some nutball thing; she might be crazy. "How do you do something like that?" He had to find out what he could from her—like her access under the building's surface, and other handy stuff—and get moving again.

She looked smug, pleased with herself. "I just do it. The trick is to get somebody up close enough to a jack I've got exclusive control of, so I can catch 'em. Like this body." She pressed her thumb against her breastbone.

184 ■ ■ ■

"This ain't mine. Well, it is *now,* but it's not the one I started out with. I got several of 'em, about a dozen, all stashed in various places around the building. It keeps me hopping, making the rounds and taking care of them all; they gotta be fed and stuff. This one's the only eveningsider I got. It took a long time to catch her; I used some old pre-War music I got out of an archive I broke open. I looped it and kept it playing from a jack I found over here that had an audio output; must've been part of some old public-address system. I just hung around for days, lurking in the wire, waiting for one of 'em to come along, hear the music, and lean up close to the jack. I'd just about given up when this one wandered by. Soon as she had her head up close, I made the jump, and zap, she was mine."

Weird shit, whether it was true or not. Talking about the leap from being a cold signal on a wire into warm, living flesh. If she could do that . . . Good thing it was impossible. He didn't want to let on that that was what he thought. "What happened to her? The person who used to be inside the body?"

Felony shrugged. "Died, I guess. You take over somebody else's body, you gotta spend a little time getting control, rooting 'em out. Then they just aren't there anymore."

"Yeah, but a dozen of them? What do you need so many for?"

"I told you—I'm a loner. I don't need a bunch of other circuit riders tagging along, cramping my action. This way, I got *physical control* of the jacks I use, plus some great big sections of the wire itself, whole subnets. I can cut 'em in and out of the grid whenever I want, so none of those little jerks can get into 'em when I'm not looking. If I tried to do that with just one body, I'd be hiking my ass all over this damn building. Twelve bodies, in twelve locations, I can just zip from one to the other, pop in as long as I need to do my housekeeping, and split to the next one. Cuts the travel time down to nothing, so I got more time to do what I want." Her smile went wicked.

"Yeah, I bet." The surreal nature of the conversation finally seeped in. Hanging on the wall a million miles from home, with all sorts of bad news hot on his tail, having a chat with some loony girl with the notion that she could pop in and out of bodies like changing her clothes. The world had assumed this quality since he'd fallen through the clouds. *Maybe I never came back up.* The usual comforting notion, assumed when things got too strange: *Maybe I'm still falling, dreaming in the bed of air.* He opened his eyes and the woman was still there.

"I suppose . . . you're going to take *me* over now. Add my body to your collection. Is that it?"

She looked at him scornfully. "Why would I want you? Don't flatter yourself. I already got one body, this one, right here in this locale. Another one would be just something else I'd have to look after. Besides, I got my standards. If they aren't young and in good shape—better than you—and female, then I'm not much interested. Why should I go back to some ugly guy's body? I had one to begin with, and I was glad when I got rid of it."

More nuts stuff. He had humored her long enough; time to get some practical info.

"Say, as long as you're here, think you could tell me if—"

She was already climbing back up the rope, with monkeylike agility. She looked back down at him. "Sorry, mac, but like I said, I'm a busy person. Maybe I'll come by again some time, see how you're doing."

In a few seconds, she was at the small opening in the wall, and vanished inside. Axxter stared after her for a moment, then shook his head and resumed his slow travel.

186 ■ ■ ■

12

He spotted him coming. Even in the night, he could see the figure in the distance, working its way toward him.

When it had gotten too dark to go on traveling, his arm and leg muscles cramping up, Axxter had drawn the pithons in tight, setting himself as close to the wall as possible. For sleeping; or at least to look as though he were.

He'd been expecting that the mysterious benefactor, the person who'd laid the bread on him, would show up sometime after the sun had gone down beyond the cloud barrier. All the time he'd been traveling across the wall, he'd had the sense that somebody else was out there, tailing him. Not the loony girl—he figured whether she was nuts or not, she had some crazed variety of errands to run. Or the Havoc Mass's megassassin; if it had been close enough for him to detect, it would've already barrel-assed the rest of the way, locked on target, and made mincemeat of him. Unless there was more than one spooky cat lurking around in this sector, it had to be the one with the food. He hoped it was; a day's worth of his hard-working progress had gotten him to the point of starving again.

There it was again. Hunger and ongoing weirdness had sharpened his senses. He could hear it, something moving closer, little clicks of metal against metal, a sidling scrape against the wall. He closed his eyes, waiting.

Breath, quiet and unhurried. Axxter felt the stirring in the air. Until it was right next to him—

He twisted about and grabbed. For a moment, he had his arm around the figure's waist, pulling it to him. It gave a heavy grunt, half from surprise, half wind knocked out by Axxter's forehead butting into its stomach.

"Sonuva*bitch*—" A fist landed against the side of Axxter's head, hard enough to dizzy him. His grip on the figure's ribs broke, and he slumped back into the pithons' slack.

A flashlight went on, glaring in his face. He shielded his eyes; past his hand's edge, he saw the other man dimly lit by the beam bouncing off the wall.

The man straightened up, sucking in a ragged gulp of breath. "Jeez—" Another gulp. "Try to do somebody a favor. The thanks you get."

Axxter could see a narrow, sharp-angled face, long, spiderlike hands holding the flashlight. Like a club, in case of any more action.

"Nice way to act." The man probed at the edge of his ribcage. "You could've killed me."

It wasn't just his hands, Axxter saw now. They were fitted with some sort of fanned hooks, strapped to his forearm and extending beyond his fingers. Not metal, but something black that bent like rubber against the man's jacket.

"Sorry." Axxter shook his head, trying to get rid of a ringing noise in his ears. "But you were the one sneaking around."

188 ■ ■ ■

"Of course I was sneaking around. I expected this kind of reaction. You morningsiders are all alike—you're just ready for a punch-out all the time."

You morningsiders—easy to figure out the rest. "You're from this side?"

"Born and bred. Name's Sai. Here, I figured you could use this." He dug into a pack looped around one shoulder and held something out.

More of the flat round bread. Axxter took it and tore a piece off. But before taking a bite— "How come?"

"How come what? The food, you mean? I just knew you'd need it. Stuck out over here like this. I didn't want to see you starve to death before you had a chance to get back home to the other side." He took a pouch of water from the bag and drank before handing it over as well. "That'd seem kind of cruel. To go that way, and all. I mean, if you're willing to take your shot at going straight through the building, you should get a real chance at it."

Axxter chewed and swallowed. "What do you know about that?"

A shrug. "I know all kinds of stuff. I know more about you—and where you come from—than you know about me, and the way things are around here. But you see, that goes back to deep psychic divisions in your head, of which the building can be seen as an exteriorized representation, a mirror-image grown large. The morningside is all light and surface, and action all the time; whereas over here it gets underneath appearances, and into thinking and knowing. Very broody."

Another loony. This territory seemed to be crawling with them. The bread was all right, though.

"Hey, don't give me that look." Sai had picked up on his thoughts. "The fact that you don't know what I'm talking about just goes to show that you're a real morningsider."

"Maybe so." Axxter had finished half of one of the flat

■ ■ ■ **189**

loaves. "I just don't have a lot of time for discussion. I got a lot of problems right now."

"This is true. Hope you don't mind, but I listened in on your agent's call. Tapped the line. That business with the megassassin is going to be a bitch. Those guys are built for speed." Sai scratched himself with one of the rubbery hooks. "It's going to be on top of your ass before you know it."

This looney seemed to be more helpful than the last. Or at least concerned. "Well, I'm trying to make some speed, but . . . it's slow going."

"That's 'cause you people let yourselves get dependent on those motorbikes. You think as long as you're making noise, you're getting somewhere." Sai held up one hand, shining the flashlight on the hooked contraption. "Simpler the better. You can make really good time with a set of these." The shoulderpack hung empty after he'd taken out another pair of the devices. The leather straps and buckles dangled from the stiff armatures behind the hooks. "Can't really show you how to work 'em until we've got some better light. They can be kind of tricky until you get the knack."

Axxter examined the hooks; they had little sensors at the tips, similar to the ones on his pithons.

"Get some sleep." Sai pulled the lines from his belt up across his chest and fastened them to the wall. "We'll head out soon as we can see." He folded his arms and closed his eyes.

"I don't get it." Axxter fastened the hooked devices onto his own belt. "What're you doing all this for? What's the deal for you?"

One eye opened and regarded him. "You're the most interesting thing that's happened around here. In a long time. You don't know it, but you're something . . . historic." The eye closed; he lowered his chin onto his chest. "You'll see."

190 ■ ■ ■

Axxter reached into his jacket and tore off a small piece of bread. For a while longer, he chewed and watched the figure sleeping next to him.

■

■

"Come on, you gotta let 'em take your weight. Get a little swing going." Sai, several meters ahead and upwall, looked back, waiting for him to catch up.

The travelhooks—as Sai called them—had been scary at first. Axxter clung to the wall, his hands flat against the cold metal, catching his breath. In the half-morning, when Sai had first strapped the devices onto his arms, it'd taken an act of wild faith for him to turn off the pithons, letting the lines retract into his belt and boots so only their triangular heads showed. His safety lines; the old nausea and fear came back that he'd known when he'd first gone out on the vertical. His head had swum, the immovable building seeming to tilt and rock as he'd looked over his shoulder, down toward the cloud barrier below. That had passed, but it had still been several minutes before he'd worked up the courage to use the hooks as Sai had shown him, anchoring himself with one of the devices while swinging monkeylike, twisting back to front, to reach for the next hold with the other.

Even with his hesitancy, they were fast; by the time the sun came over the top of the building, Axxter figured that he and Sai had covered twice the distance he'd made in his previous traveling. Once the rhythm was established, the peculiar torsion of the hooks as they anchored and then bent around themselves . . . The few times Axxter had screwed up and missed catching the next hold, his gut had clenched in fear as the image of himself falling snapped into his head. Then Sai had taken pity on him and explained the devices' interlock system; the previous

■ ■ ■ **191**

anchoring point wasn't released until a microsecond after the new one was locked onto.

"Come on—" Sai's voice called back to him. "You don't have time to lose, man."

Another hour of traveling; Axxter caught up to where Sai had snugged himself in close to the wall. Axxter's arms ached, deep into his shoulders; he rubbed them in turn after reeling out the pithons and latching himself secure.

"You'll get used to it." Sai nodded toward Axxter's hand kneading his bicep. "It's more the novelty of the motion than anything else. The hooks really do most of the work." He took bread and water from his shoulder-bag. "Break time."

Munching away, Sai pointed out to the sky. "Hey, there's your little friend."

Axxter turned his head and saw the distant figure of the gas angel. Lahft; as she came closer, he recognized her, smiling happily.

She dangled in air next to him, close enough to touch. "Hi. Hello. Falling?"

He leaned back against the pithons, and shook his head. "No. Not yet, at any rate."

With little swimming motions, she turned around. She looked over her shoulder and the top of the spherical membrane. "Do more. Do the pretty."

The designs he'd programmed into the biofoil he'd implanted into her were still there. *She's gotten bored with them.* One of the unfortunate qualities of time: everything got old eventually. He wondered if he'd done her a favor by letting her know that, ending even that small bit of her innocence.

"I guess I can . . ." He hadn't tried sending out any signal from his transceiver; since the Small Moon's orbit didn't include this side of the building, there hadn't seemed any point. But with the target right in front of him— "Okay.

192 ■ ■ ■

How's this?" He pulled a tiger playing with a butterfly up from his archive, coded and sent it over the distance of less than a meter. As the screen display dropped from his vision, he saw the image blossoming across Lahft's membrane.

"Nice." She turned from admiring herself and looked at him.

"Yeah, it's nice." The sunlight coming through the membrane made it radiant, a smooth glowing rose. "That's the best display I've ever had."

Beside him, Sai nodded. "It's kind of a shame that all this stuff usually just gets wasted on a bunch of big ugly guys."

Lahft wasn't listening to them, letting the breeze slowly draw her away.

"Hey—" Axxter called out to her. "Come back around again sometime—whenever you want—and I'll do another one for you."

She considered this, putting a finger to her chin. Then that same unalloyed smile appeared. "When *you* want. You here, and me—" She flung her arm out to indicate some distant point in the sky. "You make you—like a pretty, but *you*—on me. Then I come here. To you." She had floated several meters away, and had to shout the last words. Before she was gone entirely, dwindling to a far speck.

Sai yawned, stretching out his arms in front of him. "Angels are okay. You could do a lot worse than being on a friendly basis with them."

He realized for the first time that Lahft had shown none of the usual angelic shyness around Sai. As if she was used to him, or just not scared of him.

"I suppose. I don't see what good it'll ever do me, though."

Sai shrugged. "It's like those old stories, you know, fairy tales and stuff, where the kid befriends the ants and the birds. And they wind up saving his ass somehow on the last page. You just never know."

It wasn't the first time Axxter didn't know what the hell somebody was talking about. "What about that other one? That girl?" He assumed that Sai, with his spying around, had witnessed that encounter. "I suppose she's got her uses, too."

"That circuit-rider broad?" Sai snorted. "You'd be smart to steer well clear of her. People like that can cause a lot of trouble."

"Yeah, she seemed pretty demented. Talking some crazy stuff about switching around into different bodies. Like she had a wardrobe of them, or something."

Sai shook his head. "That's not what I meant. If she were crazy, then she wouldn't have such a potential for trouble. But she can really *do* all that stuff—that's why she's such bad news." He tightened the straps on his travelhooks. "Come on. We gotta get moving."

∎

∎

"There. That's it." Sai pointed ahead of them.

Catching his breath, Axxter looked across the wall. The building's surface was tinged red by the sun setting at the limit of the clouds. The entry site appeared as a black hole in the middle of reflected fire.

Sai had been pushing to reach the spot before sundown. The speed of their travel, accelerated by his own growing skill with the hooks, left Axxter dizzy, his arms aching underneath the leather straps.

"Told you I'd get you here." Sai clapped him on the shoulder. "Come on."

He led the way to the curved edge of the site. Axxter grasped the lip and peered inside. Nothing but dark.

"There should be some of my buddies around. I told them to wait for me here." Sai leaned his head inside and

194 ∎ ∎ ∎

let out a high-pitched, whistling cry. It echoed inside the building for several seconds. After it died away, yelping whoops came bouncing back in reply. "All right—let's go on in." He unstrapped the travelhooks from his arms.

Axxter pulled away from him. "Wait a minute. Your friends—people like you—are inside there?" He glanced again at the darkness inside the building.

Sai slung the hooks onto his belt. "Well, sure. Where else?"

He pulled away, a sudden horror prickling across his scalp and arms. "I thought . . . I thought you were an eveningsider. I thought you lived out here." He gestured around at the building's exterior.

"So?" Sai peered at him. "What difference does it make?"

Then he knew. "You're from *in there*." He pushed himself back from the other, the words *Dark Center* unspeakable, filling his mouth. This one, the smiling figure who'd popped up from nowhere, and all the ones like him, inside, calling back and forth like wolves—

Sai reached for him. "Come on—don't be an idiot—"

Axxter slashed at him with the travelhooks. Sai jerked back to avoid their sharp-pointed tips.

"Stay away from me." Axxter crawled backward, his belt pithons securing him to the wall. He kept the hooks lifted between himself and Sai, as though he were brandishing a knife. "Don't come near me. I know what you are. I know what you want."

Sai looked at him in disgust. "You don't know shit." He shook his head, then turned and slipped inside the entry site, into the dark.

■

■

"That was one of your dumber moves."

The voice came from behind him; startled, Axxter

turned his head and saw Felony latched to the wall, re-garding him with her level gaze.

She nodded toward the entry site where Sai had disap-peared. "What'd you flip out on that guy for? He was doing you a favor. Bringing you all the way here, and stuff."

Axxter glanced at the dark hole, then back to her. "Isn't he . . . isn't he one of them?"

"'One of them'—one of them what?"

"You know." He still didn't want to say it aloud.

"You mean, the Dead Centers?"

He nodded.

"Christ almighty." Felony rolled her eyes upward. "Is that what you're all freaked out about? What if he is? You're spooking yourself for no reason, man. Those Dead Center folks aren't anything to worry about. They're harmless."

Proves she's nuts. Or ignorant—she hadn't seen some of the things that he had, such as the burned-out sector over on the other side. "Well . . . I know different."

That got a derisive snort. "There's a bunch of stuff you think you know. And none of it's true."

Irritated, Axxter looked away from her, scanning the building's surface. The last of the twilight was fading, the clouds ebbing to a darker red. He wanted to get well clear of the entry site, but still close enough to keep it in view; if Sai and his Dark Center buddies came swarming out, he wanted to have as much warning as possible.

Plus there was other business he needed to take care of. His fright at discovering Sai's true nature had also ebbed away. "You know where I can find a plug-in jack around here?"

"Gotta make a call? No problem. I know where all the jacks are."

He followed her on a diagonal upwall; she seemed much clumsier moving with her pithons, as if she'd spent little time with them on the building's surface. A kilo-meter away from the entry site, he spotted the jack's con-centric yellow markings.

"Here you go." She secured herself close to the jack.

A taped call was waiting for him as soon as he inserted his finger. NY—YOU CAN GET MEGASSASSIN LOCATION INFO DIRECT FROM A & R. KEEP IN TOUCH. BREVIS. That was cool; his agent had known exactly what he needed to find out. The Havoc Mass was probably making the megassassin's progress public, just to work up au-dience interest and add to their reputation: *You can run but you can't hide*—that always played well.

Ringing up Ask & Receive revealed that the meg-assassin was only a little ways out from the Left Linear Fair, having crossed through the day before.

That's weird. Axxter broke the connection and leaned back against the pithons. He'd figured the megassassin would've been much closer than that; he wouldn't have been happy to find out that it was just about to clear the curve of the building, spot him, and come barreling across the wall to kick his ass, but he wouldn't have been sur-prised. Weren't those big fuckers supposed to be faster than that? He'd always heard that once they got going, they were unstoppable, building up speed, creaming their target as much by force of impact as by all the other good-ies grafted into their formerly human bodies. This one seemed to be taking some kind of tourist route to get to him.

"So what's the problem?" Felony had managed to listen in. "Just means you got a little breathing space."

Axxter worked at a fingernail. "It just doesn't make sense. If the Havoc Mass wants to dramatize their lethal effectiveness, they'd want that thing to be on top of me *fast*. Not sauntering around out there on the wall some-where."

■ ■ ■ 197

"And you're the guy who knows so much. You didn't get filled in on this one, did you?"

"Meaning what?"

She spread her hands out, palms upward. "Hey— maybe these megassassins aren't all they're cracked up to be. Or maybe they *are* rough, but they're deficient in some other skills. Like they're not the world's greatest trackers, maybe. It might be having a hard time picking up your trail—you arrived on this side by air, remember."

He shook his head. "It should've had my last location pinpointed by the plug-in jack I used. Still doesn't make sense."

"Sense, shmense; you gonna worry about every little thing, good or bad? Just consider yourself lucky. For the time being, at least."

Easy for her to say—Axxter regarded her. "Hey, how long were you trailing along after us?"

A shrug. "Long enough."

"Did you hear what we were talking about?"

"You mean, did I hear what that Sai character said about me? Yeah, I heard. So what?" Her smile broadened. "The guy's right. I'm not crazy—but I could be trouble." She reached out, grabbing a new hold. "I got business to take care of. I'll see you around."

■
■

Through the night, he debated calling up Ask & Receive again, in case any more handy info had come in. Finally deciding against it—he already had enough to go on; anything else would probably have confused him even more.

As soon as it was light enough to see, he headed back toward the entry site. Through the hours of waiting in the dark, he had listened for any sound of Sai or the other Dead Centers, their high-pitched wailing calls to each

198 ■ ■ ■

other; there had been nothing but the building's eternal silence. Now, leaning over the lip of the site, he peered into the darkness, searching for any sign of movement within.

Still nothing. *Go on.* The rounded metal edge grew slick with his perspiration. *Go on in, and see what you find.*

Maybe the girl Felony was right; maybe the Dead Centers were nothing to be afraid of. She seemed to know more about what was going on around here, on the eveningside, than he did. Her "business" brought her here, brought her—maybe—to a lot of places around Cylinder; she was in some ways an authority. *If she's not crazy*—the other possibility. He only had Sai's word that she wasn't crazy, that all of her wild talk wasn't just the wind whistling through the cracks in her skull. But if Sai was a Dead Center, then how much of what *he* said could be trusted? Maybe Sai had his own weird reasons for wanting him to believe that Felony could do those things; some spooky mindbend that he hadn't figured out yet. And if you didn't trust what Sai said about Felony—and why should you?— then you couldn't trust what Felony said about the Dead Centers . . .

It went around and around, not in a circle, but more of a spiral, into a darkness as deep as the entry-site hole. He'd have to either trust both of them, Sai *and* Felony, or neither of them.

He was wasting time, he knew, trying to work it out. Either way, he was still on this side of the building and everything he wanted—his whole life—was on the other, with a long walk in between. Worrying about who was lying to him—as if that were some novel state of affairs— was just a way of avoiding climbing into the entry site's shivery black. Out of the light, as much of it as there was at the this hour of the eveningside's half-dawn, and into the night inside the building, which never ended. Heavy spook territory.

Or he could starve to death out here. Axxter sucked in his breath and pulled himself into the entry site. He slowly got to his feet and stood up, feeling a solid horizontal surface under his feet; it had been a long time. The constant tension of moving around in the vertical world ebbed out of his spine, a sensation so pleasant that it sapped away most of his fear.

Cautiously, he walked forward, away from the circular light of the opening. Whatever the intentions of Sai and the other Dead Centers might have been toward him awhile ago, he probably hadn't improved the situation by chasing Sai off with the travelhooks. That sort of thing could piss off the friendliest person, especially when it came in return for various favors performed. He'd have to watch out.

That worry aside, it wasn't so bad inside the building. There was even light, parallel rows of faint blue radiance up on the ceiling; he hadn't been able to see them from outside.

Maybe I'll make it. He thought about that as he walked. Maybe he just had to keep putting one foot in front of the other, keep going; maybe he'd find some Dead Center cache of groceries, a big pile of those round loaves, or Sai or one of the others would take a liking to him again, and drop off little presents while he slept . . . He rolled that thought around as the entry site's opening grew smaller and smaller behind him.

He smelled it first, coming from a smaller tunnel branching off the main one. Like gasoline, sharp and pungent. Pushed into the air by a wave of heat. Some kind of machine; he only had a second to consider what that meant, when it came out of the dark beside him and hit a blow straight to his chest. He fell backward, flying

200 ■ ■ ■

for a moment, until the back of his head and his shoulder struck the floor of the tunnel. He shook his head, dazed, eyes refocusing. In front of him was the megassassin.

He didn't know it could smile.

All black, darkness inside darkness, a raw machine stench of oil and heated metal, and at the same time the human smells of sweat and shit. From Axxter's angle sprawled on the floor, the thing's bulk blotted out everything else, as though its massive shoulders rubbed against the limits of the tunnel's ceiling.

It looked down at him, with the little red dots that had been its eyes, and smiled as its chest opened to reveal the sharp and the blunt things moving into readiness. At the center was the death ikon, the image spiraling into view.

At least it's not mine. Somebody else's work, a mandala of skull-headed black maggots, grinning with needle teeth as they writhed around a thorned heart. It would've been too much to be killed by something with his work on it.

Then again—his brain had dropped into an odd lucidity, tranquil and slow—*it might've been nice.* To have his own stuff be the last thing he ever saw.

He looked up into the megassassin's grin. The whirling devices at the end of its arms converged toward him.

Then the explosion hit, and all he saw was flame and smoke.

"What the fuck—" The floor of the tunnel had rocked hard enough to knock the megassassin off its feet. Axxter found himself slung against the wall, a curved section split open beside him.

A hand came through the smoke and grabbed his arm. "Come on—" A voice he'd heard before. "This way—"

He let himself be pulled through the jagged opening. Felony's grip tugged him into a staggering run. Behind him, he heard the grinding howl of the megassassin echoing through the building.

13

"I think we'll be safe here. For a while."

She had led him through tunnels smaller and smaller, conduits branching off the main course. A world behind the smooth walls; ending finally in a tiny cubical space lined with pipes and a maze of wires. They both had to crouch under the space's low ceiling.

The scramble on his hands and knees left Axxter panting. Head lowered, he saw his hands covered with oil and cindery ash. His jacket smelled singed. "What—what was all that? That explosion?" Maybe everything around him could go up in flame and smoke the same way.

Felony leaned back against the wall, arms wrapped around her knees. She shrugged. "No big deal. There's some heavy-duty power lines running in spots, and the insulation has gotten old and unstable. All you gotta do is short 'em together, and you get a pretty messy bang—lots of smoke and stuff. I just did it to throw that big hulk on its can and make a hole big enough to grab you."

He grunted his thanks. The slap of the explosion was still echoing inside his head. *Alive*—that amazed him. He'd never heard of anybody being shown a megassassin's death ikon—not under the circumstances, at least, of its being out to get you—and being around later to talk about it.

"I thought . . . you'd taken off. To go take care of your business."

Felony pushed a strand of hair away from her eyes. "Yeah, well, I was just on my way; I got some safe spots around here where I usually stash this body—you know, so nothing happens to it while I'm over on the other side. And I spotted that thing lurking around; lurking around as well as something that big is able to. I figured it was just waiting for you to come cruising by so it could jump out and do you over. There wasn't time to come out and warn you; plus—hey—I didn't want that sonuvabitch scoping *me* out and going after my ass."

"Thanks, I guess." He rubbed his hands on his trousers, smearing the black stuff. "Didn't know you were that concerned about what happened to me."

"I'm not. I just don't like some ugly asshole like that lumbering around on my turf. Pisses me off."

"I still don't get it, though." Axxter gazed back the way they had come. "That thing shouldn't have been here. Not this quick; it was reported as having crossed over to this side just a day or so ago. Those things don't travel that fast."

A shrug. "Maybe they were wrong. About when it crossed over."

He shook his head. "That can't be—I got the info straight from Ask & Receive. Paid top dollar for it, hundred percent reliability. They can't be wrong about stuff like that. It's their business to know."

"So? Maybe they lied to you."

"Lied?" He stared at her. "You mean, didn't tell me the truth?"

"Yeah, that's the general idea; that's what the word means."

It meant more than that. Axxter rocked back on his heels where he crouched. *They lied?*—meaning they hadn't just *not* told him the truth; the info agency had cooked up something, a statement about the megassassin's location, a lie, and told him that instead.

"If they did that—" He mused aloud, the conjecture and its ramifications too big to hold inside. "If they're capable of doing that . . . that would mean . . . everything."

Felony regarded him with distaste. "What're you getting into such a sweat for? So they fed you a line—what's the big deal?"

"Don't you see?" He leaned forward onto his hands. "It would mean that Ask & Receive couldn't be trusted." It astonished him as much as the first time he'd seen the sun setting beyond the clouds. "They're an impartial source of information; that's their whole reason for existence. You have to be able to trust what they tell you."

"Impartial, huh?" She sneered. "They weren't so impartial in this case, were they? What they told you led you right into that thing's ugly face."

Once you accepted this one possibility, you had to follow it through. The lie Ask & Receive had told him had worked only for the benefit of the Havoc Mass; it had handed him right over to the agent of their implacable vengeance. The megassassin hadn't had to waste any time snooping around for him. He'd walked blithely into its clutches, looking over his shoulder for no more than Sai and the other Dead Centers. All of which, the lie and his

204 ■ ■ ■

reliance on it, his faith in the info agency, would mean that Ask & Receive had somehow been contaminated by the Havoc Mass. If the info agency wasn't impartial, it wasn't on his side, either; it was on *their* side. The people who wanted to kill him.

"Then I'm screwed." He looked up at Felony and announced the result of the equation. "I'm fucked all the way. If I can't trust them, then I've got no source of information that I can rely on. I never did; nobody ever has. For all I know, Ask & Receive's been feeding shit to people for years. Handing poor suckers like me right over to the Mass. Only nobody's ever found out, because the only way you could find out—getting the info from Ask & Receive—is screwed up the same way."

She seemed unconcerned. "So? That's what you get for believing everything they told you in the first place. You should've been going and finding things out for yourself, about what was true and what wasn't."

"About the whole world? Everything inside or outside the building? You can't do that; nobody can. There's just too much stuff."

"Maybe. But you could've checked out the parts that concerned you a little better."

A bleak, formless hole was growing in his gut. "I trusted them . . ."

Felony shook her head, pityingly. "So you die—trusting 'em. That's the way it goes."

It was the way it went for everybody, though; Axxter didn't know whether to regard that as some sort of comfort, or as an even more chilling consideration. If everybody in or on Cylinder was relying on Ask & Receive's tainted information—and that information was tainted to the Havoc Mass's advantage—then that meant the Mass ruled Cylinder without anybody else even being aware of it. Or was about to rule the building; perhaps the corruption of the information agency was a fairly recent event, and the Mass was still setting up all its pieces on one great chessboard, encircling its old doddering rival, the Grievous Amalgam. No matter; however far along the process was, the Havoc Mass was the most powerful force on Cylinder. They had a direct pipeline, via Ask & Receive, into everyone's brain. The part that dealt with facts and real things. The Mass had managed to usurp reality.

"Hey, cheer up." Felony smiled at him. "At least you're better off than you were a little while ago. Now you know how you were getting screwed around with."

"Yeah, great." Axxter stared glumly at the tiny space's wall. "Fat lot of good that does me. I won't die ignorant, I suppose." Of the big picture; there were still a lot of the small details that kept niggling at the far corners of his brain. Like why the megassassin had had a different death ikon graffed on it, instead of the one he had worked up for General Cripplemaker's commission. Even if they had all taken out this great blood oath on his head—and the vigor with which they were pursuing it, the lengths to which the Mass was going in order to kill him, was also somewhat puzzling—it still didn't seem likely that they would miss the chance to rub his face in it. Make his own work be the last thing he saw before he had his arms and legs plucked off, one by one. That went against everything he thought he knew about warrior psychology: they loved cheap, effective irony like that.

"So get off your dead butt and do something about it."

"Yeah?" The puzzle of the ikon faded against more practical concerns. "Like what? I'm stuck out here a million or so miles from where I need to get to—and from where the information I'd need to get there is kept. I can't just go calling up for the info I need; not anymore."

"No big deal. I can get you what you need."

Axxter tilted his head, studying her. "What do you

206 ▪ ▪ ▪

mean? Are you saying you can go on-line and crack open Ask & Receive's restricted-access, high-security archives, and just haul out whatever info you want?"

She looked back at him, wide-eyed. "Of course not—why do you think they call those archives high security? It's because people can't get into them. They wouldn't be *high security* otherwise, would they?"

"Oh." Disappointed. "I thought you circuit riders and hackers and all were supposed to be able to do that kind of stuff."

Felony sighed and shook her head. "What a load of shit you've got between your ears. Of course we can't do that. Some little assholes, like that D:Fex crowd, they like to talk as if they can. But it's all just talk. They can only screw around on open lines, unshielded ones, or networks that nobody else is using or that nobody cares enough about to boot them off of. All the valuable stuff—like the Ask & Receive archives—that's all locked away tight. Nobody can get in there without permission, bullshitting hackers to the contrary."

"Then what're you talking about? About me being able to get info I could use?"

"Simmer down, will ya? I'm talking about going down to the dumps and picking up some stuff. You see, these little wiseacre hackers can't really get in anyplace where they're not wanted, but they *can* still make nuisances out of themselves—static on the line, prank calls, shit like that. So to keep them all romping around somewhere out of everybody's hair, for years now Ask & Receive has been dumping outtake footage of any real good violent event that they've gotten tape of, all into an open-access file. What they sell as entertainment is the edited-down, hyped-up, and glamorous version that really snaps along, keeps people's attention. But the circuit riders can go rummaging through the dumped footage and come up

■ ■ ■ 207

with all the little nuggets they want, incorporate them into their little on-line war games. They love playing war."

"What good does that do me? A bunch of raw footage of warrior skirmishes?"

She nodded sagely. "Well—I've done a little checking around of my own. Just because I'm interested in your . . . unusual situation. And it seems to me that all the shit you're in started after you came across that sector over on the other side, where some heavy action had just happened. If I were you, I'd want to know all I could about that little scene."

He shook his head. "There wouldn't be footage of that in there. That didn't have anything to do with any of the warrior tribes, so there wasn't any coverage prearranged for it."

"Oh?" She leaned back, smiling. "You're sure about that?"

"Don't get all mysterious with me. Not now. Just tell me what you're talking about."

"Hey—like I said—the time's come for you to check some things out on your own."

■
■

He watched as she hooked one alligator clip onto a length of bare wire, the other clip pinching the end of his finger.

"What I'm going to do—" Felony licked the end of her own finger and dabbed spit on the connections. "I'm going to go on-line myself, and then patch you in. That way, anything that's looking for you—like Mr. Big-and-Ugly out there—won't know it's you on the line and come stomping in here. At least not right away."

"How am I going to find what I'm looking for?" He was starting to get cramps in his legs from squatting so long in the tiny space.

"It's just a simple chrono stack, no fancy indexing or anything. You'll just have to go back to the date when you found that place, and root around from there." She hooked a couple of wires together. "Good luck."

■
■

This is hopeless. A loop of numbers had crawled up across Axxter's vision. He scanned down the list of dates, finally tagging a clutch of them.

The first file he opened up was a collection of outtakes from a low-intensity raiding party; the participants, a couple of nothing gangs he'd never heard of, seemed more interested in making faces at each other than in actual bloodshed.

He opened the second file. It was the raid on the burned-out sector. He recognized the sharp edge of the metal, the way the explosion had twisted it out into the air. A glance up at the map coordinates in the corner confirmed it.

Jesus— Axxter stared at the scene. Smoke and red light billowed out of the opening. *This wasn't supposed to be here. All of this stuff—* There was a lot of it, taped from several different angles; he fast-forwarded through it, the recorded screams having raised the hairs on his arms and back of his neck. He stopped at a good shot of the raiders, froze the scene, and zoomed in on them. All in black uniforms that he didn't recognize, without any insignia. They operated with cold, destructive efficiency rather than the usual warrior swagger and guffawing laughter. Two meg-assassins, towering over the rest of the cohort, were in the middle of the slaughter, clanking forward with grim inevitability.

He went back to the start of the file. Before any explosion or smoke or flames: the black uniforms were gathering, checking out their weapons and setting up equipment . . .

■ ■ ■ **209**

on the outside of the building. Axxter watched in amazement as one of the camera angles shifted, revealing the edge of the building, dawn light breaking over the clouds. At a signal from a commanding officer, the raiders swarmed toward the smooth, unscarred lip of an entry site. The explosion followed a few seconds later, ripping the metal into the great jagged edges that dangled out into the air.

They came from outside. Axxter stopped the tape. That meant—

He zipped toward the end of the file. Everybody dead now, the horizontal sector's inhabitants reduced to ash and blackened meat. And, at the farthest awaylight limit, an unbroken barrier wall to the building's center regions. Which was soon taken care of: more explosions, then a team of the raiders grabbing hold of the smoldering metal and bending the shards out toward them.

So it would look like they came from inside the building. That's what it meant. Axxter stared at nothing, thinking it through. *They set it up that way.* Who?

Back into the file. He found the best shot of one of the two megassassins; for a moment, there had been three separate cameras trained on it. He switched through the angles. The last one was a full-on frontal shot. Its chest panels were open, revealing the death ikon. Death's-head cobras writhing in a circle. The same as he'd seen here, less than a meter away, looming over him in the tunnel.

Well, well, well—an interesting discovery. Axxter rested his chin on his knees, arms folded around his shins. *The things you find out.* The Havoc Mass was going around blowing open horizontal sectors and letting those old boogeymen the Dark Centers take the rap. Bad business— military tribes weren't supposed to do shit like that. They were supposed to stay out on the vertical, bashing each other's heads and having a rollicking good time scheming for control of the toplevel, or a little farther up the wall, closer to the good sweet things that power brought. Not slaughtering defenseless people who stayed on the horizontal precisely to be safe, to stay out of harm's way. Those were the rules; anybody breaking them was playing a harder game, one that stopped at nothing. Including the secret taking-over of the one sure rock that everybody depended on, the supposedly impartial Ask & Receive? Once you break one rule, you might as well break them all.

He played the last tape in the file. The raiding party, work done, went back out to the building's surface. Framed in the now-jagged entry site opening was a gas angel, suspended in air and smiling curiously at the scene inside. He winced when he saw her familiar face; a gout of flame from one of the men's weapons knocked her out of the sky. Laughter on the soundtrack.

On the tape, an equipment vehicle was parked on the wall, waiting for the men. Easy, relaxed joking-around as they stripped off the black uniforms and slid into olive-drab fatigues. Axxter zoomed in on the commanding officer, on his shoulder patch turned toward the camera. The rocker bar below the main patch read RECONNAISSANCE. Above that, circled around a golden sunburst, were the words GRIEVOUS AMALGAM.

That can't be— Axxter stared at the image in his sight. *No, they're Havoc Mass; they have to be.* Because of the death ikon on the megassassin's chest, on the tape; if it was the same as the one that was over here chasing him, and it was the Havoc Mass that wanted him dead, then a megassassin bearing that ikon had to belong to the Havoc Mass. It was the only way it made sense.

Unless—a new, chilling thought crept into his head— unless the Grievous Amalgam also wanted him dead. And they'd sent their own megassassin to do the job.

Work it out. Why would the Grievous Amalgam want to kill some poor schmuck graffex who hadn't done shit to them? Maybe for the same reason their raiding party would shoot some inquisitive little gas angel out of the sky for poking her pretty face into something they wanted to keep secret. If they'd wanted people to know it was the Grievous Amalgam doing it, they wouldn't have been wearing the black uniforms. And if some freelance graffex comes strolling into the scene, lah-dee-dah, while the metal's still hot, there's no telling what clues he might glom onto as to who did it—best to ice him, too. The Amalgam had probably been wanting to kill him for some time now, ever since he'd reported his finding of the burned-out sector to Ask & Receive and they'd realized that somebody had stumbled across the aftermath of the raid. His getting the commission, and landing up in the Havoc Mass camp where the Amalgam couldn't get at him easily, was probably the only thing that had kept him alive. Until they'd heard he was over here on the eveningside; then they'd sent the heavyweight gun over to snuff him, to keep him from blabbing any giveaway he might have spotted at the burned-out sector that would pin it on the Amalgam. Of course, nobody would have known that; so Brevis, when he'd heard the report of a megassassin crossing over Linear Fair to the eveningside, had naturally assumed it was the Havoc Mass's machine, coming to settle their grudge against him.

The thoughts whirled faster in his head, too fast to catch. *Then it's not the Havoc Mass that's taken over Ask & Receive; it's the Grievous Amalgam. That's how they stay in power—*

Too much to work out now. He'd have to think about all this, if he lived long enough. Once he'd loaded all the files on the raid into his own archives, he broke the connection.

"Felony?" He looked around the cramped space. She wasn't there.

14

"**S**he's not here." The voice came from behind him. "She had her little errands to run."

Axxter turned and saw Sai leaning against the wall of the space.

"What?"

Sai smiled and spread his hands. "You're not going to pick up something and hit me over the head with it? Scream and run? I was looking forward to a little more action from you."

He shook his head, watching and waiting.

"Good." Sai nodded, visibly pleased. "Now maybe we can carry on a discussion like sane people. You know, that's the main advantage of finding out exactly what kind of a shitty situation you're in: that kind of knowledge lessens the otherwise freewheeling activity of your imagination. You're less likely to go making weird accusations against people who're just trying to do you a favor."

"I had my reasons."

"Yeah, but they weren't *good* reasons. Just a lot of crap other people have told you, that you've heard so many times that you believed 'em without thinking them through. Everything you thought you knew . . . You gotta be careful about stuff like that." Sai pointed with his thumb behind himself. "You've already screwed it up with a whole bunch of folks who could've done you some good. Not everybody around here is as interested in your case as I am. Dead Centers—as *you* call us; I think the term's a little offensive, myself—they've generally got enough to keep them busy."

Axxter was tired, his brain frazzled with trying to squeeze in all the new, upside-down, and backward info he'd gotten off the line. Sai's cool, rational voice soothed him; he could listen to it for hours. He knew there wasn't that much time left for him, though.

Sai knew it, too. "You'll have to think about these things later. If there *is* a later for you. It doesn't do any good to save your ass if you just go through life being an ignorant fuck and not thinking about the important things."

Axxter opened his eyes. "Like what?"

"That's the problem with you." Sai shook his head. "Not just you, but all of you morningsiders. There's so much that you don't know—so much that you've forgotten—that you don't even know where to begin, what to think about, what questions to ask. You guys out on the vertical are as bad as the ones on the horizontal. You think you're hip or something just because you're out there scrambling around, chasing up and down the wall, and you don't know what's going to happen from one day to the next—but you're still just as ignorant."

Hectoring rather than soothing; it had gotten under his

214 ■ ■ ■

skin. "You know so much, then? Why don't you tell me? If you feel so bad for me, and all."

"It wouldn't do any good. We can't teach the blind to see. I mean, you don't even look around you; you never have. Like this building, Cylinder itself." Sai gestured toward the walls, and all the ones beyond. "You live in it, or on it, but you never think about it. It's obviously constructed, a thing put together, but you never wonder why, or by whom."

Axxter shrugged. "That was all done before the War."

"There you go again. If there's anything you don't know, you can just say *before the War,* and you're off the hook. You don't even know anything about this so-called War—it's just a handy way of getting rid of all the stuff you don't want to think about."

"So what'd be the point? Dinking around with a lot of old crap like that isn't going to help me with my problems. And I had enough of them before all this other shit happened."

"Correction." Sai pointed a finger toward him. "You had all the problems you wanted. *Wanted,* man. You liked having them, so you wouldn't have time on your hands and wind up thinking about all that other stuff, the big stuff that you've forgotten. Cylinder was built for a reason; its construction and ongoing operation violates at least a dozen laws of physics—the thermal problems alone connected with a structure of this size are pretty unbelievable. The air you breathe, if you think about it at all, you spout some mumbo jumbo about *atmospheric bonding,* as if knowing the words means you understand how it works. Now, the physical transgressions in themselves are no big thing—anything can be worked around, if somebody knows what they're doing—but you still gotta ask *why* they bothered. It's not easy, doing impossible stuff."

■ ■ ■ 215

"If it's impossible, how could they do it?" This sonuvabitch wanted to play word games, fine.

Sai's wolfish smile returned. "Maybe you just think they did it. Maybe they just did something to make you think a building big as a world exists, and that you're living in it or outside of it."

Axxter could taste his own disgust. "Screw that. I hate shit like that. Looking at your own navel until you fall in—I've got lots more important business to take care of. Hate to remind you, but there is some huge ugly bastard clanking around here, looking to smear me into jelly. I gotta worry about what I'm going to do about *that* before I can sit on my can and screw around with bullshit philosophical questions. All right?"

The other shrugged. "Have it your way. That's why I came back around here—just to give you a helping hand. What'd you think of that stuff you found in the dumps?"

He touched the bare wire beside him. "You were tapped in?"

Sai nodded. "But I knew all that stuff already. I just wanted to see if you'd stumble across it. Pretty interesting, though, wasn't it?"

"Pretty dangerous, you mean—for them. Why would they leave shit like that lying around, where anybody could stumble across it?"

Sai smiled. "Because they don't know they've left it lying around. One of the problems with big organizations like the Mass—to survive, they have to compartmentalize more and more of their actions, make them routine and automatic. The mechanism for dumping tapes like that was set up before they got involved in dinking around with Ask & Receive. Nobody in the Mass exec levels has caught on to this leak until now because nobody but a bunch of adolescent-mentality circuit riders has ever come

216 ■ ■ ■

sniffing around it. You're the first who has some reason to make real use of it."

"Yeah? Like what? I don't see how it helps me any. It just means I'm in deeper shit than I already thought I was."

"Eh, just hang on to it. Having info like that—*real* info—you might be surprised the use you'll find for it sometime." Sai pushed himself away from the wall. "You want practical? I'll give you practical—come with me."

He led Axxter down a low-ceilinged tunnel. "You got a bit of a break, being in here. Those megassassins aren't equipped for tracking in this kind of environment— there's a lot of heat and electromagnetic sources that throw their sensors all off. This one that's tracking you is still recalibrating itself, learning the ropes. Soon as it knows which end's up, though, it'll stop blundering around and be right on your tail. So we really ought to stop jerking off and see about getting you on the road." He stopped beside an empty panel in the tunnel wall and drew back a tattered, oil-stained cloth hung in the opening. "Take a look."

Axxter lowered his head, eyes straining in the darkness; after a few seconds, he made out Felony, curled up on a bed of rags. Her breathing was slow and shallow.

"That's not her." Sai let the curtain fall back into place. "Like they used to say about dead people: she's not here anymore. She just left her body behind. One of them, at any rate. See?" He pointed to a phone line running under the curtain. "She's off taking care of business over on the other side, in one of the other bodies she's glommed into her stable. She's quite a collector. If she found out I know about this little hiding place of hers, she'd be righteously pissed."

"Is this what you wanted to show me?"

■ ■ ■ **217**

"Naw—just something I thought you'd be interested in, is all. Come on."

After following Sai long enough to feel his back going into spasms, Axxter was finally able to stand straight up. They'd stepped out of the low tunnel into a larger space, the ceiling, if there was one, beyond his sight.

"How's that?" Sai's voice echoed off the nearest wall.

"What is it?" He watched the beam of Sai's flashlight moving across a flank of metal.

"Transport, man. Wheels—well, sort of; in the metaphoric sense, at least. It actually works on mag-lev technology, just zooms along, no friction. If you're into pre-War high technology, this one's a beauty; it's the fastest thing in or on Cylinder." Sai looked around and caught Axxter's uncomprehending look. "It's a *train,* man—that's what things like this were called. Runs on tracks. See?" The flashlight beam played along two massive girders, tall as a man, stretching out in front of the machine's bullet nose. "Like transit cables, only on the horizontal—you understand that much?"

"Yeah, I guess." Axxter looked up at the windows set flush in the train's front cabin. "Where's it go to?"

Sai smiled. "This is your lucky day. Finally. You're looking at part of Cylinder's former transportation network. There used to be hundreds of these babies running straight through the building. That's how people and stuff used to get from one side to the other."

"Wait a minute. This thing—right here—goes to the other side? The morningside? Is that what you're saying?"

"Yeah, it'll get you within a couple kilometers of the surface. The tracks run right up to where the barriers were constructed. You'd have to hoof it the rest of the way from there."

"But it's out of commission—is that the deal? It doesn't work anymore, it's just a hunk of rust sitting here."

218 ■ ■ ■

"Oh, no. It works fine." Sai stepped over to the train and rapped it with his fist. "We've kept it in good shape—me and a couple of my friends. It wasn't hard to do. It's got a lot of autonomic maintenance equipment built in."

Axxter looked at him in amazement. "You mean to say, you've got this thing sitting right here, it's ready to go, it can zip me back to the other side *now*—and you've been wasting my time, gassing on about a bunch of weird metaphysical junk? I don't believe this."

"'Gassing on'—" Sai snorted. "You know, you got this problem: people try to do you favors, and this is how you act in return. Saying rude things. That other stuff is important, too. More than you know. You're going to have to think about it sometime."

"Yeah, right; anything you say." Axxter stood on tiptoe, trying to peer into the train's window. "How does this thing work?"

"It's simple, practically runs itself. You'll have no problem with it. People like you have a knack for ripping off other people's technology. You're like magpies with brains, or something. If it's metal and flashy, you glom right onto it."

Axxter ignored him, walking around the front of the train to the other side. "What's this other stuff over here?"

Sai followed him. "You know, just getting over to the other side isn't going to solve all your problems. You're still going to have the same people looking to kill you. More now than you originally thought you had gunning for you."

"I'll worry about that when I get there. I can only deal with all this one step at a time." Axxter squatted down beside another machine, a smaller one. "What's this?"

The flashlight beam played over it, revealing the lineaments of wheels and engine, chrome and black enamel. A

■ ■ ■ **219**

motorcycle of a make—either the original or a replica—that Axxter didn't recognize. There was no emblem painted on its tank, or other identifying mark. The machine hulked, brutish and dangerous-looking, in the darkness.

"What's it look like?" Sai pointed the flashlight away from it, down a line of other machines. "There's tons of this pre-War technology around here. See what you've all been missing by being afraid to come inside and look around? Think of all the fun you could've been having with this stuff." The sarcasm was plain in his voice.

"Does this thing run, too?"

Sai reached past him and pressed a starter switch below the handlebars. The engine roared into life. "Pretty big displacement—" Sai shouted over the noise. "This thing's built for speed." He switched off the engine. "Probably not a good idea to call attention to where we are."

Axxter ran his hands over the motorcycle's tank. "I could use this. Over on the other side." The memory of his poor Norton, crumpled and spinning through the air, was still strong. "I'd have to get it adapted, get the grappling wheels put on and stuff . . ."

"You're getting way ahead of yourself. You're not at the point where you need to be scoping out a new set of wheels. You can bet that the Havoc Mass has already figured out your plan of action and where you're going to pop out on the morningside. It's a sure thing they've sent their own megassassin around to that entry site you're aiming for. You show your head over there, and you'll be hash in a minute. It won't matter that you've managed to get away from the Grievous Amalgam megassassin that's stomping around over here."

He knew it was true. Deflated, Axxter leaned his weight against the motorcycle. It was exactly the sort of thing that General Cripplemaker and the rest of the

220 ■ ■ ■

Havoc Mass would think was funny, to stake out the entry site with the megassassin that he'd worked on.

Sai switched off the flashlight, leaving them in the gloom provided by the intermittent blue fixtures above. "What you need—right now—is some way of getting the Havoc Mass off your ass. Then you could head on out of here, and you'd be home free."

"Sure—" He nodded glumly. "That'd be real fine. But you can't talk with people like that. They're all nuts, and hopped up all the time. A simple apology, or an explanation or whatever, isn't going to cut it with them."

"So? You just have to come up with something else. Something that's so valuable to them that it wipes out whatever grudge they've got simmering against you. Think about it."

Think— His brain shifted reluctantly into gear. It'd be so much easier to just lie down on the floor and wait for whatever was going to happen. Even if it was going to be gruesomely unpleasant. All the stuff he'd found out had fatigued his head, as though it had been crammed to the bursting point with useless knowledge. What good did it to do to discover these things? . . .

He saw it then, perfect and luminous, right in front of him. He raised his head, looking straight at Sai. "They don't know. The Havoc Mass—they don't know. *They don't know what's going on.* And I do. About the Grievous Amalgam screwing around with Ask & Receive. About all the information they rely on being contaminated. And I'm the only one who can tell them."

In the darkness, he saw Sai's smile.

Axxter looked above him, as though the idea had become buoyant, floating over their heads. "And if I told them that—then they'd believe me, about being set up." Another realization had hit him. "Because it wasn't DeathPix that screwed me over, that overrode the animating signal for the graffex work I did. It was the Grievous Amalgam. They wanted to snuff me, to shut me up about whatever I might've seen where they raided that entry site, only they couldn't get to me inside the Havoc Mass camp. But they found a way; they just had to get the Mass pissed off enough at me, and the Mass would kill me. They'd have done the Amalgam's work for them."

Sai nodded, pleased. "It takes you awhile, but you get there eventually. You still don't know everything you need to know, but you got the process started, at least."

The little light going on inside his head had carried its own sparking circuit, a trickle of excitement, seeing one small bit more clearly. "Right—I still don't know *why*. I mean, why they did it in the first place, what the Grievous Amalgam got out of sneaking around and burning out that sector—"

"That's unimportant; that's not what you need to know. Stuff like that, the reason shit happens, you can just make your assumptions and let 'em ride. Maybe the people in that sector you ran across had gotten a little uppity, and needed their chain given its ultimate yank; or else whatever factory they ran had been working under contract, and it was easier for the Amalgam to pay 'em off like that. Plus, you got to remember that the Grievous Amalgam's an old organization; they've been sitting up on the top-level for a long time. Long enough to get fat and lazy, to lose that warrior's edge, the hungry feeling, that put them up there. They've got to substitute cunning for what they've lost, if they're going to hang on. You don't know how long they've been pulling this shit, and on how many people; they've got a lot of alliances to keep in line. And good PR is ninety percent of that process. For all you know, the Amalgam might've been generating false reports of all the battles they've won, opposing tribes subdued, areas conquered—all of them nonexistent. Then

222 ■ ■ ■

they use Ask & Receive to distribute the phony accounts, and everybody else thinks it's fact, just because they got the info from a supposedly impartial source. And who's going to find them out? You're talking a lot of territory; practically anything—or nothing—could be going on, and nobody would know the difference. The only ones likely to discover that something's not quite kosher are freelancers like yourself; you're the only ones who might blunder into a sector reportedly raided by the Grievous Amalgam and find a completely different reality from the one everybody's been handed by Ask & Receive. You might not be the first poor bastard who's gotten into this kind of deep shit—you just might be the first one to have gotten this much of a run out of it."

That was a chilling thought. There were always stories going around in the loose fraternity of freelancers about one or more of their number whom nobody had seen in a long time, too long a time. The final assumption being that *Something* had happened to them—unspecified as to what—or else they had taken the big step of their own free will, cutting free from the wall and embracing the clouds below, depressed at some negative turn in their ramshackle careers. You just never saw them again, never knew. But this meant that the spooky Something might not have been accident or suicide, but murder.

"Yeah, well, that may be for all I know—" Axxter peered closer at the other. "But what do *you* know? I mean, if you knew what I was going to find in that dump . . . and you've got so much stuff figured out . . . then what else do you know?"

Sai laughed. "You're wishing for something, but I don't think I can give it to you."

"Come on. The way you know what's going on . . . how you can just tap in on whatever lines people are using . . .

■ ■ ■ 223

how the building works, all this high-tech stuff you and your friends keep running . . . You must be able to do it."

"Do what? That hacking shit? Go on-line and break into restricted access files—is that what you're talking about?"

Axxter nodded.

"As they used to say in another time, another place—boy, I despair of you." Pity in Sai's voice. "It just goes to show how hard old mythology dies. Especially myths that serve somebody's purpose, and that key right into some little need inside people's heads. That hacking bullshit goes back a long way—not just before the War, but before Cylinder itself. You gotta ask yourself, who did it benefit to have people believing that restricted-access data files and operating systems could be broken into by some bright thirteen-year-old with a dime-store terminal and a fast hand on the keyboard? That was a line of crap from the beginning; the only basis for it was a brief historical period right at the beginning, before the really good methods of locking up stuff were invented. Some little hacker punk would manage to get into someplace on-line where he wasn't supposed to be, and then go around bragging about it. But it was like somebody going to a sector where everybody leaves their doors unlocked, and then claiming to be a master burglar because you lifted somebody's toaster. Soon as everybody started locking their doors, that penny-ante stuff was *over*. But it was an interesting coincidence that right at the time when that kind of information-handling technology was taking over the world, a bunch of stuff started showing up in the popular media that depicted it as essentially harmless because teenage kids could crack it open—so what's there to worry about, right? People were less likely to worry about the files being kept on them in massive, crosslinked data banks as long as they could be made to believe that the machines

224 ■ ■ ■

running the info were just kinda cuddly and easily fucked with."

Axxter shook his head. "You lost me there somewhere. All this ancient history jazz—"

"Sorry. Didn't mean to give you a lecture. Just one of my pet subjects, is all. I wonder about the people who got involved in handing out that line of crap—there were so many of them, they couldn't all have been on the payroll. Some of them, maybe most of them—hell, maybe even *all* of them—must've actually believed that bullshit. Because they wanted to. So they wouldn't have to deal with the scary stuff that was actually happening." Sai switched the flashlight on again, drawing a circle with its beam across the train. "So anyway, you don't get some magic key to everybody's deepest secrets. You'll just have to do with what you know already."

15

He had to laugh. At the way things had worked out, the set of the teeth in the vise around his ankle.

"I'm sorry—" Axxter wiped his eyes. His laughter had bounced wildly back and forth in the high-ceilinged space. "It just all seems so funny. I'm not only sitting on the info that would save my own ass, but it'd also blow everything on the other side to pieces—I mean, stuff like this would go off like a bomb right in the middle of the Grievous Amalgam hegemony—I've got all that tucked right inside my head, and there's no way I can use it. Eventually, their megassassin is going to track me down and waste me, and that'll be the end of it. I might just as well have never found out what's going on at all."

"Is it as bad as all that?"

Axxter stared at him. "Are you joking? I can't just call up the Havoc Mass and tell 'em, can I? If I get on the

226 ∎ ∎ ∎

phone line again, the Grievous Amalgam megassassin will pinpoint my location, and it'll be all over—I might have enough time to blat out some of what I know, which I'm sure the Havoc Mass will appreciate knowing, but a fat lot of good that'll do me. And if I climb on board this thing here and head straight for the other side, without telling the Havoc Mass what I've found out and getting off the hook with them, then their megassassin creams me. Either way, I'm dead."

"What you need is some other way of getting hold of the Havoc Mass. Instead of the phone line."

He grunted. "Yeah—too bad they're the only game in town."

A smile in Sai's voice. "Sure about that?"

All this hinting around was getting on his nerves. "Yeah, I'm sure. The Small Moon relay satellite doesn't come around on this side of the building; it's stationed permanently over on the other side. Otherwise, I could possibly transmit a signal and bounce it off, get it to the Mass that way. But since the Small Moon doesn't come in sight here, that just can't be done."

"What about using something else besides the Small Moon to bounce your signal off?"

Axxter sighed. "You're driving me crazy—there isn't anything else."

"Come on, man—you gotta think about the ants."

Maybe he wasn't the one who had gone crazy. "Ants? What the hell are you talking about?"

"Like in the story—when you befriend the ants, they do you a favor in return. Come on, *think;* for whom did you, once you got past your cynical self-interest jive, ever do a good deed? Hm?"

It took a second to remember. "You mean—the gas angel? Is that what you're talking about? What the hell good is that?"

"You could use her to send a message."

"Oh, yeah, sure; that'd work just great. Let a gas angel play mailman—are you out of your mind? How long do you think it'd take her to go drifting around on the wind currents from here all the way over to the Havoc Mass camp? I don't have that kind of time; that megassassin is on my tail *right now*. Plus I can just imagine her bobbing into the camp—if there were some way of telling her how to find it—with a letter from me in her hand; I'm sure she'd get a fine reception from those guys." Axxter shook his head in disgust. "If this is your idea of helping me out, you might as well just forget it."

"You're still not thinking, man; that's not what I meant at all. Show some imagination. You could use the angel the same way you'd use the Small Moon if it were available: as a relay satellite, something to bounce your signal off to get it where you want it to go. Think about it: the Small Moon's not much more than a reflective metal surface, suspended out in the atmosphere. Same thing with that angel, after you grafted that foil onto her—granted, she doesn't have the encoding and narrowcasting facilities that the Small Moon does, but the principle is the same. All you'd have to do is have her station herself at the right spot out there, and you'd be able to clear the curve of the building and bounce a signal off her for the Havoc Mass to pick up. It's simple."

"Yeah, it's simple—simpleminded. You're forgetting one little thing. The signals that get relayed by the Small Moon are encoded to channel them to the person you want to talk to. You can't just throw a raw signal out in the air and expect it to trigger the reception mode on the right party's comm line."

Sai spoke slowly, patiently. "But you don't need their comm line. You've got another way of communicating with the Havoc Mass. The graffex work you did for the

Mass—you control the animating signal for it, as long as something like the Grievous Amalgam isn't overriding it. And they're long done with that now. All you have to do is change that animating signal to incorporate your message, transmit it, bounce it off the angel, and it'll get picked up by your graffex work at the Havoc Mass camp. They'll be able to read what you have to say to them in the patterns on the biofoil; hell, you could include sections from the tapes you loaded out of the dumps. Whoever's wearing that foil you worked on will be turned into a walking video receiver."

He stood speechless for a moment. "That's the most absurd plan I've ever heard in my life. There's about a dozen different reasons something like that wouldn't work. I'd have to depend upon the angel getting into exactly the right position out there; the Mass might've already had all that work I did for them torn out and replaced—they weren't exactly thrilled with it to begin with, remember?—so even if I got the signal bounced to them, there might not be anything to pick it up . . ."

"Sure—" Sai seemed unfazed by the objections. "You don't want to do it, fine. I wasn't offering it as some kind of foolproof suggestion. I'm just telling you: it's the only option you got. Other than just curling up and waiting for the megassassin to find you."

"You know, I've gotten really sick of people telling me I've got no other choice. I seem to hear that a lot."

"You got some other bright idea? Let's hear it, then."

He didn't. The pisser was that there never was one.

Sai waited for him to speak, seconds ticking into a full minute, then finally nodded. "Okay, look—if you're going to do this, you're going to have to work fast. You're not going to have much time: that megassassin has been having a hard time tracking you down inside here, but you get out on the surface, it'll be right on you before you know it. That's what its sensors are geared for. You're going to have to have your message to the Havoc Mass all taped and ready to go, so you can just let it rip as soon as the angel's in the right position. So you sit down right now and work that up—make it the pitch of your life. Fast and snappy, but with everything in it, all the evidence you got out of the dump. You do that, and I'll go check out the territory between here and the surface, see if we're all clear to proceed." He switched on the flashlight, the beam darting ahead as he moved away. "See you in a bit."

Axxter watched the cone of light diminish, and then he was alone in the dark.

■
■

"You sure that thing's not around?"

"Stop worrying." Sai shielded his eyes with his hand, looking across the sky. "You got a margin. The megaassassin's several levels inside the wall—even if he got a fix on you right now, it'd still take him awhile to work his way out here."

Axxter bit his lip. "This sure seems to be taking a long time."

"Like I said, don't worry; she'll show up. She's got a crush on you."

A dot appeared in the sky, growing larger until it had arms, legs, the sphere of the flight membrane behind. Then at last her smile radiating toward him.

"Hi. Hello." Lahft dangled in air a few feet from where Axxter was latched onto the wall. She turned, looking over her shoulder at him and displaying the image on the grafted biofoil. "Good to see you." She laughed, like bells falling.

Axxter looked at the picture of his own face that he'd transmitted. The sunlight glared off the shining curve

230 ■ ■ ■

of metal, obscuring the black dots ordered into eyes, nose, and chin. It was the first self-portrait he'd ever done; he resisted the temptation to work it over now, to rotate it to a three-quarter profile, so it wouldn't look so full-on stupid. *Like I'm waiting to get killed. This is accuracy.*

"Come on." Sai nudged him in the ribs. "Tell her what you need her to do. You don't have *that* much time."

He couldn't tell if he was getting through to her; she just bobbed and listened, eyes wide.

"You got it?"

She tilted her head, her gaze drifting past him. Axxter prayed that there was at least one gear meshing with another behind her brow. "Here . . . now." She nodded, then pointed off into the sky. "There. *After* now."

"Yeah, that's right. Right out from the Linear Fair; I mean, the big line. Go out as far as you can. And *stay* there. You got it?"

She smiled at him.

"Jesus flipping Christ." He turned toward Sai. "This is hopeless. This isn't going to work."

"How do you know?" Sai returned the angel's smile. "She's smarter than you think. She's just on a different wavelength."

Lahft reached out and touched Axxter on the shoulder. "When is now? Is now now?"

That took a moment to decipher. "Yeah—I want you to go there now."

"Now good-bye." She drifted away, still smiling. Axxter watched her go, his heart leaden.

"You might as well start transmitting—that way, it'll get bounced off as soon as she's in position."

Axxter nodded. He called up the file he'd prepared from his working archive and sent it out. On the display he flicked on REPEAT UNTIL INTERRUPT. Beyond the glowing words, the angel's form dwindled slowly against the sky. "How long we gonna stay out here?"

Sai settled back against the wall. "As long as we can."

■
■

The sun was setting, turning the cloud barrier red. Axxter watched the deepening color. The hours of inaction, latched to the wall while the transmission had gone beaming out, over and over, had seeped exhaustion into his muscles.

Sai's hand on his shoulder jostled him out of a semi-doze. "You hear that?"

"Hear what?" Then he did: a low rumble vibrating through the building's metal and into his flesh.

"You stay here. And keep transmitting." Sai clambered toward the lip of the entry site. He was back in less than a minute. "Okay, show time's over. Time to move."

"It's here? It's found us?"

"It's on its way. Come on, let's go."

He could smell it again, the choking odor of oil and hot metal, as they slipped inside the entry site. The mega-assassin was there, somewhere in the darkness inside the building. And coming closer, a straight line toward him; he had to resist the impulse to scramble back out onto the building's surface.

Sai peeled back a panel from the tunnel wall, just wide enough to squeeze behind. He gestured for silence with a finger to his lips, then pushed Axxter through the opening. He turned and peered over Sai's shoulder, out to the empty tunnel.

Empty for only a second; then a black shape, stooping under the tunnel's ceiling, filled the space. It stopped, the pistons of its arms contracting, the shining hands opening and closing, fists clenching.

232 ■ ■ ■

The massive head turned, and two red lights, small dots of blood, bored into Axxter's gaze.

"Go!" Sai was shouting, pushing him ahead. Axxter stumbled, then got back onto his feet. "Move it!" Behind him, he heard the wall of the tunnel being ripped open.

When he reached the high-ceilinged space, he pitched forward onto his hands and knees. For a moment, all he could do was hang his head and pant for air. Past the throbbing of his own pulse, he heard Sai's own laboring breath close at his ear as the other pulled him onto his feet.

"You gotta hit it, man. Get in the train and *go.*"

"How—how's it work?" His mouth had dried; he couldn't swallow.

Sai pushed him toward the machine. "It's programmed—it's only got one speed, and it's only got one way it can go. Just punch the green button, and you're outta— Where you going?"

He walked around the front of the train to the other side. In the space's dim light, he found the motorcycle he'd spotted before.

"Jesus Christ—you don't have time to screw around with that now—"

"I want it." Axxter pulled the motorcycle off its centerstand and rolled it toward the train. "I've got to get *something* out of all this." It was too heavy to push up the steps into the front cabin; he squeezed past the front wheel and climbed up. "Come on, give me a hand with this thing."

"You're out of your goddamn mind—" Despite his protests, Sai got behind the motorcycle and pushed. The two of them managed to wrestle it up into the small space behind the train's control panel.

Panting with the effort, Sai stood outside the cabin,

■ ■ ■ **233**

both hands gripping the sides of the door. "You happy now? Like I said, all you gotta do is—"

Then he was gone. A hand of dark metal, wide as his ribcage, knocked him aside, sending him sprawling across the floor. The megassassin's bulk filled the doorway.

"Shit—" Axxter scrambled backward. The motorcycle toppled over and pinned him against the cabin's wall. As the megassassin grinned and reached for him, Axxter's hand fumbled about on the control panel. His fingers found something round that yielded to his pressing it.

A high-pitched whine vibrated the train. Beneath him, he could feel it gliding into motion as the megassassin snarled and lifted the motorcycle away from Axxter. The machine's tank rose off his chest, then fell back as the train picked up speed, leaving the megassassin behind. A roar of frustration sounded, the megassassin's metal fingers scrabbling at the side of the train.

The train's speed increased, the whine of its engine singing in Axxter's ears. The motorcycle toppled over, its wheels skidding on the cabin's floor. Its weight slammed the back of his head against the wall. For a few seconds more, as the cabin tilted and went dark, he heard the megassassin screaming its rage in the distance.

■

■

A little red light flashing. He saw that out of the corner of his eye before he saw anything else, or even knew that he could see. The red pulse nibbled at the gray fog swimming around him.

Axxter raised his head, feeling another pulse inside his skull. The rhythmic pain peeled back the fog in layers, until the front cabin of the train was revealed. The flashing red light was above him, up on the control panel. He pushed at the toppled motorcycle pinning him to the angle

234 ■ ■ ■

of the floor and the wall behind his shoulders; slowly, he managed to pull himself free of the machine's weight.

He had to lean on the control panel with both hands to keep from falling over. The red light was a small rectangle with words printed in the center. END OF LINE. It went on flashing as he straightened up and stumbled to the door.

The side of the train was scarred, part of the metal sheathing torn loose where the megassassin had clawed it. Axxter looked around the space. It seemed tattered by neglect, with coils of wire and other debris scattered about. A smell of burnt things drifted in the air.

After some searching, he found what he was looking for, marked by the same concentric yellow rings. He wriggled his finger inside the plug-in jack to make contact.

He called up the Havoc Mass camp; when he ID'ed himself, he was put right through to General Cripplemaker.

"Axxter—good to hear from you!" The general's voice in his ear sounded genuinely pleased.

"Did you get my message?" He leaned against the wall by the jack for support.

"Loud and clear! Clever of you—we didn't know what the hell was going on at first. But when we saw what you were transmitting, with those tape excerpts you dug up and all—well, I can assure you that it certainly changed some minds around here. I owe you a personal apology, my boy."

"Yeah, yeah, that's great . . . wonderful . . . What I really want to know is whether I can come on through. To the outside. I mean, I made it this far, but I need to know whether it's safe for me out there."

Cripplemaker laughed. "You don't have to worry about that anymore—what with the info you relayed to us,

■ ■ ■ 235

you've got yourself quite a hero's status with us. We've got a welcoming reception all worked up for you."

Axxter breathed out his relief, leaning his head against the wall. "Well, I might not be in shape for your kind of party right now; you might have to put it on hold for a little while. But I guess I'll see you in a little while, then."

He disconnected and pushed himself away from the jack. His legs were still weak beneath him as he walked back toward the train. Several meters ahead of the point where the bullet nose had come to rest, he found the torn metal of the barrier between the building's interior and the horizontal sector beyond. He climbed up onto a mounded stack of rubble and looked. For a moment it was like a replay out of his own archive: the burnt-out sector, ashes and bones. Seen from a new angle, a long shot of destruction, the sharp edges rounded with the passing of time, decay setting into whatever soft bits had been left by the raiders. And in the distance, a patch of blue sky.

Something held him back. All he had to do was to climb on over and walk toward the sky, and he'd be there, on the morningside again. It was the smell, the odor of dead things, still hanging in the sector's air; it would be there, he knew, long after it could no longer be sensed. Anyone would be able to feel it, as though it had seeped right into the metal of the walls.

Movement, out toward the exit; Axxter saw it. Hard to miss, something big . . .

He fell back from the barrier. The shock of seeing a megassassin out by the sector's farthest limit had hit him like a blow to the chest.

Jesus Christ—what's that thing doing here? It couldn't be the one that had been on his tail, over on the eveningside; he'd left that one far behind. And even if it had somehow gotten here—if it had hung on all the way to the side of

236 ■ ■ ■

the train—it wouldn't have strolled past the barrier to hang around in the burnt-out sector; it would've just stomped around to the front cabin once the train had stopped, reached in and dragged him out, then unscrewed his head like the lid from a jar.

Axxter cautiously raised his head over the bent ridge. The thing was still there. Facing him this time, its mass blotting out most of the sunlight from the opening just behind it. The two red dots of its eyes looked straight into his; it had spotted him. It didn't move; Axxter was frozen to the spot, expecting the megassassin to come rushing toward him, its cruel arms flashing the sparks of bared steel.

A smile. If cats could smile when they had a mouse trapped in an angle of floor and wall . . .

The megassassin's chest opened up, the metal panels folding slowly to either side. The death ikon blossomed over its oil-fed heart, the image spiraling out toward its throat and groin.

He saw it. His work. The one he'd done, General Cripplemaker's commission. Black within black, darkness so deep you could fall into it forever. The work of his own hand turned in its mesmerizing glory.

It's mine. He couldn't turn his eyes away from the image, though his thoughts had gone skittering around inside his head. If it was his work, then the ones he'd done the work for— *It's theirs. It's the Havoc Mass—it's their megassassin.* They had sent it here to wait for him. For him to just come bumbling out, singing and thinking all his worries were over; this was the welcome Cripplemaker had said they'd prepared for him.

It didn't make sense. Cripplemaker had said they'd gotten his message—they should've called off their megassassin, put it back in whatever brooding deep storage it usually resided. Instead of leaving it here, waiting for him

■ ■ ■ 237

to show up. And then when it'd opened up its chest, displayed its ikon—that meant it still had its assignment to do, the only one it was designed for. Soon as it was no longer amused at the sight of him frozen in place, with nowhere to hide, it would come rumbling down through the burnt-out sector, past the barrier . . . and do its little job.

The view of the megassassin, silhouetted at the sector's entrance, stirred something in his memory. Another time . . .

He moved back from the barrier. In the building's darkness, he called up the files he had loaded from the dump. He fast-forwarded through the tapes until he found what he was looking for. The two megassassins that had been there in the middle of the raid on the sector. The ikon that marked one of them as belonging to the Grievous Amalgam was clearly visible; he worked through the camera angles, trying to get a clear frontal shot of the other one.

Nothing; the cameras had only caught the second megassassin from the back, working away, the great hands flashing and cutting. Beyond it you could see the faces of its victims, their faces contorted as they looked upon the megassassin's death ikon, the last thing they'd see . . .

He stopped the tape, and magnified the frozen image as far as it would go, centering on one poor bastard about to be reduced to ash and pulp. His sight filled with the image of the man's face; he magnified again, centering on one eye.

There it was. A reflection, curved by the round surface of the eye, but still visible. The death ikon. Axxter recognized it; he had almost known beforehand what it would be. The same one he had seen before, up in the Havoc Mass camp, that he'd replaced with his own work.

Which meant—it flashed perfect through his head—

238 ■ ■ ■

that it was the Havoc Mass's megassassin. The second one on the tape, back there in the raid on the sector. It hadn't been just the Grievous Amalgam's doing; the Havoc Mass had been in on it, too.

The sonsabitches. Axxter blinked away the file, leaving him gazing into the darkness in front of him. They were all in it together; they had always been. One more universally assumed truth had turned out to be a fiction. The Grievous Amalgam and the Havoc Mass weren't rivals for power—they were in league together. It made sense, once you followed it all the way through: why stop at reducing Ask & Receive to a charade? Once the only reliable source of obtaining info had been corrupted, there'd be no way of detecting all the other frauds and conspiracies that could be devised. Except for the occasional dumb bastard who stumbled onto something he shouldn't have—and those could be easily eliminated. His clever message to the Havoc Mass had served only as a confirmation that he'd found out too much. So naturally General Cripplemaker had told him to come on through. Where their little reception committee would be waiting for him.

"Screw this." His voice was loud in the darkness. No longer afraid; the angry pulse at the hinge of his jaw had driven everything else out. *Let's just get it over with.*

He went back to the barrier. "Hey!" He cupped his hands around his mouth as he shouted. "Give me ten minutes, okay? Think you could do that? Then I'll be ready for you." He thought he saw, out at the sector's exit, the megassassin smile; at any rate, it didn't move from its position at the metal lip. Axxter nodded and headed back to the train.

It took less than ten minutes; there wasn't much that had to be done. He'd found an operatable welding torch

■ ■ ■ **239**

in the train's maintenance compartment; that, plus the coils of cable scattered around the area, simplified things.

One section of the blown-open barrier was low enough to wheel the motorcycle over. The metal edge was fused smooth, with nothing to snag the thick steel cable trailing behind the bike from where he had spot-welded the cable's end to the frame. The cable snaked over the barrier and back to where the other end was welded to one of the protrusions jutting out from the train's undercarriage. He glanced over his shoulder—the megassassin was still waiting there, as if watching his antics with amused puzzlement. It was in no hurry.

The engine's roar echoed through the sector as Axxter straddled the motorcycle and switched on the ignition. In the distance ahead of him, the megassassin tilted its head, the red-dot eyes glaring at him. He dropped the machine into gear and rolled on the throttle. He glanced back over his shoulder, to see the steel cable unwinding behind the rear wheel; then he lowered his head over the handlebars as the machine's speed battered the air into his face. His eyes locked with the megassassin's as it spread its arms wide and braced for impact.

It looked so big the last few seconds, as the sector's charred ruins blurred past on either side, that it seemed like a wall, a wall with eyes and a spiraling black image, dark within dark, at its center. He could already see himself smashing into bone splinters and jelly; that would have been fine as well, anything that happened now was fine, as long as it happened, no more fucking around—

Then he hit. For a moment he felt the megassassin's fingers folding over his spine, as the motorcycle's front wheel crumpled and sparked against the thing's chest. Then he was surrounded by light and air, wind rushing against his arms and legs, and he knew he was sliding beyond the megassassin's grasp. It howled, and he heard

240 ■ ■ ■

it; not rage, but fear and shock as it spun and fell, knocked clear of the entry site's edge. It had thought it could never die.

Red webbed over Axxter's eyes; some metal piece from the motorcycle had torn loose and stung his brow. He held on, wrapping his arms around the tank. The motorcycle kept on its course, flying straight out from the building.

The motorcycle twisted about; he could see back toward Cylinder. The steel cable slowly lost its slack, becoming a straight line. Then for a moment it was straight, a dark perfect line incised through the air. He gripped the motorcycle tighter, arms and legs squeezing hard onto the crumpled metal. If he could hold on, if the cable held, if he survived the arc back down to the wall—

With a sharp bell note, louder than the roaring wind, the cable snapped.

He pushed himself away from the motorcycle. The megassassin was long gone, falling toward the clouds; now he wanted to be free of everything else. He opened his arms wide, head tilted back, the heart beneath his breastbone pulling him on with a sudden joy.

Another figure, its form silhouetted against a halo of light, rushed from the clouds to meet him. He reached out for her, though she was so far away, and fell.

16

He was making progress, slow but steady, heading upwall, when he heard the motorcycle from down below. He looked over his shoulder—wincing—and saw a familiar face smiling over a set of handlebars.

"Hey, Ny!" Guyer Gimble lifted one hand and waved. "Hold it right there!" She leaned over the motorcycle's gauges and gunned toward him.

She pulled up alongside him and killed the engine. Her smile grew even wider and fiercer in complete delight. "Christ, Ny, I was hoping I'd find you out here. How the hell are ya?"

He leaned back against the pithons, shrugged, and managed a smile. "I'm okay, I guess. In one piece, at least." He hadn't felt that way when he'd come to, strapped to the wall, the day before; every part of him had seemed to have come loose, held together only by the bag of his

242 ■ ■ ■

skin. That was the aftereffect of his head-on impact with the megassassin. He'd been glad when there hadn't been any more blood welling up in his mouth to spit out.

"You sly sonuvabitch—you been having adventures right and left, haven't you? You got any idea how famous you are?"

He shook his head. "You mean for coming all the way through the building?" She must have been following the story, he figured, watching the entertainment broadcasts.

Guyer barked out a laugh. "That, plus other things. You heading up to the toplevel?"

"Yeah." Axxter nodded, the motion sparking a flare of red in his eyes. "Gotta see my agent." He'd already come across a plug-in jack and tried making a call, but had gotten only dead silence. All this slamming around had put something out of commission.

"It'll take you a long time, crawling up there like that. Come on, get in; I'll give you a ride. That's where I'm heading, too."

He managed to climb into the sidecar and strap himself in. Guyer eyed the mottled bruise covering one side of his ribcage, revealed when his jacket rode up.

"You okay? You look kinda messed up."

"I'm okay." He wedged his legs down among her stowed gear. "Mostly."

She started up the motorcycle and headed upwall. Axxter looked back over his shoulder. He hadn't gotten very far from where he'd started. He could still spot the dangling, ragged lines with which Lahft—or maybe another angel; he hadn't been conscious when he'd been helped—had fastened him to the wall. Maybe it had become some kind of sport among them, catching him every time he came falling toward the clouds. Twice was lucky enough; he didn't feel like trying it a third time.

"You're gonna be strolling into some heavy action,

Ny." Guyer shouted over the engine noise and the rush of wind. "The whole building's in an uproar, from the top-level all the way down the wall. Everything's upside down now, man."

He leaned toward her. "Why? What's going on?"

She grinned. "You'll see, man. When you get there. Your agent will fill you in."

His head ached too much to try to figure anything out. He sat back, gazing straight up the wall, and closed his eyes.

■
■

"Ny—Jesus Christ, it's good to see you." Brevis came around the side of his desk and grabbed Axxter's hand. "I didn't know what the hell had happened to you, whether you were dead or what. But I kept hoping."

He let his agent deposit him in a chair. "What the hell's going on out there?" He pointed his thumb toward the door. "It's like a riot or something." Not like, but was, he knew; getting from where Guyer had dropped him off to Brevis's office had been harder than he'd expected, with shouting crowds surging in waves, and the crackle of distant gunfire and explosions. He'd spotted at least a dozen different military tribes, all engaged in freestyle grappling with each other. Sticking close to any handy walls and sidling through had seemed the wisest course of action. Something big was up, obviously.

"Haven't you heard?" Brevis sat back down behind his desk. "Uh, guess you wouldn't have . . . what with your being in transit, as it were." He gestured toward the walls with both hands. "This is it, Ny: the big one. Revolution time. Everything's up for grabs. Cylinder's whole structure of power has collapsed. Alliances, treaties . . . everything. There's going to be a lot of scrambling around for a while." He leaned back, hands clasped behind his head.

244 ■ ■ ■

"No matter what happens to you personally, Ny, at least you'll always have the satisfaction of knowing you made an impact on the way things work."

"Me? What'd I do? I didn't do anything to cause all this." He tilted his head toward the door; from beyond the sounds of the rioting could be heard.

"Nobody's told you? It was your little broadcast, Ny. I mean, that was a great idea about bouncing your signal off that angel—when the signal hit this side, everybody wondered what was going on, so they traced back and figured out what you'd done. And when I say everybody, I mean *every*body; every military tribe that'd ever had graffex work done for them, or anybody else with access to programmed biofoil."

"What're you talking about?"

"Don't you see, Ny?" Brevis smiled. "You didn't just send that little transmission you'd cooked up to the Havoc Mass; you sent it to everybody. The signal wasn't encoded the way that the Small Moon encodes everything it sends out—the coding is what limits the signal's reception to the intended target. Without that coding, your signal went completely wide-band. Every piece of active biofoil on this side of the building got its usual programming overridden, and started showing all that stuff you'd put together, those tapes and everything. It wasn't some little secret between you and the Havoc Mass anymore; *everybody* saw the proof about the conspiracy between the Havoc Mass and the Grievous Amalgam. Soon as their respective allies and treaty partners saw that, then the game was up. Thus all this foofarah going on outside."

"Jeez." A vague wonder moved inside Axxter's chest; all he'd been trying to do was save his own ass. And all this had come about because of it . . . "So what's going to happen now?"

"Oh, some new order will emerge. Eventually. That's

how things always go. The only thing that's certain is that it won't be either the Grievous Amalgam or the Havoc Mass calling the shots up here. They've already gone through mass defections, all their ranks scrambling around for position with somebody else. If they can; a lot of old grudges are going to get settled at their expense."

Cripplemaker would probably do all right, sneaky shit that he was. But the general's fate wasn't of any concern to Axxter. "Well . . . whatever comes down, money's always going to come in handy. Right? Now that I made it on through, it's time to rake it in. What's the payoff come to?"

Brevis's smile disappeared. He looked sadly at Axxter. "There isn't any payoff, Ny."

His heart went cold. "What do you mean?"

"No payoff. No money, no nothing. That was the other effect of your broadcast. Remember?—your evidence completely indicted Ask & Receive, too. They're bankrupt, washed up, kaput. They were completely liable for the validity of the info they had been supplying, so now everybody's got a suit against them. Fat lot of good it'll do, though, since they've already rolled over."

"But—my money—"

"Ny—you sold the rights to Ask & Receive. I've been telling you: they're bankrupt. Those rights you sold them are part of the assets that the vultures are picking clean. When they get done—if they ever get done; a mess like this takes years to clear up—you'll be lucky if you realize enough out of it to buy a sandwich."

Inside his head, some cool lobe, separate from the rest, admired the rigorous efficiency: to get back here, to collect the money for getting back here, he'd had to destroy the thing that would pay him the money. *That's marvelous*. Perfect in its way.

He got up out of the chair.

246 ■ ■ ■

"Hey—where you going?"

The noise outside rushed over him as he pushed open the door. "I'm going for a little walk. I'll see you later."

■
■

There was no answer. He pushed the button beside Ree's door again, and got only silence in return. Plenty of silence down in the horizontal sectors, far removed from the uproar at the toplevel. Things always stayed the same on the horizontal.

"She's not there, man."

Axxter turned around and saw a woman standing behind him in the corridor. Dark-haired, almost pretty; he'd never seen her before. "Do you know where she went?"

The woman smiled. "I think she's gone for good, fella. She got married."

"Oh." Somehow he'd never expected that.

"Ny—" The woman leaned against the corridor wall, regarding him. "Don't you know who this is? Who I am?"

She'd known his name. That, plus her voice, lower in pitch but with the same laughing inflection in the words. "Felony . . . ?"

She nodded. "You got it. Inside here, at least. This is the body I keep around these parts."

"I didn't know if I'd see you again—"

"I asked around, decided to look you up; figured you'd come around here. Your neighbors where you used to live told me where. I just wanted to see what kind of shape you were in, after all that."

Axxter returned her smile. "What kind of shape am I in?"

She shrugged. "Same as before, I guess. By the way, Sai told me to say hello. He's a little dinged up, but basically all right."

"Glad to hear it."

Felony pointed her thumb toward the door. "Your girlfriend's run out on you?"

He nodded. "I guess she had somebody else on the line, and decided to go with that when she found out I wasn't going to be getting the big bucks."

"Well . . . I did a little checking around on my own; just public record stuff. Here, take a look." She dug out a folded sheet of paper and handed it to him. "That's a printout from the registry office."

He found himself looking at the date of Ree's marriage. It took him a moment to figure it out. "Oh. That was while I was still over there. On the eveningside."

"That's right. Before she knew whether you were going to make it back, alive or not. Nice, huh?"

He crumpled up the paper and threw it away. All along the corridor the doors were shut, silent. "I guess that makes sense. She's just that kind of person."

"Hey—so no loss, huh?" Felony pushed herself away from the wall. "I gotta run; things to do. You take care of yourself, okay?"

"Sure." He watched her striding away, not looking back at him.

■
■

He walked and walked, until there wasn't any place to walk. Until he was outside again. On the vertical.

Smoke and flame, and distant shouting from far above, as he climbed out the small exit site. It was the first one he'd come to.

His boot-pithons sang out and locked onto the wall's surface as he stood up. Straight out, perpendicular to the building's steel skin, tilting his head back to look across the sky and the cloud barrier below. His hand touched his belt, but then drew away, leaving the pithons at his waist

248 ■ ■ ■

still coiled inside their little nests. He didn't need them now.

He stood on the wall, the old fear and nausea gone. He stood and gazed down, over the curved empty territory of the vertical world. A bright, cold wind surged against his face, stinging his throat and lungs as he drank it in. The clouds boiled silver, tearing his eyes.

His arms spread wide, hands gathering in even more air.

A long time to get there, but now he was home.